GIDEON GREEN IN BLACK AND WHITE

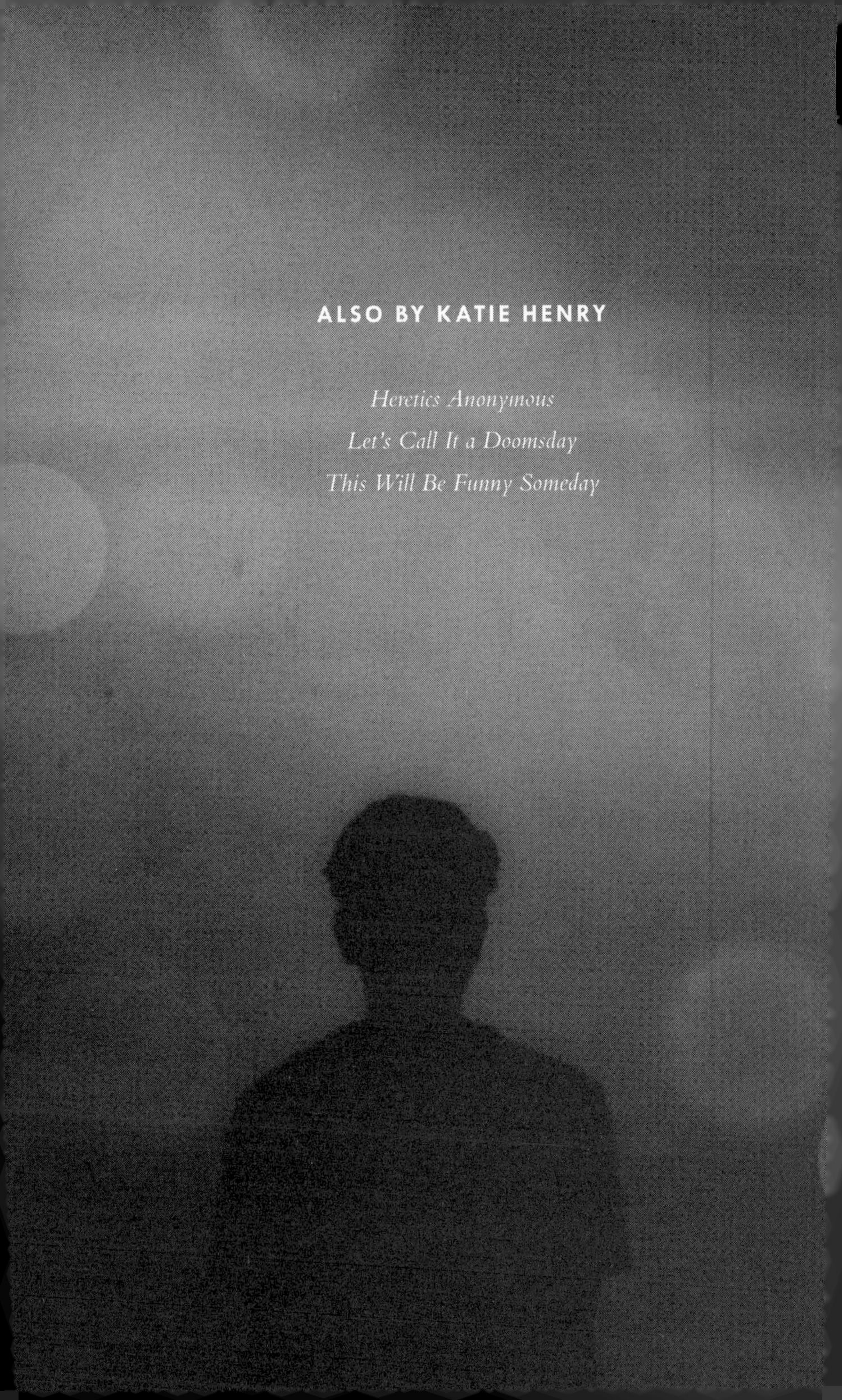

ALSO BY KATIE HENRY

Heretics Anonymous

Let's Call It a Doomsday

This Will Be Funny Someday

GIDEON GREEN
GREEN
IN
BLACK
AND
WHITE

KATIE HENRY

KATHERINE TEGEN BOOKS

An Imprint of HarperCollins Publishers

Katherine Tegen Books is an imprint of HarperCollins Publishers.

Gideon Green in Black and White

Copyright © 2022 by Catherine Henry

All rights reserved. Printed in Lithuania.

No part of this book may be used or reproduced in any manner whatsoever without written permission except in the case of brief quotations embodied in critical articles and reviews. For information address HarperCollins Children's Books, a division of HarperCollins Publishers, 195 Broadway, New York, NY 10007.

www.epicreads.com

ISBN 978-0-06-295573-9

Typography by David Curtis

22 23 24 25 SB 10 9 8 7 6 5 4 3 2 1

First Edition

For Mom,

who read me countless stories and always listened

once I was ready to start telling my own

DISCLAIMER TO THE DISCLAIMER

The statement below is a parody of the "all persons fictitious" disclaimer, which emerged as the standard please-god-don't-sue-us boilerplate language after Princess Irina Alexandrovna of Russia successfully took MGM to court for libel over the 1932 movie *Rasputin and the Empress*.

This book will contain no further educational content.

DISCLAIMER

This story is a work of fiction, which you probably guessed when you picked it out of the fiction section. All characters, locations, and organizations are a product of the author's imagination, except for the ones that aren't. Any resemblance to real events is purely coincidental and would honestly be pretty surprising.

The investigative procedures used by the teenage protagonists are not condoned by the author, the Society of Professional Journalists, or any known legal system and should not be attempted by anyone. You will go to jail.

CHAPTER 1

THE THIRD-GREATEST TRAGEDY of my life is that I don't live in a film noir.

The second-greatest tragedy of my life is that it's 498 days until my eighteenth birthday, which means 498 days until I get to leave San Miguel, California, more specifically, Presidio High School, and, more broadly, my holding pattern of a life here.

Don't worry about the first-greatest tragedy, because it happened a long time ago and isn't interesting or special at all. It happens to lots of people, and I prefer to focus on the ways I'm not like most people.

Here are two examples:

Everyone else at lunch is wearing shorts and T-shirts, and I am wearing a trench coat.

Everyone else is eating lunch together, and I am eating alone.

Which is fine. It's good, actually, because it gives me space to think about things.

Like how nobody would ever eat a brown-bagged lunch in film noir. I can't think of any noir I've seen where the private investigator eats a chicken focaccia sandwich, and I've seen pretty much every movie in the genre. Nobody goes to high school in film noir, either, but no matter how many times I ask, Dad won't let me drop out. So here I am.

You're probably picturing me in a school cafeteria with a lunch line and tables fiercely guarded by rival cliques, but you shouldn't. That's a trope. Every kind of movie has its tropes—the things you know you're going to see, the things you start to expect—and is there a bigger one for teen dramas than cafeteria cliques?

Maybe there is. I don't watch a lot of them.

But this is Southern California. Nothing is indoors if it doesn't have to be, so benches and metal tables are scattered across the open-air campus. Everything here is sprawl, from freeways to lunch spots. And the only person who seems particularly attached to any given table is me.

Someone clears their throat. When I look up, there's a whole crowd of someones gathered around my table.

Like I said, high school cliques are a trope, not reality, but if I had to sum this particular group up, I'd label them the Future Ivy Leaguer Overachievers. Perfect GPAs. Lots of extracurriculars. Would murder you with their bare hands if it meant moving one spot up on the class rank. Maybe that's not fair, I think, when I see Lily hovering in the back, looking uncomfortable. But after what she did to me . . . maybe it is.

And standing in front—so close her legs are touching my table, clearly in charge, clearly the one who cleared her throat—is Mia. I'm not sure exactly where it falls on my list, but the existence of Mia McElroy is definitely some type of tragedy.

If my life were a noir, Mia would be described in the script like this:

```
MIA MCELORY (F, 16): a real knockout dame with
legs that go all the way up to her pelvis
(because that's 000how legs work) and a slash of
red lipstick two shades darker than her hair.
```

But this is just high school, and Mia's just a girl with the personality of a piranha.

"Hi," Mia says, drawing out the word over five seconds so I can better hear the *go fuck yourself* subtext underneath. "We're going to need the table."

You're probably imagining her in a cheerleader uniform, but you shouldn't. That's another trope.

She clears her throat again. "Did you hear me?"

"Yes."

"So . . . ?"

"So, I don't agree." I take a bite of my sandwich. "You don't need the table."

"We do need the table, actually."

"Shelter is a need. Food is a need. Are you going to eat the table?"

"Oh my God," Mia mutters.

"Mia," I hear Lily say, but I refuse to look at her. "Maybe we could—"

"We need the table because, unlike you, we have actual things to accomplish this lunch period," Mia says. "We're planning the Key Club's community food drive, which I know you couldn't possibly care about, because you don't care about helping the community, or like, anyone besides yourself."

I point at the lumbering guy at her shoulder—her boyfriend, I can't remember his name—who's texting on his phone, oblivious. "Really? *He's* helping with the food drive?"

Mia looks behind her. When she swats at her boyfriend's arm, he jumps out of his skin. "Could you get off your phone and do something about him?"

Mia's boyfriend shoves his phone in his pocket so fast you'd think it was on fire. He looks at me, then back to her. "But . . . he's just sitting there."

"Yeah, exactly," I say. "Thank you, Hired Goon."

"What?" he says.

Lily leans closer to Mia. "We could go on the lawn. If Gideon doesn't want to move—"

That's the first time I've heard Lily say my name in five years. Which wouldn't be remarkable, except she used to say it every

4

day, when we were still best friends.

"No." Mia folds her arms. "We need a hard surface, and we need the space. He doesn't. There are plenty of other tables he could use—"

"But this is my table," I say.

"Smaller tables, more appropriate tables for one person—"

"I always sit at this table."

"—that would work just fine if *Gideon* would stop being so *selfish*."

I don't know what else to say to her. I chose this table in my second week of freshman year and I've sat here every single day since and so I have to sit here now. It makes perfect sense in my head, but I can tell from the way they're all staring at me it makes no sense to them.

"Why are you being so weird about this?" Mia snaps. "Just pick a different table."

"I'm not being weird."

"Of course you are," she says, then gestures at . . . well, all of me. "Who the hell wears a jacket when it's eighty degrees?"

"It's a trench coat. I always wear a trench coat." This gets no reaction. "People used to wear stuff like this all the time. And fedoras. And shoes that weren't made of plastic." I can tell I'm not helping my case, but I can't stop. "If someone from the 1930s or the '40s saw the way *you* dressed, they'd think *you* were the weird one. Not me."

"Wow. So you're really still doing it." When she smiles, it's toothless. "You're still playing detective."

I didn't play a detective, I was one. Was.

"I'm not a detective."

"It's almost cute," she continues, "how committed you are. Almost."

"You know, Mia, why don't you ask somebody else for their table?"

"Because you're the one eating alone."

"I always eat alone."

"Yeah. You do." Mia locks her sharp eyes on mine. "Have you ever wondered *why*?"

Maybe I could have left it there, if she hadn't said that. Or if it was someone else saying it. But after what they all put me through—Mia included, Mia *especially*—it's out of my mouth before I can stop myself.

"Your boyfriend is cheating on you."

Mia's eyes bug out. The aforementioned boyfriend's mouth drops open.

"*Excuse* me?" she says.

"Oh." I blink at her. "That means he's seeing somebody else."

She puts both hands on my table. "What the Jesus *fuck* is your problem, Gideon?"

"It's not my problem," I say. "It's your problem. Yours and—" I turn to her boyfriend, who still hasn't closed his mouth. "I'm sorry. I can't remember your name. Colton, Ashton, Braxton . . ."

"Matt," he says.

Okay, so I'm not batting a thousand.

"Matt," I repeat, "I'm sorry to be doing this to you, Matt—well, not that sorry, you *are* cheating on her." I take a breath and focus back on Mia. "Did you see how panicked he got, when you interrupted him before? I bet that's been happening a lot, lately. Right, Mia? He's all jumpy?"

Matt's phone rings in his pocket. Just once, a high, musical alert. He ignores it. "And see, *that's* interesting," I say. "That text alert, it's not the default tone. And no offense, Matt, but you seem like a default kind of guy."

"Dude," he says. "Don't do this."

Mia whirls around on him. "Don't do *what*, Matt?"

"I'm betting he programmed a special tone for one contact," I say. "A very special contact."

"Give me your phone," Mia says. "I want to see your phone."

"What? No!" Matt's hand rests protectively over his pocket.

"I just want to see your phone," she repeats, deadly calm. "Why can't I see your phone?"

"You don't need his phone," I assure her. "There are other clues."

Matt throws up his hands. "Clues? Nothing is happening!"

I point at Matt's face. "He's trying to grow a beard, too. Can you see that? I mean, it's not working, but—" I shrug. "Do you *like* beards, Mia? I bet you don't. So who's *that* for, do you think?"

"Shaving was irritating my skin!" Matt protests.

"His clothes are new, too, like he's trying to impress

somebody." I gesture at his pants. "Forgot to take the size sticker off."

Matt looks down at his jeans, swears, and rips off the sticker.

"What the hell is going on?" Mia yells at him, though she's pointing at me. "Is that little asshole right?"

Five feet six is exactly average height for a sixteen-year-old American male, but I don't think she's in the correct mental state to hear that right now.

"Babe, of course not," Matt pleads with her.

"It's Ava Clark, isn't it."

"Does Ava Clark wear pink lip gloss?" They stop and turn to stare at me. "Like sort of a peachy color, kind of neutral, little bit of glitter?"

"Why?" Mia, vibrating with rage, bites off the word. *"Why, Gideon?"*

"Oh, no reason." I point to my own shirt collar. "Just the stain on his jacket."

Mia looks for it. Finds it. And that's when she really explodes, a volcanic ball of righteous fury erupting in the middle of the open-air quad.

"What is that, Matt?" she demands. "*Whose* is that?" She gestures to her red lips. "Because it's definitely not mine!"

"Mia," he says, eyes shifting around the crowd that's started to gather around us. "I can explain." She waits. He flounders. Then— "Did you know humans were never meant to be monogamous?"

Swing and a miss, Hired Goon.

"I can't believe you!" she shouts at him. "You are, you're cheating on me!"

"Yeah. He is." I lean forward and smile at her. "Have you ever wondered *why*?"

For a second, Mia almost looks like she's going to slap me. Then she does slap me.

CHAPTER 2

MR. WALLACE WOULD be a terrible detective.

He chose to be a high school principal, so it doesn't matter, but detectives have to be organized. They can't have papers covering every inch of their desk or folders piled up to the windows. How can you find clues if you can't even find a pen?

Another reason he wouldn't be a good detective: he doesn't have any clue how to lead an interrogation. He hasn't asked me a single question yet, and this chair is very comfortable. There's even a cushion. It's like he doesn't know the basics.

Maybe it's not an interrogation. It shouldn't be. It wasn't my fault.

Mr. Wallace types for a moment on his computer, then cranes his head around the screen to look at me.

"Gideon . . . ?"

"Green."

He types some more. Then stops. Then rolls his wheelie chair away from the computer, so that he and I are eye to eye.

"Have I seen you before?" he asks.

Here's something I like about noir movies: they don't blur the background. In most classic cinema, the camera focuses only on the person in the foreground and whatever they're saying and doing and feeling. And whoever's in the background . . . they're a washed-out blur. In film noir, the people in the background stay in focus. They still matter.

Lots of movies blur out anyone in the background. Lots of people do, too.

"Have I?" Mr. Wallace prompts me. "Seen you in my office?"

I shake my head.

"Your name sounds so familiar," he says. "Gideon Green."

I shrug. He folds his hands on his desk.

"All right. Can you tell me what happened at lunch?"

"I told Mia her boyfriend was cheating on her. And then she hit me." I pause. "And then her boyfriend pulled her off and she started yelling at him—I mean, she was already yelling, but she yelled louder. And then he started yelling back at her, and then Mia called Ava Clark a home-wrecking trash bag, which isn't accurate because Mia doesn't have a home."

"Okay. Well—"

"Obviously she has a *home*, but not one with her boyfriend. Ex-boyfriend. So how could Ava Clark be a home-wrecker, is what I'm saying."

He stares at me, unblinking, so I must have missed a step.

11

"Lunch ended," I add. "And then I went to chemistry. And then your receptionist came and got me and then it's right now."

"Do you . . . ?" He scans my face, looking for something and not finding it. "Do you have any thoughts about what happened today?"

"The average person has about forty-nine thoughts every minute," I say. "But I'm pretty sure I have more than that, so."

He does another scan. "I mean, do you feel responsible at all, for what happened at lunch?"

I scoff. "I'm not the one who cheated on her."

"Don't you feel like it was cruel," he asks, "to tell Mia something like that? To embarrass her like that, in front of everybody?"

I wonder if he even considered *she* might have been cruel. A person can be class president and in the running for valedictorian and still be hell on wheels, too.

But he knows Mia. He likes her. And he's never seen me before.

"You know," I say, "*she's* the one who hit *me*."

From the look he gives me, it's clear he thinks I deserved it. And maybe I did. But only for the last thing I said. Not for the other stuff, not for telling Mia the truth. That's a detective's job. Telling the world what's real, even if people don't want to hear it.

I'm not a detective anymore, but I still care about the truth.

"Mia was . . . remorseful," he says. "About that."

Please. The only way *remorseful* is in Mia McElroy's vocabulary is as an SAT word.

"But she did seem concerned this was part of a pattern, for you."

"Pattern?"

"She said—" He checks his notes. "'Gideon thinks he's like Sherlock Holmes, but the only way he's like Sherlock Holmes is being a high-functioning sociopath.'"

I didn't want to get into this, but of course Mia would make sure I had no choice. "She means my detective work."

That sends his eyebrows sky-high. "I'm sorry, you're . . . a detective?"

He's using the wrong tense. Just like Mia.

"I *was* a detective. Not anymore." I cross my arms. "I retired."

It was called Green Private Investigations and I founded it in the summer after fourth grade. I had a sign and an office and everything. I'd wanted to get a real business license, too, like Dad had with his restaurants—his first one was just going up then—but he said the county clerk's office would never do it.

I charged clients a dollar a day and commission if I recovered something valuable. I usually didn't. It was all sentimental stuff, and it's not like Jennie Burke's mangy stuffed rabbit was insured. But I can still remember the way she flung her arms around my waist when I got it back for her.

I found a lot of lost toys. Recovered missing bikes and stolen game controllers and things like that. Figured out who was stuffing mean notes in desks or who told on somebody for flooding the bathroom sink at school or whether someone was cheating at heads up, seven up. And then—

"Wait," Mr. Wallace says, and it dawns on his face. "I remember you."

All the tendons in my body tense at once. He doesn't remember *me*. He remembers one single thing I did when I was ten, and that's if I'm lucky.

"Gideon Green, I knew I remembered that name," he says slowly, like it's coming back to him in pieces. "You were on the local news. Five years ago, something like that? Someone's necklace had gone missing, and you led the cops right to it. That was you?"

"It was actually a necklace and earring set."

"And they did a little mock ceremony for you, right? Gave you a medal, the police chief shook your hand, they put you on the local news. My wife taped the segment, she thought it was so cute."

Yeah, just what every detective wants. To be adorable.

Then he stops. Frowns. "Or . . . were you on the news twice? Once with the medal, and another time later—"

"Nope," I interrupt. "Just once."

You can find yourself on the other side of adorable in a flat second.

He nods, though, so I guess he believes me. One more reason

Mr. Wallace would be a bad detective: his memory sucks. I wish everyone's did.

"When did you retire?" he asks.

I take a deep breath before answering. "Middle school."

I never saw it coming. I should have, when the whole summer between sixth and seventh grades passed with no customers. Just me and Lily in my dad's garage, boiling in the heat until Lily would force me to go back to her house, which at least had AC.

What's going on? I remember asking her. *Why aren't they coming back?*

I don't know, Gideon, she said. But she knew.

Here's what happened: puberty had hit everyone else like a freight train, and I didn't even notice. When Lily started updating me with who had kissed who and who had broken up, I didn't hear her. Or I didn't understand what it meant, I guess.

That August, Lily went to sleepaway camp. We'd spent every whole summer together since we were seven, but all the other girls were going. When she came back, she had different clothes and stiff shoulders and a look in her eyes that was far away.

She also had a lot of excuses, mostly for why she couldn't come over. And when seventh grade started—a blur of new buildings and new teachers and triple the kids of our elementary school—she started avoiding my eyes and practically hurtling herself out of earshot whenever the bell rang. By the time I got out to the quad, she'd already be at a table with a bunch of girls who stared daggers whenever I got too close.

15

Finally, Mia took it upon herself to deal with me. And being Mia, she did it with all the subtlety and compassion of a hand grenade.

Don't you get it? Mia snapped at me after she'd cornered me by my locker. *She doesn't want to hang out with you. So stop coming over, already.*

She's my best friend, I protested. *Why doesn't she want to—*

Mia flicked her eyes from my thrift-store fedora to the Dashiell Hammett paperbacks spilling out of my locker. *Yeah. It's a real mystery.*

I didn't talk to Lily again.

This isn't the first-greatest tragedy of my life. Tragedies are bad things that happen without anybody clear to blame, which is what makes them tragic.

This was a straight-up betrayal.

Mr. Wallace shuffles papers around on his desk, watching me out of the corner of his eye. I think I was quiet for too long. I think I was supposed to say something, even though I didn't have anything to say.

"Well. Obviously, the events of today were . . . unfortunate," Mr. Wallace says.

"I'm sorry," I say. It's a little bit true. "I didn't know Mia was going to flip out like that." That's all the way true.

"Maybe you two could talk it through," he says, sounding hopeful. "We could set you and Mia up for peer counseling."

"Wouldn't we have to be peers first?"

He closes his eyes. Sighs. Opens them again. "Just . . . please keep your deductions to yourself in the future."

I nod. "Okay."

He gets up, leads me to the door, and gestures out into the empty hallway. "I sincerely hope I don't see you here again."

He won't. I know what I am. Just a blur in the background.

San Miguel is like a bunch of cities in San Diego County, in that it is not a city.

I mean, it is, technically. It says so on the "Welcome to San Miguel" sign by the freeway and also on Wikipedia. But it isn't a real kind of city, with skyscrapers or subways or dark alleys. It's a medium-sized suburb-ish kind of place that isn't close enough to the ocean to be a beach town.

Dad says I don't know how lucky we are to live here. And fine, the weather is perfect and the food is fresh and the sidewalks practically sparkle, but it's like—who do you have to kill for a little grit around here?

My neighborhood does have one big upside: I can walk to and from school. Sure, it's up a gigantic hill, but being able to get myself home every day, without needing a ride or trying to dash across the freeway like a raccoon with a death wish? It's basically like owning a unicorn.

Inside, I hang up my keys on the hook in the kitchen, above the phone. I'm sure we're the only people under eighty who still have a landline, and the only calls we get on it are from telemarketers and my grandma Felicitas. She refuses to learn a new phone number, which means Dad can't ever disconnect it.

Then I make a beeline for my room, shutting the door as quietly as I can behind me, kicking my shoes into the footwear graveyard under my bed, and dropping my backpack by my dresser. There's a rustle next to me, then a series of irritated squeaks as my chinchilla gnaws at the bars of his habitat.

"Okay, Asta, I'll take you out." I unlatch the door and scoop him out. "You don't have to scream about it."

Asta resumes gnawing, this time at my fingers.

I lie down on my bed, letting Asta curl up on my chest. Every inch of the four walls around me is covered with posters of my favorite movies. Dad told me he doesn't understand how I can relax with so many pictures of guys in fedoras with pistols glaring down at me. I told him I don't understand how jogging is relaxing, but I don't make a big deal about him doing that.

The truth is, there's nowhere in the world I feel more relaxed than here. It's hot outside, but my room is dark and cool. Getting through seven hours at school is hard, but Asta's fur is soft under my fingertips. Everything I like and everything I need is right here, in this tiny space that's only mine.

There's a knock at my door. Before I can say, "Come in," Dad has already pushed it open and is standing in the doorway.

"Hey, kiddo," he says.

"Hey," I say, but I keep my eyes on Asta, gearing up for the rest of our daily two-minute conversation. He'll say, *How was school?* and I'll say, *Fine.* And then I'll say, *How was last night?* and he'll say, *Oh, you know,* and I'll nod as if I do.

I know getting a new restaurant off the ground takes a lot of work, because I've seen Dad do it before, but he seems more tired this time around. When I see him. Which isn't that much, because by the time Dad gets home at night—after the last guest pays their tab, the kitchen gets cleaned, and the staff piles out—I'm asleep. And when I leave for school early in the morning, *he's* asleep.

It didn't use to be like that. He used to be home more, and I used to spend more time at the restaurant—his first one, which had burgers, not the new one, which has nothing on the menu a child would eat. I liked his first place, as a kid. All the college-girl waitresses snuck me desserts, and it was way better than hanging out with a babysitter or staying at school for aftercare. It felt like I was home.

But I'm not a kid anymore. So now I just feel in the way.

Dad steps in through the door, moving my backpack out of the way with one of his clunky, nonslip clogs.

"Can you put Asta in his cage? I want to talk to you."

"It's not a cage," I say, lowering Asta back in. "It's a habitat."

Dad shakes his head. But it isn't a cage. A cage is somewhere you don't want to be but are trapped in anyway. A habitat is a place where you have everything you need. Where you're supposed to be.

"I'm heading over to Verde for dinner service."

"Okay," I say, when what I really mean is, *Duh*.

"What's your plan for dinner? There's plenty in the fridge." He lists on his fingers. "A bunch of mole, a quarter of a quiche . . . a whole branzino entrée."

"Is that an animal or a fish?"

"Fish are animals."

That means it's fish. "Maybe I'll make fries."

His mouth slides into a frown.

"People pay good money for my branzino," he says, "and you want freezer fries."

I'm glad they do. I like living in a house, I think about saying. *But I don't like fish. You know I don't like fish.* I decide not to say anything at all.

Dad clears his throat. "Fries, and?"

"Just that."

"Eat a vegetable."

"Technically," I point out, "a potato *is* a—"

"You're killing me," he says. "A *green* vegetable."

I nod like I'm considering it—which I'm not—but he keeps staring at me. I stare back at him, trying to figure out what he wants me to do. Then he looks away. Takes a deep breath in through his nose.

"Gideon . . ."

"What?" I ask, warily, because when he does that—makes my whole name a giant sigh—the rest of the conversation never seems to go my way.

"Aren't you tired of this?"

I don't say anything, because I don't know what he means. He sweeps his hand across the room until it lands back on me. "Every afternoon, it's the same."

I like it the same.

"You hole yourself up in this room—"

I like my room.

"Draw all the curtains—"

He acts like I'm a vampire, but it's just practical. "It has to be dark so I can watch—"

"Movies," he cuts in, sounding like he just ran a marathon. "Yes, I know, your movies. And look, it would be one thing if they were different movies, okay? If you were, I don't know, making your way through the whole Criterion Collection. Preparing for film school, or something. But it's the same movies, every day."

"I cycle through them."

"It's either the one where the gas station owner goes to Mexico—"

Out of the Past.

"Or the one where an insurance salesman strangles a man, and there's the girl with ugly bangs—"

"Double Indemnity, and he snaps the guy's neck."

"My point is: you're in a rut. And you need to get out."

One person's rut is another person's routine. And there's nothing wrong with a routine.

21

"Whatever, fine. So I'll watch a new one."

"I mean you *literally* need to get out."

This didn't work when I was twelve and he signed me up for Sports Adventure Camp (outfielder + poor hand-eye coordination = broken nose), and it didn't work when I was fourteen and he tried locking me out in the backyard all afternoon (summer in the desert + no shade = mild heatstroke). I wonder what he'll try this time. And how I'll injure myself.

"You could come work with me," he suggests. "I was your age when I got my first kitchen job."

That's worse than a broken nose. "The kitchen?"

Kitchens are loud, hot, and chaotic, with people calling out orders and scrambling around each other and ten burners going at once. I can't think of a place I'd like to be less.

"Or as a server," he says. "You'd make good tips."

Has he *met* me? Waiters have to be nice to people even when those people are mean to them. They have to apologize for things that aren't their fault. You don't make good tips by being honest.

When Dad looks at me, I wonder how much of what he sees is actually me and how much is some ghost of who he hoped I'd be, instead.

"Fine." He shrugs. "Thought I'd make it easy on you, but if you want to find something on your own, that's okay, too."

"What do you mean, find something?"

"I mean come up with anything else to keep you busy and

22

out of this dark little room. A job, a sport, a hobby—it's up to you. But otherwise, you're coming to the restaurant with me. Got it?"

"But—"

"Nope," he says. "I asked if you got it."

If I tell him I do, he wins, and if I tell him I don't, he'll only keep talking. So I throw my hands up and say: "This is so unfair!"

"Just once I'd love a simple 'yes' from you, Gideon." He checks his watch. "I'll see you tomorrow. Don't set the house on fire."

One time. It was only the stove. And did he ever acknowledge how good I turned out to be with that fire extinguisher? He did not.

He leaves without shutting my door, and I listen to his footsteps down the hallway, the jingle as he grabs his car keys, and the click of the lock behind him.

Once I'm sure he's gone, I get up and slam my door closed. It doesn't make me feel any better. It's always the same thing with him: the things I like aren't the things he likes, and somehow that makes the things I like wrong.

He didn't use to mind, so much. When I asked for pasta with butter every night in first grade, he accepted we might not ever have the same taste in food. When it turned out I couldn't swing a bat to save my life, he accepted I wouldn't be the varsity baseball captain, like he'd been. But the older I get, the more differences there are. It's like they're the giant bags of flour I've helped him carry into his kitchen. When you can carry them one by one, it's doable. But pile them on top of each other, and your knees buckle.

The doorbell chimes. I don't get up right away, because sometimes our mail carrier does that to let us know he left a package. But then it chimes again, so I guess Dad forgot his keys or his phone or some other aspect of my personality he wanted to criticize.

As I'm walking to the entryway, the doorbell rings a third time.

"God, *okay*," I say as I twist the knob, "would you just give me a—"

But the moment I open the door, I stop dead in my tracks.

Because it isn't Dad standing in front of me.

It's Lily.

CHAPTER 3

THE FIRST THING Lily says is: "I need your help."

The second thing she says is: "Oh God, that's not how I meant to do this."

And then, before my brain catches up with my vocal cords, she's burying me under an avalanche of words. "I planned this, you know, because I like planning things, and when you answered the door I was going to say 'Hi,' and then you were going to say 'Hi,' and I was going to ask if I could come in and the whole help part of it wasn't going to be a thing until way later."

She takes a breath. I seize the opportunity.

"Do you want to?" I ask her.

She blinks. "Want to what?"

I move out of the doorway. "Come in?"

"Oh. Yes."

When she steps through into the entryway, she turns all the way around.

"Wow," she says as I'm locking the door again behind us. "I haven't been here in forever."

My shoulders stiffen, and I turn around so we're face-to-face. "Whose fault is that?"

Her eyes go soft and sad. "I didn't mean—"

"It's fine."

"All I was trying to say—"

"Do you want something to drink?" I interrupt her again. "Water, or . . . ?"

Lily looks relieved. Maybe she didn't actually know what she was trying to say. "Water would be great. Thanks."

I look down the hallway. "You remember where it is, right? My room?"

"Yeah. Of course." Then she turns and heads toward it.

As I fill up her glass at the kitchen sink, I keep replaying the words. Four of them. One syllable each. *I need your help.*

Nothing in my life is like a noir. I don't have an agency with my name on the door. I don't go looking for leads on foggy nights or walk alone on wet sidewalks. It only rains like forty days a year here. Another tragedy. Constant sunshine really destroys the aesthetic.

Nothing in my life is like a noir . . . except this.

Because this is always how it happens: a detective in his office. A knock at the door. And a girl who needs help.

Well, okay, they're *women*, not girls. Femmes fatales, if you want to get technical with trope names. Complete with dark pasts, hidden motives, and skirts so tight I don't understand how they even walked.

This is my bedroom, though, I think as I step through the door. And this isn't just any girl. It's Lily.

"Your room looks just like I remember it," she says, taking the glass. "Exactly the same."

I almost ask her to try to figure out what's changed, like that game you find on kids' menus. Spot the differences.

"Isn't yours?" I ask.

"What?"

"The same."

She laughs. "Since sixth grade? I still had my doll collection on display."

I frown. Then she frowns.

"No," she says. Quieter. "I—it's changed, a lot. Since then."

I don't know what I'm supposed to say to that, and I guess neither does Lily, because there's only silence for a moment.

"Well," I say finally, "Asta's new, anyway." I nod my head over her shoulder, at Asta's habitat.

Lily turns. Then gasps. Then rushes over to plop down beside the habitat. "Oh my God. She's so cute."

"He's a boy."

"I'm sorry for misgendering you, Asta," she says.

He sniffs at her fingers, apparently unoffended.

Lily looks back up at me. "Why is he named Asta?"

"It's a movie reference." I gesture at my wall of DVDs. "I'm kind of into them."

"No kidding." Lily squints at the wall. She never liked wearing her glasses. I guess that hasn't changed. "Do you only own movies that were made in the past?"

"All movies were made in the past."

"You know what I mean."

I think life would be a whole lot easier if people would just *say* what they mean and not force me to guess.

Then, out of nowhere, Lily says: "Oh my *gosh.*" At first, I think she's overcome with how soft Asta's fur is (understandable) until I see her eyes aren't on him, but on the bulletin board above my desk.

I know what photo she's seen, without even having to ask. It's the one on the pushpin in the corner, the one with curled-up edges. The one where Lily and I—the kid versions of ourselves, anyway—are standing in front of my garage and the "Green Detective Agency" sign we made out of butcher paper and paint. We're small, and smiling, and still friends.

Lily gets to her feet, walks over, and takes the picture from its pushpin. "How old were we here? Nine?"

"Ten."

From this angle, I can see both Lilys at once, the one in the photograph and the one standing in my room. And I can see all the differences, too. Her dark hair shorter and swept up into a ponytail instead of two braids. The freckles on the bridge of her nose all faded. Taller and willowy instead of just skinny.

I'm taller, too, obviously, and my hair's more brown than red at this point, but . . . Lily looks one step away from adult. And I barely look different at all.

"I can't believe you still have this," she says.

"What, a picture?"

"A picture of us."

It isn't a picture of us. It's a picture of me and my detective agency. She only happens to be in the frame. I get the angle she's going for. She wants that photo to be evidence I missed her, and I didn't. I don't.

I clear my throat. "You said you needed help."

She leaves the photo on my desk and comes back to sit on the bed. I stay leaning against the door frame.

"So," she says, suddenly sounding nervous. "As you may or may not know, I'm the Features editor for the *Herald*."

I look at her blankly.

"The newspaper."

My face doesn't shift.

"The school newspaper. Of our school."

"Oh." I nod. "Yeah. Sure."

"I take it you're not a regular reader."

"There's a crossword puzzle, right? I think I've done the—"

"Anyway. I'm the editor of the Features section."

Features is another word for full-length films. Maybe we still have something in common. "Is that movies?"

"No, Entertainment covers movies. Features is more like human-interest pieces. Profiles of people or clubs. Highlighting stuff that's interesting but isn't going to get a big flashy news headline. You know?"

I don't know. I nod anyway.

"And I really like it. I mean, I definitely joined in freshman year just for my résumé, but it's my favorite thing I do now—and I do a lot, so that says something. I would totally edit Features again next year, but what I'd really, *really* like to be is . . ." She hesitates, like it's hard to say it out loud. "Editor in chief."

"Oh." From the faraway look in her eye, I guess this means something, to her. I can't relate. Nothing that happens in high school actually matters. "I hope you get it."

"Me too, but—" She shakes her head. "At the beginning of the year, I thought I was a shoo-in. It's only me and the Opinion editor and one of the News editors who are even interested, and I'm the best writer of all of us, by far. Not to mention, the current editor in chief basically acted like it was already mine. But then lately—" Lily makes a frustrated noise. "I don't know. It's like she's not sure anymore. Maybe it's because I don't really write stuff that's hard-hitting. I barely ever make the front page and the one time I did it was a total disaster, which wasn't even my *fault*—" She takes a breath. "I just know I have to do something. Something really big. And I think this piece could be it."

"What piece?"

30

Lily takes a moment, then says: "Do you know Luke Dobson?"

I shake my head.

"He's a senior, he goes to Presidio. Well—*went* to Presidio. Until recently."

"Dropped out?"

"Not exactly," she says. "He got arrested."

That makes my ears perk up. Presidio has over a thousand kids, so there are bound to be people who get transferred to the alternative school for having weed in their locker or something, but an actual arrest? That's rare.

"For what?" I ask. "Drugs?"

"Vandalism, as far as I can tell. He's still seventeen—that kind of stuff isn't public if you're a minor—but that's what he said, when I called, after I heard. I only got to talk to him for a minute, but that's what he said. That the charge was vandalism." She pauses. "And that he was framed."

Well, duh. Nobody's ever guilty in prison, are they?

"You know him," I say, and it isn't a question. "He's not just some kid who goes to Presidio. He's your friend."

"Family friend," she says. "Our moms formed this kids' playgroup together when we were little, them and a couple other families. So we all saw each other a lot—it's a pretty small club, kids of gay moms in East County—but we never hung out at school, or anything."

"So friends, but not best friends," I clarify. "Like we were."

She looks down at the bedspread. "Right."

"But you care about him enough to want to . . . what? Exonerate him?"

"I wanted to do this Features piece," she explains, "like a deep-dive, long-form investigation on kids getting caught in the juvenile justice system and all its failings, and obviously I wanted Luke's experience to be the centerpiece. A San Miguel kid, just like all of us, who because of one nonviolent crime has his whole life upended. Anyway, I pitched it to our editor in chief and she completely shot me down. Killed the story and let it bleed out on the floor."

It's not the kind of thing I'd read, but that doesn't mean it's bad. "Why?"

"Tess said the administration would never go for it, having some story about a Presidio student who turned out to be a criminal. But I know her, if she'd believed in the story, she would have fought for it." Lily looks down at her hands. "She just didn't believe I could pull it off."

"So how'd you convince her?"

Lily hesitates. "I didn't. Haven't. Yet."

A loose-cannon cop on the edge is a pretty standard trope, but I've never heard of a loose-cannon teenage journalist before.

"I wasn't ready to let it go," she continues, digging a battered blue notebook from her backpack. "So, I thought, maybe if I can show her this issue is bigger than my family friend, maybe I can convince her there's something really newsworthy here.

That's when I started looking at the overall crime stats. And they were . . . weird."

"Weird how?"

"San Miguel is a very consistent city—"

"That's about the only thing you can say for it."

"Crimewise. It's consistent." Lily flips through the notebook. "From year to year, the crime rate stays steady. Not that much better, not that much worse. Until . . . this year."

She holds the open page out to me. And without really understanding why I'm doing it, I move from the doorway, sit next to her on the bed. It's a giant graph—hand drawn—with lines in all colors. Some arching steeply upward, but some totally flat.

I point them out. "Those don't look like they're changed."

"And that's what's so weird! Violent crime—assaults, muggings, domestics—they've stayed the same, and pretty low. It's the nonviolent crimes that shot up." She points. "Burglaries up seventy percent, vandalism up almost a *hundred* percent, more car break-ins than we've had in three years combined—"

"There goes the neighborhood."

"Yeah, and people have definitely noticed. It's become a whole thing, for the mayor, all these suburban moms sending him petitions to 'Save Our Streets.'"

"Okay, so . . ." I shrug. "The city's going downhill. It happens, right?"

"Not that suddenly," she says, shaking her head. "Not for no apparent reason, and not in only *some* crimes, the kind that aren't violent."

"And the ones without witnesses."

"What?"

"None of those crimes have witnesses," I point out. "People don't get burgled when they're sitting in the living room watching TV."

Lily thinks about this. "We do have a witness, though."

"We, what *we*—"

"I finally convinced Luke to talk to me about the whole thing, and if he thinks he was framed, there must be something connecting him to this weird pattern."

"I don't see what any of this has to do with me."

"I tried going through the proper channels first," she says. "I put in a public records request for the arrests, but that can take months. I even called the police department directly, to see if they could give me some kind of explanation."

I could have told Lily from experience taking anything to the SMPD was only going to get her condescended to. At best. "I'm sure that was a dead end."

"I asked for the press liaison, but I guess the closest thing they have is the police chief's assistant, and she just gave me some line about the department's *commitment to the community*, then hung up before I could ask a second question."

"Yeah, they're useless and they're dicks about it, that's kind of their MO," I say, starting to feel impatient. "But it's not like I can help. I don't know anything about crime rates, or journalism, or any of this stuff."

"Maybe not." Lily folds her hands in her lap. "But you do know how to solve a mystery."

When I finally get it, my first thought is: Oh.

My second thought is: Hell no.

"Lily—"

"It might not seem like a mystery, not the ones you're used to, but I know it is. I know there's an explanation, but my last name isn't Woodward. Or Bernstein."

"Yeah, I know, it's Krupitsky-Sharma."

Lily closes her eyes. Shakes her head. Opens them again. "What I mean is—I'm a good writer, but I'm not a detective."

"You heard me tell Mia. Neither am I."

"You might have taken the sign down off your garage. But yeah, I *was* there, at lunch, with you and Mia, and that's how I know."

"Know what?"

"You're still solving mysteries," Lily says. "You're just doing them in your head."

For a moment, the only sound in the room is Asta, burrowing into his wood shavings.

"I know we haven't been . . . close." Lily picks at my bedspread. "In a long time."

That's the understatement of the century.

"And I know you might not totally trust me."

No, actually, *that's* the understatement of the century.

But . . . Lily came here knowing I might not even let her inside. She took a chance, and Lily isn't a risk-taker. She always had to be coaxed into it, usually by me.

That's its own kind of evidence: Lily wouldn't do any of this on impulse.

"I think there's something here. And I really think that together, we could solve it." She's looking up at me, half hopeful, half impatient. "What do you say?"

What *should* I say? You ditched me? You're only here because you think I'll be useful? You stood right behind Mia today and didn't say a single thing?

No, I'm not thinking about this logically. That's where detectives go wrong, if the story turns out to be a tragedy. They get too caught up in their feelings and stop seeing the facts.

Fact 1: The more I'm out of the house, the more Dad will get off my back with his whole "wasted potential" dramatics.

Fact 2: If Lily's wrong, and this is nothing more than a big clerical error and a juvenile delinquent with delusions of innocence, I've lost nothing but my time.

Fact 3: If Lily turns out to be right, and this is something big, I can solve it. And that would change everything.

If I figure this out, if I'm right and everybody knows it, it would mean I was right about other things, too. It would mean I was right to consider myself a detective—a *real* detective—even when I was ten. It would prove this was never just a game, like

Lily thought it was, or a phase, like Dad thought it was, or the start of a criminal record, like the police department thought it was. If I was right all along, that I really was born to do this, then Lily was wrong to abandon me, Dad was wrong to be disappointed in me, and everyone else was wrong about . . . well, all of me.

If I'm right, if I solve this, I can prove them all wrong.

"Okay," I tell Lily. "I'm in."

CHAPTER 4

ON THE RARE Mondays Dad takes a night off from Verde, you'd think he would want a break from worrying about the restaurant and we'd order takeout or something. But you'd be wrong. He likes to use these nights to try out new ideas, using me as a guinea pig.

You'd also think me sitting at the table, silently eating a cheese enchilada, would be impossible for Dad to criticize. You'd be wrong about that, too.

"You can't even taste it when you eat that fast," he complains.

I swallow a bite. "Yes, I can."

"Well, how does it taste?"

"Um. Good?"

"'Good' doesn't tell me a lot. What does it need?" He pushes forward the salt and pepper stand. "Does it need salt, does it need spice, is there too much lime?"

"I don't know."

He makes a sound in the back of his throat. "Could you think about it for more than a second?"

It's food. It tastes like food. I don't know how to be helpful. "More salt, I guess?"

He nods. "Okay. Good note. I'm thinking about adding it to the menu."

"You should. It's good."

"If you like it," Dad says, then hesitates. "I could show you how to make it. It isn't hard."

I take another one off the plate. "You're always going to make it better than I would, anyway."

His eyebrows knit together, like he's somehow *more* annoyed now. I don't get it. That was a compliment.

"So." Dad puts his fork down. "I've been talking with Mario— he's my general manager, you remember?—about where we might be able to fit you in."

"Fit me in where?"

"At the restaurant." And then before I can say anything, he's already launching into it. "I told you, you can't stay in that room every day, and if you didn't think I meant it—"

"I found something," I interrupt him. Which he doesn't like. But it does stop the lecture.

"You found something," he repeats.

"Something to do. That isn't in my room."

He looks skeptical. "And what is it?"

I hadn't thought this far. It's not like I can tell him I'm

39

investigating again. Not after how that all ended. But I have to say something, so I blurt out the first thing I think of:

"I joined the newspaper."

He looks even more skeptical. Which I understand, because I have also met me.

"The newspaper."

"Yeah."

"You. Joined the newspaper."

I wish he'd stop repeating everything. It makes me feel like he thinks I'm lying. And fine, I *am* lying, but only because he backed me into it, and that will be my defense strategy if I get caught.

"Lily asked me to." This is what you're supposed to do, if you're being interrogated by the police or the CIA or your dad, who knows you almost failed ninth-grade English and would never join a newspaper. You tell as much of the truth as you can, lying only about what's totally necessary.

"Lily?" Dad's eyebrows shoot up. "I didn't even think you still talked to her."

"Yeah, I didn't, until last Friday, when she came up to me and asked me to join. She's an editor. For . . . Features? Anyway, I guess they're super understaffed and kind of desperate and since you said I had to do something, I thought . . ." I shrug. "Why not, right?"

"Well. Okay." He sits back. "Sure. I bet that looks great on a college application."

"Yeah."

"No, you know, it's a great idea. Especially if you're doing it with Lily." He picks up his fork again. "She was always a good influence on you."

It takes me forever to find Lily the next day after school. It's not like I know her schedule, and I don't even have her number, so I can't text, either. I finally spot her in one of the locker bays.

"So, where are we going?" I ask her.

She frowns. "Going?"

"Yeah. To investigate."

"Oh," Lily says, turning away. "Well, we can't really do anything until the weekend."

"Why?" I ask, hurrying to catch up with her as she sets down the hallway at a rapid clip. "You said this was important."

"It is, but so is Late Night."

"Late Night?"

"Production week," she explains impatiently. "For the paper. All the editors stay late the whole week, so—"

"You're going to think this is funny," I cut in. "I actually told my dad I *joined* the paper."

She stops midstep. "You did what?"

"I had to give him some reason I wasn't going to be at home, while you and I are investigating, if we ever actually *start*—"

Lily gasps. "That's perfect!"

"I mean, I wouldn't say it's a perfect lie, but—"

Before I can finish the thought, Lily has snagged my coat

sleeve and is already dragging me down the hallway. "I spend all my time in the *Herald* office and if you're there, too, it'll be so much easier to work together."

It takes me a second to work out what she's already decided: I should join the newspaper. Not as a lie or a cover but *actually join*. It takes me another second to start panicking.

"Wait, Lily—"

"And you'd learn stuff, because it doesn't seem like you've got a clue about journalism or writing or anything that isn't detective movies, no offense."

"Yeah, some taken, actually—"

"This might be the smartest idea you've ever had."

"I've had good ideas before."

She counts off on her fingers as we walk down the hall. "Trying to make ginger ale out of seltzer water and powdered ginger from your dad's spice rack."

"It didn't taste that bad."

"Sprayed PAM all over my mom's kitchen floor so you and I could go 'indoor ice-skating.'"

"If you're going to try and tell me you didn't have fun, you are a *liar*."

"The time in fifth-grade math when Ms. Miller was super mad at everyone, asked us when exactly we'd all stopped listening to her, and *you* told her: 'Around October.'"

I throw my arms up. "It was true!"

"But not smart." Lily stops us in front of two large double

doors. The sign on the wall reads: "H102: Newspaper/Yearbook."
"Here we are."

She pushes open the door and ushers me through.

If my life were a noir, the only way to capture the chaos we walk into would be one long, continuous pan shot. Like:

INT. *HERALD* ROOM—DAY

A large, busy classroom, bursting with the
noise of computer keys clacking, the voices of
a dozen kids talking and laughing and arguing,
someone's phone going off somewhere, and the
whir of an ancient printer spitting out pages
by the wall.

A bank of desktop computers sits against one far
wall, while a sagging beige couch that looks like
it was pulled from the municipal dump occupies
the other, with a collection of six big wooden
tables in the middle. The *HERALD* STAFF (various,
teens) sit mostly in pairs, working around
laptops. And at the table in the center—

CLOSE ON: A dark-haired GIRL with holes in the
knees of her jeans and a T-shirt with the UCSD
triton in the center stands over a set of

printouts, neatly lined up, so she can see them all at once.

LILY

(V.O., calling out)

Hey, Tess!

STILL ON: the GIRL—long-limbed, clear-eyed, and not that it matters but also very pretty—looks up from the table and across the room.

LILY waves her over. GIDEON wonders why his palms are suddenly sweating.

When the girl reaches us, she looks me up and down, then she sticks out her hand and says, "Hi. I'm Tess Espinoza."

For a half second, I can't remember why I know that name. Then I do. And before I can stop myself, I look down at her other hand, the one she didn't offer. Her left hand, with a woven bracelet around the wrist, and empty air where her index and middle fingers would be.

"Were you hoping for the Tess Espinoza with ten fingers?" she asks lightly.

My head jerks up, and I can feel all the blood rush to my face. That was so stupid. I'm so stupid. Why did I *look*?

"I'm sorry," I say, rushing the words out as fast as I can. "I didn't mean to—"

44

"It happens. What's your name?"

"Seriously," I say, "I'm so sorry."

"That's a very unusual name," Tess deadpans.

I swallow. "Gideon. My name is Gideon."

"Nice to meet you, Gideon." She flicks her eyes to Lily. "And why am I meeting you?"

"We need a new copy editor, right?" Lily asks.

"Eternally."

Lily pushes me forward an inch. "I thought he could take the test."

I swivel around to stare at her. "What?"

"Have you ever edited something before?" Tess asks.

I shake my head.

"Do you like English class?"

I shake my head again.

Tess sighs deeply. "Do you know what a copy editor *is*?"

I think it's obvious from the way I look at her that I don't. She throws up her hands. "Lily, come on."

"A copy editor looks for problems," Lily tells me. "Typos. Tense switches. If someone's name is spelled with two *r*'s in the first paragraph but then one *r* in the second. They *detect* things that aren't *right*." She pauses. "Get it?"

I get it. Lily doesn't just want me close by—she thinks I might actually be good at this.

I look back to Tess. "I'll take the test. If that's okay with you."

"Your funeral." She turns on her heel and heads toward the back of the room.

Once she's out of earshot, I drop my voice and say to Lily: "You should have told me it was Tess Espinoza."

"She's the only Tess at this school," Lily hisses back.

I hadn't even realized she *went* to my school. I think she's a year ahead of me and Lily, and I know she didn't go to our elementary school, because that's when it happened. It was all any of our parents talked about that whole summer, how a little girl got hold of a firecracker at a Fourth of July party and it blew up in her hand. I don't know how many times Dad reminded me of the story over the years, how careful you had to be with explosive things.

I saw a picture of her in the newspaper once—a real one, not the *Herald*—a few years ago. She was at the beach, with wet hair and a surfboard. I can't remember the headline.

Tess returns with two stapled sheets of paper and slaps them down on the table. "I'll be back in five minutes." She points to Lily but talks to me. "If she tries to help you—"

"I wouldn't let her," I promise.

"Good instinct." Tess smiles conspiratorially. "She's the worst speller on the staff."

I laugh. Lily glares at me. I concentrate on the test.

The instructions are simple: *Identify all errors.* Or as Lily said: *Detect what's wrong.*

The typos are easier to spot than I thought they'd be—dessert when it should be desert, manger instead of manager, lose instead

46

of loose. I don't know a lot about grammar or baseball, but I do know you need an apostrophe after the *s* when talking about the Padres' starting lineup. And I notice tons of little things—numbers spelled out in one paragraph but left as numerals in another. A quote that doesn't seem to belong to anyone. An acronym with no explanation for what it means.

When I'm done, Tess scores it, her eyes flicking back and forth between my test in one hand, the answer key in the other.

"You missed every single comma splice," she says. I don't argue, mostly because I have no idea what a comma splice is. "But whatever, that's teachable."

"Sounds like he's in," Lily says, and when Tess nods, Lily grins and punches me in the shoulder.

"Ow, Lily, God." Then I look to Tess. "Really?"

"Yeah, congrats," she says, "you just narrowly beat out the other candidate: absolutely nobody."

"That's a very unusual name," I say.

Then we just look at each other for a while, both sort of smiling, until Lily steers me away by the elbow. "Why don't I introduce you to everyone?"

I'm annoyed at her and have no idea why. "Okay."

"Maya and Araceli are the News editors." She points out two girls huddled around the same computer, heatedly debating something on the screen. Next to them is a thin guy with glasses and a serious look on his face. "And Jason is in charge of the Opinion section."

47

It's a blur of names and faces and sections as she introduces me to everyone. I had no idea a newspaper this short could need so many people. Finally, she walks me over to the far corner and the old, extremely gross couch. Two guys are sitting on it, arguing over something on their shared computer. One of them is blond and tall and I don't recognize him, but the other—short, stocky, wearing a band T-shirt with THE RABID PANDAS on it—I've had classes with before. Ryan.

"Hey," Lily cuts in. "Guys, this is Gideon, he's the new copy editor."

"What's up?" says the blond one.

"Welcome to hell," Ryan says.

"Stop," Lily says.

"We do the Entertainment section," Ryan says. "That's Noah, and I'm Ryan."

"Yeah, I know," I say, "we have a class together. Last year we had two."

I can feel Lily cringe beside me. That probably wasn't the right way to say it.

Ryan seems unfazed. "My bad, dude. Don't know why I didn't recognize you."

The answer is I sit in the back of every class and never talk, but Noah jumps in with an alternate theory. "Probably because you're always high."

"Slander," Ryan says. "Vicious slander." He looks back up at me. "Wait, which class?"

"Chemistry."

"Shit," he says. "I am always high in chemistry."

"And then Will does Sports, but I don't see him." Lily looks around. "He must be moving his car."

"Shouldn't there be like . . . an adult here?" I ask.

"We have a staff adviser. Ms. Flueger."

"So where is she?"

Tess sidles up alongside us. "If I had to guess, having sex with her husband in the back room of his Honda dealership."

"Tess," Lily groans. "Don't say that, you're going to scare him."

"Why would that scare him? He's not the one trying to sixty-nine on a bed of defective car keys."

"Ugh," Lily says.

"I'm not scared," I say. And I'm not. That isn't the right word for it at all.

"Ms. Flueger and her husband are trying to have a baby," Lily explains.

"Yeah, so, whenever she's ovulating, she finds some 'errand' to run, disappears for the whole afternoon." Tess, reading the question on my face, adds: "She left her Google Calendar up one day. Ryan took screenshots."

Noah walks past, calling over his shoulder to Tess and Lily: "Hey, my mom's here with the food."

Tess checks her phone. "Already? It's so early."

"I don't know, she's got other shit to do today."

"I'll help bring it in," Lily offers, and goes off with him, leaving me and Tess alone in the center of the room.

"So what do you think?" she asks. "Maybe you'll stick around longer than our last copy editor. Or last . . . several."

"What's the record?"

"Longest?" She thinks about it. "Three months."

"I can beat that."

Dad's always saying my mouth moves faster than my judgment, and I should give it a chance to catch up, occasionally. This has to be one of those times, because why would I say that to her? No way I'm sticking around longer than three months. This whole thing is just a cover. But for some reason . . . I feel like I mean it.

She brushes hair out of her eyes with her hand—her right hand, the one I *didn't* stare at—and I'm seized with shame all over again.

"I just wanted to—" When Tess looks at me, the embarrassment only gets worse. "Um. I shouldn't have stared that way. Before."

She shrugs. "Like I said, it happens."

"I'm sorry, though."

"You mentioned," she says. "Look, I'm not planning to dwell on it. And neither should you, or this is going to be a really awkward dinner."

"Dinner?"

"Yeah, and if you want any fried rice, you're going to have

50

to shoulder-check Ryan for it." She starts to walk away. "Fair warning."

There's the sound of a door being kicked open, and then Lily and Noah are at the front of the room, arms filled with paper grocery bags. They set them down on the center table, and everyone else rushes to unpack the cartons of takeout food and six-packs of soda.

Huh. Lily did say this was a "late night" for the paper. I don't know how long they're staying, but it must be late enough to need dinner. And they're eating it together.

I could leave, if I wanted to. Nobody would notice, except Lily, and this whole thing was so unexpected I don't think she'd hold it against me. I *should* leave. If you asked me to list the things that made me most uncomfortable, numbers two through four would be hanging out with people I don't know, hanging out with people I *do* know, and eating food I didn't pick myself.

Number one would be bears. That's not important.

I think about how awkward it would be, to eat with all these people I've just met, whose names I can barely remember, who are voluntarily giving up their night for a school newspaper I've never even read.

I think about the dinner I'd have at home. In my room, with a movie on. Alone.

I could go. But I don't. I walk over and sit down at the table.

CHAPTER 5

IF MY LIFE were a noir, we'd be conducting this interview in some grim, gray prison visitation room. In the script, it would read like:

```
INT. VISITATION ROOM—DAY

GIDEON and LILY sit on one side of the metal
grate separating them from LUKE DOBSON, wearing
the prototypical black-and-white-striped uniform
and probably smoking a cigarette, because they
let people smoke anywhere in the 1940s, even
while giving birth.
```

But this isn't a noir, so the scene looks more like:

INT. LUKE'S BEDROOM—DAY

GIDEON and LILY stand on the one patch of carpet
that isn't occupied by dirty clothes and half-
used cans of spray paint. Across from them is
LUKE DOBSON, wearing a hoodie and pajama pants
even though it's 4:00 PM, and smoking a joint
because why not, I guess.

And as it turns out, he never ended up going to juvie.

"It's called like . . . a diversion program?" he tells us. "Where
if I don't fuck up for the next year everything basically goes
away."

"Just like that?" I ask.

"No, I mean, I had to allocute, which is just saying to the
court yeah I did it, and instead of going back to Presidio I have
to finish up at the alternative school and do this bullshit art
therapy program where I *learn to use my creativity productively.*"

He mimes blowing his brains out, then takes another hit.

"But no drug testing, I guess?" Lily wrinkles her nose.

"Blessedly . . ." Luke exhales. "No."

I'm starting to regret agreeing to this. Luke doesn't seem like
the kind of guy you'd build a case around. Luke doesn't seem
like the kind of guy you'd trust to feed your goldfish.

"So I don't really get why you want me to go over the whole

story again," Luke says to Lily. "In a year, it's going to be like it never happened."

"I think it's part of a bigger picture," she explains. "Especially since . . . you told me you were framed."

"Yeah." He runs his hand through his hair. "That's maybe not totally accurate."

"Shocker," I say. Lily shoots me a look.

"I meant more like I was put up to it. You know?"

And then even Lily looks skeptical. "Someone told you to vandalize a store?"

"Someone *paid* me to *tag* it," he says. "You make it sound so criminal."

"It was," I remind him. Lily elbows me.

"All I knew is my friend said he had a job for me, easy money, not going to be a problem with the cops."

"Well," I say. "Obviously *that* was wrong."

Lily glares at me. Luke just stares.

Then he asks: "Who are you, again?"

"Gideon."

"Green," Lily rushes to add. "Gideon Green—he went to Emerson Elementary, too. Do you remember in fifth grade—you would have been in sixth—there was a kid who helped the cops catch a thief?"

Luke doesn't seem impressed. "Maybe."

"It was on the news," Lily says, because obviously eleven-year-old Luke was a huge fan of local TV. "Gideon saw someone

54

coming out of the back door of his neighbor's house one afternoon and he knew it seemed suspicious."

"I didn't *know,*" I correct her. "Not for sure."

"So he walks right up to this guy and asks who he is, and the guy says he's the neighbor's son. But Gideon knew they didn't have a son, so he called the cops—"

I groan. "That's not how it happened at all!"

"Fine, then you tell it," she says.

It's been years since I've told this story to anyone. But I remember every moment.

"The guy said he was Mr. and Mrs. Cabot's son. And I didn't know if they had a son either way, but then I noticed his eyes."

Luke frowns. "His eyes?"

"They were brown. And Mr. and Mrs. Cabot have blue eyes, so it wasn't biologically possible for him to be their biological son."

"So he was adopted," Luke says with a shrug.

"Possible, but statistically unlikely. Still possible, though, so I said to him, 'Oh, the one who lives in Florida?' and he kind of blinked at me for a second before saying, yeah, that was him. That's when I knew he was lying. And that's when I noticed he was wearing a really heavy letterman jacket with really big pockets even though it was really hot."

"So what, you tackled him?" Luke asks, looking me up and down with an insulting but accurate amount of skepticism.

"No. I went back to my house like I didn't care at all, watched him leave, and then called the cops."

"Who thought it was a prank call," Lily adds.

"Didn't take me seriously at all," I agree. "So I just told them they were going to get a report about something—something small, that could fit in a pocket, but something valuable—stolen from that house. And when they did, the culprit was going to be someone who used to play number seventeen on the Presidio football team, drives a red truck, and probably works for the home security company the Cabots hired a couple months before, because I was in the front yard the whole time and the alarm never went off."

Lily smiles. Luke just stares.

"Anyway. Mrs. Cabot found some jewelry missing, the cops got the guy in two hours flat, and I got . . ." I shrug. "Credit."

"So you can see why I'd bring him along," Lily says to Luke. "Even if this isn't ringing a bell—"

"Wait." Luke leans one hand on his desk and points at me with the other. "Weren't you the kid who got stuck on the roof of the high school?"

Of course that's what he remembers. Not any of my victories, but my one horrible, humiliating failure.

"I wasn't stuck on the roof," I say. "I'm not a *cat*."

Lily scrambles to redirect the conversation. "You were talking about your friend," she reminds Luke. "Who gave you the job. Which friend? Someone from Presidio?"

"No, he's older. His name's Jackel. He's a good dude."

56

"What's his real name?"

"Don't know. He just goes by Jackel."

"Do you have a picture of you guys together?" Lily asks. "Or just him?"

"Oh, sure." Luke pulls out his phone, types for a while, then hands it over to Lily.

It's a profile page for some social media thing I don't have. The handle is @thejackel_sd.

The pictures stop abruptly, which tracks with the arrest date in the article, but there are plenty before that, mostly of him on his motorcycle, or him and his buddies in a bar, or ads that are clearly for his personal drug-dealing service.

I especially like the photos you can tell were all taken like half an hour apart.

Jackel pounding shots.

Jackel flipping off a bouncer.

Jackel drunk driving a Vons shopping cart through the produce section.

While I'm scrolling, Lily's flipping through her folder. She emerges, triumphant, with a printout of a news article. She holds it up for Luke, pointing out the mug shot in the center.

"Is that him?"

Luke's eyebrows shoot up. "Yeah."

"John Ellington," Lily reads off the page, then hands it to me. "Jack-El. Cute."

I skim the article, picking through for the most important

parts. *John Ellington, 23* and *petty larceny* and *recent string of night-time car break-ins* and *neighborhood families terrorized*, which seems kind of dramatic for getting sunglasses stolen out of your Volvo, but whatever.

"Wait. He got picked up too?" Luke asks.

"Yeah." Lily closes the folder. "You didn't know?"

"I didn't give him up, the whole time. Even during allocution, when you're supposed to lay it all out or they could arrest you all over again. And now I figured it was safer if I didn't call or text him or anything. Safer for *him*."

Luke might not be the sharpest tool in the shed, but there's something to be said for loyalty.

"So Jackel brought you this job," Lily says. "Did he say who it was coming from?"

Luke shakes his head. "Probably thought it was better I didn't know."

"I just don't understand. . . . Why would someone *want* you to graffiti a building?"

"He said it was an insurance thing. If the place was trashed, the owner or landlord or somebody could write it off their taxes, I don't know."

"So that's all?" I press him. "You tagged the front door and then bailed?"

He looks uncomfortable. "And kicked in a couple windows. What was the problem? They asked me to."

"Weren't you worried you'd get caught?" Lily asks.

58

"Jackel said he'd done a few of these jobs already. Nothing had happened to him."

Yeah, but he did car break-ins. I wonder if Luke knew that, or even asked. Insurance scam is one way that could play, I guess—if people left valuable stuff in their cars on purpose—but it's not the only way.

I put the article down. "And you didn't wonder if he was telling you the truth?"

"He's my friend."

"It's amazing how easily friends can screw you over."

Beside me, Lily stiffens but recovers fast.

"Who was the arresting officer?" she asks. "Do you remember?"

Luke shrugs. "Some big blond dude. Harris, or something."

"No, wait." I stop him. "Go back to the beginning and take us through the whole night. Chronologically."

"It doesn't have to be chronological," Lily tells Luke.

"Yes, it does," I say.

"I'm perfectly capable of leading an interview," Lily snaps at me.

I throw up my hands. "Then why am I here?"

"Fine." Lily gestures at Luke. "Chronologically, then."

Luke takes us through everything, from meeting Jackel at some dive bar to get the details on when and where the job needed to be done—"I told him Thursday was tough, could it be Friday, and he said no, it *had* to be Thursday night"—to planning the artwork—"he said go for it, the guy didn't care what it looked like, I guess"—and finally, getting only halfway through the piece before a squad car showed up, lights blaring, and Luke "with a can of red paint in my hand. Literally red-handed, like some kind of fucking metaphor."

"Isn't that a simile?" I ask.

"Oh my God," Lily says, "it is an *idiom*."

"And then they cuffed me and took me down to the station and processed me and it was the longest night of my entire stupid life. Especially because the cop was such a dick."

"'Harris, or something,'" I say, remembering. "Big blond dude."

"Yeah, and kind of unstable, too."

"Unstable?" Lily repeats. "How do you mean?"

"Like when they first got the cuffs on me, he was smiling and joking around with his partner and basically being a cocky asshole about it all. But then when he got my ID out of my pocket, he went really still. He asked me how old I was, and I told him, and he asked me *again*—like I was going to give him a different answer! And after that, he just seemed pissed."

"Because you were a minor," Lily says.

"And he wasn't expecting you to be," I add.

"Yeah, I guess it's more work for them if you're not eighteen. They have to let you talk to a lawyer before they can start questioning you, and stuff like that. But it seemed kind of over-the-top, how mad he was about it."

Bad reactions—even just weird reactions—say a lot. Either it's in this guy's nature to fly off the handle for nothing . . . or he had some reason to lose his shit. Something we don't know yet.

I lean forward. "Did anything else feel weird?"

"I mean," he says, "I got arrested, dude. That was pretty fucking weird."

"Anything else that felt off, the way the cop being so mad felt. When you were thinking back on it, later, anything else that didn't seem right."

Luke stares at the carpet and is very still for a moment. Then he looks up at me. "The timing was perfect."

"Perfect," Lily repeats.

"Not for *me*. For them. I'd already kicked in the windows, I'd just finished the outline, I had the paint *in my hands*, and there they were, at the exact right moment. Seriously, what are the odds? It was almost like . . ." He trails off, as if it's too unbelievable to say.

"Almost like . . . ," I prompt him.

"It was almost like," Luke says, "they knew I was going to be there."

CHAPTER 6

THE *HERALD* PUBLISHES an issue every other Friday, so the schedule goes in two-week blocks. The first week is devoted to assigning stories to reporters and photographers, but I don't have to be there for that. The second week—after all the stories have been turned in and the editors have planned out their sections for the issue—is different. Monday through Thursday afternoons are Late Nights, when the whole editorial staff stays after school and through dinner to lay out their sections digitally and put together the paper as a whole.

There's so much that goes into creating a sixteen-page paper that I can barely keep it straight—text wrapping and gray boxes and pull quotes—but luckily, I don't have to. All I have to do is go through each laid-out, printed page and look for everything that's wrong.

Tess gave me what she called a style guide, and I read through it in one night. It's not like it was fascinating or anything—just a long list of rules for what should be capitalized and what shouldn't, which numbers should be written out and which ones left as numerals, that kind of thing—but I'd sort of forgotten what it was like to use my brain.

After every report card, Dad gives the same lecture about me "not living up to my potential" and "barely making an effort." And maybe he's right, but it seemed so pointless in class. Like, I *could* memorize the number of electrons in a sodium molecule, I'm *capable* of learning the causes of the Revolutionary War, but why would I, except to spit it back out on a test?

This feels different. Like a job. I've missed having a job.

There are some things about the *Herald* that take getting used to. They've all spent hours and hours together in this room, so when they all talk, it's loud and overlapping and 80 percent inside jokes. It takes two weeks before I finally ask Tess what's up with the giant list taped to the far wall, by the window.

"Oh, it's our rules," she says, smoothing down a curled-up corner. "I started a running list last May, when I became editor in chief."

The first few rules are normal enough, but then—

#4) THE COUCH MAY NOT BE USED
FOR ONE-NIGHT STANDS.

I throw a glance at the couch. "Gross."

"Right?" Tess says. "It's basically got springs poking out."

Ryan sidles up alongside us. "You know what else was poking out—"

Tess claps her hand over his mouth. "No."

"I'm guessing that one was written for a specific person?" I ask.

Ryan peels Tess's hand away. "All of them are. That one was because of Max."

"The Entertainment editor last year," Tess explains.

"He's gone now," Noah says, very seriously, from a table nearby. "Gone like the unicorns."

"He went to college," Tess says. "He didn't go extinct."

"Neither did unicorns."

Another thing that's taken getting used to is the dinners we have on Late Nights. I didn't grow up with siblings or cousins or really anyone but Dad, so it's a new experience to eat surrounded by people shouting over each other and fighting over the garlic bread Jason's mom made—which, to be fair, is worth fighting over.

Tonight's dinner is pizza and Caesar salad, which is fine with me. The pizza, anyway. I don't like Caesar dressing. Or any dressing. It makes everything feel so slimy. But I figure, more for everyone else who does like it.

So when Lily passes me the salad bowl, I hold it right out to Ryan. But he doesn't take it.

"You don't want any?"

"No."

"Are you sure? There's enough."

"Oh, um." I can feel my face getting hot, because I know this is weird. "I don't like dressing on my salad."

"Wait, so you eat lettuce . . . plain?" Ryan asks.

Tess gestures at the salad bowl. "Take a little. It's good for you. What would your mom say?"

"Hey, Tess," Lily jumps in, but the panicked look she throws is to me. Not Tess. "Did you ever get in touch with the owner of that art gallery? For the feature I pitched?"

"Yeah." The second Tess moves her eyes from me to Lily, I practically shove the salad bowl into Ryan's hands. "A few San Miguel people are in the student show. Becca Carroll, some sophomore whose name I got. And—" She clears her throat. "Ethan Kincaid."

"His art is so weird," Noah says.

"It's abstract," Tess says.

"Sculptures with no heads and like, screaming faces in the torsos and everything's covered in glitter. It's weird."

"Did he ever make you weird art?" Ryan asks Tess.

She serves herself two slices of pepperoni. "We actually don't need to talk about my ex-boyfriend this much—"

Noah grins. "Cool, yeah, let's talk about Clara Fleck instead."

"Let's say neither of my exes are appropriate dinner table conversation."

I know Clara and Ethan—I know who they are, anyway. Clara's in my grade and she's a super-athlete, and Ethan is a senior, and I know his name because the school's always putting his art up in the student gallery.

Tess dates girls, and she also dates guys. She dates outgoing basketball captains and quiet, sensitive painters, and that's evidence she doesn't have a type.

I don't mean evidence. It isn't evidence. It would have to matter in some way to be evidence, but it doesn't, because there's no reason for me to care who she dates or why. It's not evidence. They're just facts. Completely, entirely irrelevant-to-me facts.

"Do you want to talk about the paper?" Tess looks from Noah to Ryan. "Or just my nonexistent love life?"

"Nonexistent" would be evidence she's currently single, if I cared at all whether she was single, *which I do not.*

"Love life," Ryan decides.

"Yeah, definitely love life," Noah agrees.

"Executive decision, let's talk about the front page."

Tess pushes some plates away from the center of the table and lays a full-sized mock-up page in front of everyone.

"This is it so far." She points to Araceli first. "We have the headliner about the warehouse fire downtown, then we have the boys' basketball team actually winning for once. . . ." She uncaps a pen and squares off a smallish area that's still white. "And some leftover dead space. Who has something?"

"We could tease my feature about prom," Lily suggests.

Tess doesn't even look up. "And I could end up with a giant hole if you pull that piece."

66

Lily's mouth gets tight, but she doesn't say anything. Just wordlessly gathers the empty soda bottles from the table.

Tess looks to Noah and Ryan. "Entertainment?"

"We're thin this week," Ryan says.

She doesn't budge. "How long is your review of the One-Acts festival?"

"Maybe six hundred?"

"And it's a decently positive review?"

"Uh—"

"I'm not having a repeat of the *Antigone* thing, Noah. Is Laurie Drew going to corner me by my gym locker and cry about how mean you were?"

Noah looks guilty but says: "Laurie wasn't in this one."

From the recycling cans in the front door, and hidden from everyone else by the hallway wall, Lily beckons me over. I get up, figuring she either wants help with the bottles or to complain about Tess shooting down her idea. It does seem like Tess is harder on her than everyone else.

"What's up?" I ask Lily.

"Not so loud," she hisses, which gives me all the answer I need: this is about the investigation, and she doesn't want anyone— especially Tess—hearing it. "Are you free Friday afternoon?"

"I'm always free. Why?"

"There's this place I want us to check out. A bar."

"Wow," I say. "Have I driven you to drink this fast?"

She rolls her eyes. "This *quickly*."

"Is that a yes?"

"No." She digs her phone out of her pocket. "I was going through John's—Jackel's—social media and he tagged himself at this specific dive bar a bunch of times. Not only that, but he tagged himself *with* another person on my list of arrests."

"Drug dealer? Another graffiti artist?"

"Arsonist, actually."

Arson. We're moving up in the world. Can't wait to meet our first murderer.

"His name's William Potter," she continues, "though he sometimes goes by Pyro, which is just *breath*takingly unimaginative, but—"

"But you think there's a link to the bar." Then I remember something else. "Didn't Luke meet up with Jackel at a bar?"

She points at me. "Bingo. I confirmed with Luke, it was this bar. Doc Holliday's." Then she holds out her phone, so I can see what's on the screen: a bad-quality promotional shot of what looks like a generically crappy dive bar: pool table, dartboard, and dented jukebox included.

"Total rip-off," I say. "How can you call it Doc Holliday's and not have a player piano or swinging saloon doors?"

She stares at me. "What are you talking about?"

Westerns. Famous gunfights. "Not important."

Lily puts the lid on the recycling can. "We'll discuss it more tomorrow. Tess is going to notice we're gone."

"Maybe you should tell her already," I suggest. "Then you

wouldn't have to be so nervous all the time."

"It's better this way," Lily says with a firm shake of her head. "Trust me."

Is it better? I think as we walk back to our seats at the table. Or is it just easier?

When we get back to the table, the front page still hasn't been settled.

"If you take half the article, then we'll have a hole on page twelve," Ryan protests.

Tess throws up her hands. "So I'll give you an ad!"

"Which ad?"

"Hardy's Hardware, First National Bank, or the yearbook. Take your pick."

"Fine," Noah says. "Yearbook."

When dinner is over, everyone goes back to their computers and I go back to my spot at the center table and my stack of to-be-edited pages. I don't hear Tess come up alongside me until she says:

"What are you working on now?"

"Uh—" I look up at her, then back down at the page, as if I've forgotten what I was reading two seconds ago. Which I actually have. "News. Something about education bonds and school funding."

"Sounds fascinating."

"It's not."

"Yeah, no, I know." Tess sighs. "Poor Araceli. She sits through every city council meeting. We should give her combat pay."

"Wouldn't she need to be paid at all, first?"

"True." Tess pauses. "You need a comma there." She points to one of the paragraphs, but I can't tell which.

"Where?"

Tess places one hand on the table, an inch from my arm. Then she leans across my shoulder and points to the spot. "There." A stray lock of her hair escapes her ponytail and brushes against my forehead. Just for a second. It smells like sea salt.

Suddenly, from the other side of the table, Noah slaps down a printout. Both Tess and I jump. "This one's ready for you, Gideon."

"Okay," I say, and my voice is higher than it should be. Which is weird. Tess straightens up, adjusting the collar of her shirt. Which is weird, too. It looked fine before. "I'll, um. Thanks."

I reach across the table and pick up Noah's new page, which is bound to be more interesting. Watching water evaporate would be more interesting than an article about school funding. But then something catches my eye.

"Wow." I look more closely. "That's . . . a choice."

Tess was a few steps away but now turns back. "What? The school board article?"

"No, this ad campaign."

"Huh?"

"For the yearbook." I hold up the printout and show her the ad.

HEY MAN,
YOU WANNA BUY A YEARBOOK?

*Only 70 dollars, c'mon, I know everything's always spelled
wrong but we are so screwed, dude, we are in so much debt. I've
got loan sharks on my ass 24/7 and if I don't pay up by the
end of the week Vinnie's going to break my goddamn kneecaps.
I'm begging you, man, I've got three kids at home and if I can't
pay—oh God. Vinnie's on the phone, oh my God—*

BUY A YEARBOOK OR THEY'LL BREAK
HIS KNEECAPS.

Tess snatches the page out of my hand and whirls around.
"Ryan!"

He ducks behind one of the desktops. "It was Noah's idea."

"Way to throw me under the bus, dude!" Noah says.

"How about I run you both over with the bus?" Tess holds
up the paper. "This is not the copy I gave you!"

"It has drama," Ryan says.

"Pathos," Noah says.

"Loan sharks," I add.

Tess glares at all three of us, in turn. Then she walks to the
board, uncaps a pen, and adds to her list of rules:

#24) AD COPY MAY NOT INCLUDE LOAN SHARKS.

CHAPTER 7

"CAN YOU TURN on the air?"

Lily purses her lips and keeps both hands on the steering wheel. "I told you not to wear that."

"What, clothes?" I say, crossing my arms over my trench coat.

"Not clothes. A costume."

"It's just a coat."

"It's a trench coat and it's eighty degrees outside, which is why you're hot."

"That's what the hat is for. Shade."

Lily pinches the bridge of her nose. "The hat is—somehow—worse."

I touch the felt fedora gently. As if it could hear her insult. "It's cool."

"Maybe if you lived in 1922."

"It's not the right brim shape for the twenties."

"I just don't understand why you couldn't put on normal clothing."

I think my clothing is normal. It's what I see in my closet every day. It's literally my norm. How does normal get decided, anyway? Is there a convention? Do they take a parliamentary vote in an all-beige conference room?

"I don't know." I look out the window. "I like what I like."

Lily sighs. Reaches over. Cranks the AC.

"I did some research on the bar itself," she says. "Just to get a feel for what we're stepping into."

"And?"

"And . . ." She shakes her head. "Mostly, I don't know how it's still open."

"What, are there knife fights in the parking lot?"

"I'm surprised it's still open because it's had like fifteen violations in the last year." She takes one hand off the steering wheel to count on her fingers. "Mice in the kitchen, serving alcohol to minors, a *ton* of structural issues—"

Forget structural issues, the fines from the food safety stuff alone would be astronomical. I think Dad is more scared of health inspectors than death itself.

She pulls into a mostly empty parking lot off the side of the highway and parks.

I lean over the dashboard. "Is that it?"

If my life were a noir, we'd be doing this at night. The

darkness and shadows would give the scene atmosphere. But my life is not a noir, so it's four p.m. and the Southern California sun is shining right on the squat, square building in front of us, its white paint chipping and the neon beer signs in the window flickering like defective Christmas lights.

"It pretty much has to be," Lily says. "With the sign."

Her eyesight's better than mine, when she's actually got her glasses on. If I squint, I can just make out the banner that says "Doc Holliday's" and a homicidal-looking cartoon cowboy dangling by one hand from the loop of the *y*.

We climb out of the car, but the closer we get to Doc Holliday's front door, the less sure I feel about this. The parking lot is strewn with beer bottles and cigarettes, all the motorcycles parked outside are intimidating, and the sounds coming from inside don't exactly scream church social, either. I'm not nine anymore, and this isn't "The Case of the Lost Teddy Bear." This is a real bar and we're really not supposed to be here.

"Lily."

"Yeah?"

"I—" But it's not like I'm going to cop to chickening out, so I say: "I feel like I should tell you Doc Holliday gets shot."

"What?"

"In the movies. And I think also in real life, Doc Holliday gets shot in the Gunfight at the O.K. Corral."

"Okay," she says. "No clue what that means."

"It means we should be prepared for the worst."

"It'll be fine," she says, but she can't hide her voice wavering. "We're just going to a"—she looks up at the sign—"bar and grill. It's practically a restaurant."

I gesture around at the trash-strewn parking lot. "It's practically a meth lab."

She squares her shoulders and faces the door. "Come on."

Lily's self-confidence lasts for all of the two seconds it takes us to step inside and look around.

If my life were a noir, there would be a long panning shot here, so the audience could see everything all at once. Like:

INT. DOC HOLLIDAY'S—DAY

A sliver of sun comes in through the still-swinging door as GIDEON and LILY walk inside. The light inside is red and artificial, illuminating the square-shaped bar, with stools around it. Smaller tables are jammed together, crowded with patrons even though 4:00 PM is kind of early to be drinking, right?

A man bangs on the jukebox in the corner, which must have eaten his quarter, or maybe he just has anger issues. The whole scene is chaotic and loud.

GIDEON and LILY realize they are FUCKED.

Lily's eyes dart around, maybe trying to pick out the best person to interview among the following inhabitants:

—A man in a leather vest who must have just lost a round of pool, judging by the one half of a broken pool cue on the table and the other half still in his hand.

—A lady casually brushing shards of glass onto the floor.

—A dog. An actual dog licking what I hope to God is barbecue sauce off one of the walls.

"See anybody you recognize?" I ask her.

"No."

As much as I hate high school, at least I know how to be more or less invisible there. Detectives are supposed to be inconspicuous. Blend in. But you can't be inconspicuous in a bar when you're sixteen, and you can't blend in with bikers when you're in a trench coat, so now I don't know what to do.

I only know what would happen in a noir, because it's the same each time: the detective bellies up to the bar like he's spent his whole life standing there—which he might actually have—orders something stiff, and then drinks it like it's water. It's simple. It's easy.

So I should know what to do. Yeah. I definitely know what to do.

"Wait," Lily whispers, "where are you—"

But I'm already walking over to the bar, racking my brain for the drink names I can remember from movies—*Manhattan, Bronx, Gibson, Gimlet—Giblet? No. Gimlet.*

But when the bartender turns to look at me, my brain somehow panics and overcommits at the same time. Which is why I lean my arm on the wooden bar, tilt my hat up, and say the first line I think of:

"Double bourbon and leave the bottle."

"You've got to be fucking kidding me," the bartender says.

Whatever. It worked in *Kiss Me Deadly.*

"No, no, we aren't—" Lily, now at my shoulder, scrambles to cut in. "He's not—"

"What are you," the bartender demands, "kiddie snitches?"

We stare back at him blankly, until he elaborates.

"Sometimes they'll send these little kindergarten cops into bars, try to see if they can get served. They tell them to order, but"—he pours something brown into a shot glass and sets it on the bar, just out of my reach—"they're not allowed to actually drink."

I lean slowly over the bar. Pick up the glass. And—like I've seen in movies—down it in one gulp.

My first thought is: I can't believe I did that.

My second thought is: I have made a huge mistake.

While I cough and splutter and try not to keel over dead on the grimy bar floor, Lily takes over.

"We're actually looking for someone," she says. "Jackel?"

"Hasn't been around in a while," the bartender says, swiping at the taps with a dishrag. "What do you want with him?"

I should be helping her, but I'm still trying to breathe after swallowing what tasted like someone mixed battery acid and tree bark.

"Just . . . to talk."

He scoffs. "Please. You didn't come here for the conversation." He looks down at me. "Or the drinks."

"What was that?" I ask, pointing at the empty shot glass.

"A double bourbon," he tells me.

"Really," Lily insists. "We just have something we need to talk to him about. Him, or maybe—Pyro?"

The bartender stops cleaning the taps midmotion. One of the guys at the bar raises his head. There's a short, deadly silence until the bartender says: "What?"

Lily falters for a second. "Sorry. William? Also known as—"

"Kind of strange," the bartender says to her, slowly, "that you're looking for those two."

"Um."

"It makes me think, why those two? What would *those two* have in common?" His eyes bore into Lily, who shrinks back. "And who would be *stupid enough* to ask around for them when she should know exactly where they are?"

Lily clearly has no idea what to say. To be fair, neither do I.

The bartender does, though.

"Get out of my bar," he orders us.

Lily's eyes go wide. "What?"

"You heard me. I don't care who sent you, but get the fuck out and do not come back."

"Okay. Okay. We're going," she assures him, one hand pulling me by the coat sleeve, the other held up in surrender.

"Jesus," she whispers as we walk. "That was—"

"Don't freak out," I tell her. "You're fine. We're fine."

As we're walking away, though, I hear a hushed conversation behind us.

"Charlie—" someone says, and based on where the voice is coming from, I think it's one of the men at the bar. The big guy, who was watching us. Sitting to the bartender's left.

"Shut up a minute, Joe," the bartender—Charlie, I guess— snaps back.

"He thinks I know them," Lily whispers as we approach the door. "The bartender—he said I should know where they are?"

I'd point out that Lily asked for them (by name) and she does know where they are (jail), but I'm too distracted. The big guy at the bar had something to say, and would have, if Charlie hadn't cut him off. I want to know what.

A quick glance over my shoulder tells me Charlie's stopped watching us leave, more focused now on keeping his friend quiet.

"Lily," I say just as her feet reach the doorway, "if I'm not out in five minutes—"

But then I don't know what to say next. Call the cops? Maybe if I hadn't just had two shots of bourbon.

Lily's pushing open the door. Charlie's back is to me. It's now or never.

So I say: "I'll be out in five minutes."

"Wha—?" Lily manages to get out before I let the door close in her face, with me still inside. Then I edge back along the wall, using the crowded high-top tables as cover, before I can finally duck behind the jukebox next to the bar.

This is the first time in my life I've been glad not to be tall. A couple of extra inches and this wouldn't work, but curled up against its cool metal back I'm completely hidden—but close enough to hear.

"I'm done talking about this," Charlie the bartender is saying.

"Well, I'm not, man! The whole thing was weird as shit."

"It happens."

"Not like this."

If my life were a noir, I'd hear what Joe says next, because I know it must be important. But instead, what I hear is:

```
Object (small, metallic) PLUNKS onto the wooden
floor next to Gideon. He looks down. Inches from
his hand, a QUARTER spins on its edge, finally
coming to rest near his right sneaker.
```

                    MAN'S VOICE
    Dammit.

The floorboard next to Gideon CREAKS, and a
RANDOM BEARDED DUDE's face appears. When he sees
Gideon, his head jerks back.

                RANDOM BEARDED DUDE
                     (stares)

                    GIDEON
                 (stares back)

Slowly, Random Bearded Dude holds out his hand.
Gideon fumbles for the quarter. Picks it up.
Hands it over. Random Bearded Dude takes it.
Stares for one second longer. Then stands up.

Silence. Gideon holds his breath. Then, we hear
the CLANK of the quarter into the jukebox, and a
GENERIC COUNTRY SONG begins to play.

I'll say this for bikers. They know how to mind their business.

It's harder to hear now, with the music playing, but Joe and
Charlie are still going at it.

"The cops were waiting around the corner!" Joe's almost
yelling now. "They knew he was going to be there."

"That doesn't mean someone here—"

"He drank here, and when he drank, he talked. Somebody knew he was going to do that job."

And then the chorus starts, and I can't hear a thing anymore. So when the coast is clear, I duck out from behind the jukebox and make a run for the exit without looking back, all the way to Lily and her waiting car.

I throw open the passenger door, scramble inside, and slam the door. Lily floors it without warning, so I'm slammed back against the seat.

Neither of us says anything for a few blocks. She's the first one to find words.

"I am," she says, voice shaking, "so mad at you."

Mad? I'm the one who risked staying. She should be thanking me. "Why?"

"That was so stupid!" she yells. "That was so scary, for me, and you, you think this is a *movie*."

"I don't think—"

"Yeah, you *don't* think before you do *anything*, and *that* has to be the worst idea you've ever had."

"You're going to be glad I did it," I promise her.

"Explain," she says.

That's what I do, recapping everything I heard between Charlie and Joe. The new info seems to take a lot of the heat out of Lily's sails—which I think Tess would tell me is a mixed metaphor.

82

"So there's an informant," Lily says. "Somebody who goes to that bar is listening to conversations and then telling the police where people are going to be committing the crimes."

"And that's why the arrest rates have gone up," I add. "They already know when and where the crime is going to happen."

"The cops catching Luke red-handed wasn't perfect timing. Someone snitched on him."

It's possible. Even more than likely. But *possible* doesn't mean *correct*, and *likely* doesn't mean *certain*. Especially not after what I heard in the bar.

"Or maybe," I say, "he was set up."

CHAPTER 8

LILY AND I reconvene a few days later, to do what she calls a "postmortem." I don't understand that term at all. No one died. Though it was touch-and-go there a couple of times.

As Asta burrows into his wood shavings in his habitat, Lily settles herself on my bed and opens her notebook.

"What we really have to ask ourselves is: cui bono," she says.

"Gesundheit."

"You're very funny," she says with an eye roll that implies otherwise. "It's Latin."

"You take Spanish."

"I take both, actually, but it's a question that people ask, in the legal world. Cui bono. It means 'who benefits?'"

"Who benefits," I repeat. "Like, who has motive?"

"Right. The key to figuring out who did something is to figure out who would *get* something. So who would get something out of what we *know* has happened? Who benefits from these petty crimes?"

"And there's a second piece," I add. "If Luke is right, that the cops were waiting for him, and if Pyro really was set up like his friend at Doc Holliday's seemed to think—who benefits from them being *arrested* for those crimes?"

"A rival drug dealer, maybe? Who wanted Jackel out of the game?"

"But Pyro was an arsonist. Luke's just a kid who does graffiti. It would have to be someone who would get something out of a bunch of different kinds of crimes. Not just one."

"Cui bono," she repeats, more to herself than me.

I shrug. "Not them, anyway."

The next week, we have Late Night, and I'm reading one of Araceli's terminally boring articles about the school board, when a paragraph in the middle catches my eye.

Councilman Fred Willets proposed additional school funding be directed toward school safety, and the hiring of additional Security Guards for Presidio High School.

"We've seen a marked increase in crime over the last six months," Councilman Willets said. "When parents are watching their cars being broken into, their business vandalized, graffiti covering the walls of what used to be a family-centered, safe

enclave—how can they feel safe sending their children to school,
without some assurance that they are safe?"

I sit up straight in my chair, reading as quickly as I can—which isn't very fast—and as carefully as I can—which isn't very carefully, because my brain's already working in overdrive, trying to process what this means.

Though Council Members Diaz and Yen stressed the
downsides of overpolicing San Miguel's high school students,
Councilman Willets remained adamant.

"We're seeing a clear abdication of responsibility in San
Miguel," Councilman Willets continued, speaking over objections.
"Not just in our schools. On every level of government, especially
within the police department, we're abandoning our home to
the criminal element. And I, for one, find it disgraceful."

"Lily." I beckon her over and pass her the article.

Her eyes move rapidly across the page, then she cranes her neck, searching the room. "Araceli!"

Araceli's head pops up from behind one of the computers.

"Can I ask you something really quick?"

When Araceli sits down beside us, Lily points out the name in the article for her.

"Who is Fred Willets?"

"A city council member," Araceli says. "I can't remember for what voting district. And he's also running for mayor next year."

"I mean more . . . what is he like? What's his deal?"

"Well, he's rich," Araceli says. "He started in tech, in NorCal, before he moved down here a couple years ago and bought a bunch of businesses around town. And I don't want to be mean, but he's kind of a jerk."

"Like how?" I ask.

"He talks *so* much, and everything he says is so clearly just to make himself look good. He's the reason every meeting goes over." She pauses. "Why do you want to know?"

Lily clears her throat. "Um. I thought I might do a feature."

Araceli looks confused. "On . . . crime?"

"No, uh—" Lily scrambles to cover. "On him. Fred Willets."

"Oh," Araceli says. "Okay. I guess the one thing I'd say is don't bring up the police chief."

"The police chief?" Lily asks.

"Yeah. I forget his name, but Councilman Willets *hates* him."

"Can't blame him for that; the chief's a total dick." Both Araceli and Lily turn to stare at me. "So I've heard."

"Well, I don't know," Araceli says, "but Councilman Willets is always going on these rants about the police department. Like how the city's become so unsafe, and there's all this property damage and graffiti and now it looks like we live in Calcutta—"

"So he's a drama queen," I say.

"And racist," Lily adds. "I bet he's never even been to Kolkata."

Araceli gets to her feet. "If I were you, Lily, I'd pick a new subject."

The second Araceli is out of earshot, Lily whips around to me.

"This is bad," she says, her voice low.

I don't see why. So some politician also knew how to read crime stats. So what? Plus, I'm inclined to feel a little kinship with anyone whose hobby is pissing off the San Miguel Police Department.

"Why?" I ask her. "Somebody else noticed what you did. All that means is you're right."

"I already knew I was right."

"So what's the problem?" I ask, doing a quick Google Image search on my phone. Fred Willets, it turns out, looks like the word "smarmy" took human form.

"The problem is he's going to scoop me."

"He's like forty; that wouldn't even be legal."

"Ew, Gideon, oh my God," she says. "Scooping someone means getting to a story before they do. It's a journalism term."

"But he isn't a journalist."

"I bet he knows some. He's an adult, with resources, and if he cares this much, he'll break the story before I do." She breathes out. "We need to work faster."

Just then, Tess and Noah burst in the double doors, each carrying a pizza box. Ryan's behind them, a heavy grocery bag under one arm and a salad bowl under the other.

"Dinner's here!" Tess shouts. Everyone instantly drops

whatever they were doing, and I help Lily push two of the tables together.

"I'm picking up the paper tomorrow," Tess says as we all start to serve ourselves. "Who's going to help fold, at lunch?"

Everyone averts their eyes. I've been here only a few weeks, but it's become clear no one likes giving up their lunch hour to fold the newly printed papers that leave ink stains all over their fingers.

"You guys," Tess groans. "It's not *torture*. I do it every time."

"I'll help," I blurt out.

She gestures at me. "Thank you, Gideon. Anyone else?"

"I'll come with you to pick it up," Noah offers.

It's also become clear—for reasons I don't understand—that picking the paper *up* is a highly coveted invitation, subject to the choice of whoever's driving.

"No, you know what?" Tess turns to me. "Gideon was the only one who volunteered. *He* can come with me."

My eyes go wide and my face goes red. I can't help it, but I can feel it. It's not fair, Dad doesn't go red when he's embarrassed, I must have gotten that from—

Nope. Not now, I'm not thinking about that now, not when I could be thinking about Tess and the fact that she chose me over everyone else. I'm not dealing with that now, when I should be dealing with the fact that my face is still on fire and everyone can see.

I run the back of my hand across my cheek in a desperate and unsuccessful attempt to cool it down, and smile at Tess. She winks.

Which only makes the pounding in my chest so much faster and my burning face so much hotter.

"Isn't there anything to put on the salad?" Lily asks Ryan, motioning at the dry lettuce in the bowl.

"Yeah." Ryan pulls a Tupperware container out of the shopping bag. "My mom packed some. We'll dress it after."

"After what?"

"After Gideon gets some."

I stop midbite of my plain cheese pizza.

"You didn't have to do that," I tell him.

Ryan blinks at me. "You said you didn't like dressing."

"But everybody else does."

"*You* don't, though." He shrugs. "So we'll wait a second. No big deal."

It might not seem like it to him, but yes. It is. It is a big deal for someone to remember the weird things I like and don't like. It is a big deal for someone to work around it, rather than roll their eyes or act like it's ridiculous.

And it's a big deal to be sitting at this table, with everyone talking and laughing and not caring that they'll have to wait for me to serve myself, first. They care more about me than the inconvenience. They don't see me as one.

I take the bowl from Lily and pile salad on my plate.

The next day, Tess asks me to meet her by the side entrance, near the gym, right after second period.

"On time and everything," she says when she sees me. "I so made the right call."

Then she pushes open the doors and walks out of school. For a moment, I'm too surprised to react. I've never skipped school before. I've never had anything to skip *for*. Until now.

"Wait, we just get to leave?" I ask, following her out the door.

"Why not?" She flips her sunglasses down. "It's a field trip."

She starts off toward the parking lot and I hurry to catch up with her. "But I mean . . . is it allowed?"

Tess looks amused. "You never struck me as a rule follower."

I never have been. "But it's important to know either way. Right? It's recon."

"Recon?"

"Recognizance. It means—"

"I'm from a navy family, I know what it means. I don't think *you* know what it means."

At some point, I'm going to come to terms with never being the smartest person in the room when that room includes Tess. And I think it's going to happen fast, because I want to be in whatever room she is.

"I meant, do I have to come up with an alibi," I say, "for where I was third period?"

"No, I'll write you a note." She stops us by a truly ancient dark green sedan, pulling car keys from her pocket. "Sign it as Ms. Flueger."

That's good enough for me. If you've already committed to cutting class, might as well follow it up with some forgery, right?

"The printer's not far," Tess says once we're on the road. "Do you want to eat before or after?"

"Eat?"

"Why do you think everyone fights to pick up the paper? You get a free lunch out of it, paid with petty cash. It's tradition. Exit's coming up—now or after?"

"Now," I decide.

Tess changes lanes, takes the off-ramp, and pulls into the parking lot of a roadside In-N-Out.

Well. Who am I to buck tradition?

"You get the table, I'll order," Tess says as we walk in. "What do you want?"

"Double-Double without onions."

"Animal style on your fries?" I shake my head. She looks appalled. "Heathen."

While we wait for our number to be called—there are more people than I'd have expected here, for a Friday at eleven a.m.—it occurs to me that this is the best day at school I've ever had, and it's entirely because I'm not at school in the first place.

"Thank you," I say to Tess.

She sips at her drink. "Hm?"

"For picking me to come with you. For . . . choosing me."

"Copy editing is the worst position on staff. You should get a perk occasionally."

"It's not that bad," I say. "I like it."

"Really?"

"Maybe not the editing itself," I admit, "but I like having a job. I like hanging out with everyone, I like seeing the paper when it's done and knowing I helped make it, I like—"

And then I stop, because I'm dangerously, dangerously close to saying the whole truth: *I like you.*

Tess waits. I swallow. And shrug. "I only did it because Lily wanted me to. At first. But . . . I'm really glad. That she made me."

"I started as a reporter on my first day of freshman year," Tess says, "so it's hard to even remember what it looks like, from the outside. I always assumed a little like *Lord of the Flies.*"

"Huh?"

"You know. Feral children who have created our own terrifying pseudosociety." She pauses. "Didn't you have to read that in freshman English?"

I was definitely *supposed* to. Better change the subject before she figures out how close I've come to failing English. Twice.

"So you always knew you wanted to be editor in chief," I say, "from the very beginning?"

"No, I kind of grew into that, but I was always interested in journalism."

"Because of that article about you?"

She raises her eyebrows. "Uh."

"I remember there being an article about you. Wasn't there?" I ask. Her mouth gets tight. "In the paper. The real paper. Not that the *Herald* isn't a—" I clear my throat. "It was like five years ago; my dad showed me. You had a surfboard in your hand."

"Yeah." She laughs, but it sounds hollow. "Which hand?"

"I . . . ," I stutter. "I don't remember."

"It's always the left hand." And when she smiles, it's more of a grimace. "For every article, they take a photo with my left hand."

I guess there were more than I knew about.

"So that's why you were interested? Because you had articles written about you, so you knew how it all worked."

"Yes." She pauses. "But not the way you're thinking."

"What do you mean?"

"I noticed what kind of questions they asked. Every time. Every time, they wanted to know what my accident was like. In detail. The most traumatic moment of my life, and they always wanted me to relive it. I didn't like that, but I guess I understood *why* they asked."

She sets her drink down and is quiet for a moment. Then she takes another breath and keeps going.

"What really started to bother me was I would talk about being angry, sometimes, that this happened to me. The unfairness of it all. But they wouldn't write that down. If they were taping me, on a recorder, they'd seem impatient. Like they were waiting for me to move on."

The way she's talking—halting and so much quieter than she usually does—I get the feeling she doesn't say this often.

"They liked asking questions about how I stayed so positive and happy, but—they were only *assuming* that was true. What if I was a super-pessimistic bitch?"

"You aren't, though."

"I could be! Sometimes I am. Because I'm, you know, a human being." She pauses. "When I was little, I would give them what they wanted, because I could tell what they were looking for, and I was a people pleaser, like that. But when my mom or my grandma would read the article to me, it would make me feel . . . terrible."

"Why?"

"Because it wasn't real! Or—it was, I didn't lie, but it wasn't the whole truth. It wasn't until I was a teenager that I figured it out. They didn't write me like a whole person because that's not how people wanted to see me."

"No, Tess," I cut in, "I'm sure that's not—"

"You're not sure, though, Gideon. It didn't happen to you."

I close my mouth, because she's right—it didn't. And I don't know, can't know how she feels. But I can do what the reporters didn't. Wouldn't. I can let her say whatever she feels. And try to actually hear it.

"They didn't want complexity, or anger, or frustration because that wasn't what I was *for*. I was a two-minute inspiration as readers sipped their morning coffee. I wasn't a person. I was a story."

I don't know, can't know how she feels. But I do know what it's like to be a story.

"Stories matter," Tess continues. "The way we tell them matters, and so does who tells that story in the first place. I was tired of being on the outside of my own. That's why I joined the newspaper. That's why I'm here, week after week, year after year. Trying to tell the truest stories I can."

"That's always what it's supposed to be about, isn't it?" I think that's why I like the paper. Honesty matters there. "Just the facts."

"But facts don't exist on their own," she insists. "They are *told* to us. By people, and those people can be biased. Then we interpret the facts we're told, the way we choose to. That's when things get complicated."

Just then, the cashier calls out a number. Tess checks her receipt and jumps up to collect the food. I sit very still, trying to remember every word she just said. Like it's a monologue in a movie. Those can be clues, too. The things people will tell you, when you let them.

There's this famous scene in a noir film called *The Third Man*. The villain is a guy who's been diluting stolen penicillin and selling it to hospitals. Which is obviously messed up, and in case you're a sociopath, the movie shows you a hospital ward full of dying kids who were hurt by the counterfeit medicine. When the hero detective and the villain finally meet, it's on this Ferris wheel. And the villain—played by Orson Welles, as cool as an eel who's fine with murdering kids—points down at all the people on the ground.

"Look down there," he tells the hero, a man who used to be his friend. "Would you really feel any pity if one of those dots stopped moving, forever?"

And he's right—from way up in the Ferris wheel, the people below are just dots. From where we see them, that's exactly what they are. That's what perspective does. It tells you how to see things. That's what Tess is trying to tell me. Stories have a perspective just as much as camera shots do, and they have the same effect. The way a shot is framed, the way a story is told, it all does the same thing. It gives you perspective. But only one.

And the world has more angles than the one presented to you.

CHAPTER 9

LILY HAD TOLD me getting any kind of records—arrests or otherwise—would take time, but I didn't know she meant this much. It's been nearly four weeks since we went to Doc Holliday's. I suggest that if we could get ourselves into a biker bar, breaking into a municipal office should be a piece of cake, but she's not having it.

I decide to let it go. Working on the *Herald* is enough to occupy me in the meantime, especially Thursday Late Nights, which are always disasters. Tess doesn't like it when anyone says that. But it's not like disasters go away just because you're too stubborn to acknowledge them.

"Tess." Noah puts his head down on the table. "It's nine o'clock."

"Thank you for that excellent impression of a phone alarm," she says, eyes still on her computer screen.

"Are you almost done?" Ryan, fully sprawled out on the gross couch, asks me. "I want to go home."

"It's not my fault *or* Gideon's you two were so late delivering your section," Tess tells him.

I hold up the paper. "Done."

Tess swivels around in her chair. "And no red flags this time?"

"The school jazz band is no longer referred to as sounding like"—I shuffle through my stack of printouts for the first draft version Noah wrote—"'a cacophony of dying frogs and the ghost of Miles Davis weeping.'"

"That's a yellow flag," Noah says. "Orangish at most."

"Cantaloupe," Ryan suggests.

"Mac and cheese," Noah agrees.

"Please go home now," Tess says.

As Noah and Ryan head out the door, Tess throws me a look I can't interpret. She flicks her eyes to the closing door, then back to me.

Does she mean: *Those two, am I right?*

Or: *Good, now it's just us.*

Or: *I've been here for six hours already, and this smile is only a symptom of my brain leaking out through my ears.*

"Can you input the edits?" Tess asks, shaking me out of it. "I'm just looking at the time."

"You type way faster than me," I point out.

"Yeah, but with a lot more typos," she says. "Eight fingers is fine for speed, not so much for accuracy."

I get up but then hesitate. It would be weird to take the seat next to her. Wouldn't it? You're supposed to leave a gap, like you do at movie theaters or buses or . . . public urinals.

Tess looks up at me, then down at the chair next to hers. "Go ahead. You can take it." She clears her throat. "Um—since Noah probably left his section up."

I sit down. Right next to her. No gap.

My phone buzzes in my pocket, one right after another, and I pull it out to see a string of texts from Dad:

Hey kiddo

After we're done with service Mario and I need to run over numbers for the month

Going to be super late getting home

Don't stay awake for me

Then a sad-face emoji, followed by a sleeping emoji. He always ends texts with representative emoji faces, which makes me want to respond with the one rolling its eyes.

"Is that Lily?" Tess asks, looking at me out of the corner of her eye.

I stick the phone back in my pocket. "Nope."

"You could tell me, you know," she says, and almost sounds nervous for some reason. "If it was."

"I would tell you." I pause. "If it was." I pause again. "But it's not."

"It's just that she's been kind of weird lately? We used to talk all the time, but now whenever I ask her a question, she gets all squirrelly and nervous and . . ." Tess hesitates. "It's like

100

there's something she's not telling me."

Oh no. Does she know?

"And since it basically started when she brought you to the *Herald* . . ."

Oh shit. She *definitely* knows.

"Look, what happened was—" I start off, even though I have no clue how I'm going to justify both Lily and me hiding this investigation from Tess, but it's like she doesn't even hear me.

"I thought maybe you two were . . ." she says, almost stuttering the last words. "Um. Dating?"

I stop. We stare at each other. Then I burst out laughing.

"Okay," Tess says under her breath as I struggle to pull myself back together. "Clearly not."

"We've been friends since we were six," I explain, conveniently leaving out the four years we were not. "It would be like dating my cousin. Except I know Lily better than any of my cousins."

"Yeah, no, I got it."

"Not that I'm opposed to dating or girlfriends, as a concept, just that Lily *isn't* my—like I could see myself having one in the future, but I don't have one now and haven't previously, so, I'm not an expert like you are. Not that you're an expert like you've had too many, but—"

"Gideon?"

"Yeah?"

"Please take a breath before you pass out."

I do. But only because she's the one asking.

"It was my dad," I say once my lungs have reinflated. "Texting me."

"Oh." She nods. "Yeah, tell him I'm sorry I'm keeping you here so late. We'll be done in like—" She glances at the computer. "Ten minutes."

"It's fine; he's still at work."

"Night shift?"

"Sort of. He's a chef."

"Cool," she says, and I think she means it, too. "That must be awesome."

When he opened his first restaurant, I overheard him say it was his "second child." I thought that was beyond weird, and told him so, and then he told *me* I didn't have to take everything so literally. As if I thought he'd *literally* given birth to a family-friendly New American dining establishment.

It was that he put us on the same level. Me, a flesh-and-blood person, standing shoulder to shoulder with . . . a building. Four walls and a door that didn't care if Dad lived or died.

I say: "Yeah, he's practically Mildred Pierce."

". . . Who?"

Another chef who wasn't a huge fan of her eldest kid. "Not important."

Tess narrows her eyes for a moment, like she's got another question or two. But if she does, she doesn't ask it. Instead, she turns back to the computer and says: "At least he doesn't mind you staying late."

"I guess yours doesn't, either?"

"What, my dad?"

"Yeah."

"He lives in Arizona, so I don't exactly run it by him," she says, then rushes to add: "He cares about my life—I'm not trying to say that—but it's in a more general way. Like, 'How's school,' not, 'Where are you going to be at nine p.m. this Thursday.' Even when I stay with him during the summers, he's pretty relaxed."

"And your mom must be, too, right? If she's cool with you coming home after nine."

Tess gets a funny look on her face. "I . . . don't live with my mom."

"Oh," I say. "Is she dead?"

Silence drops like an anvil.

"What?" Tess's eyebrows shoot up. "Jesus *Christ*, Gideon, *no*."

Like an anvil I dropped right on Tess's foot.

"I'm sorry," I stutter. "I—"

"She's not dead, she's just a flake. In tenth grade, I decided it was easier to live at my grandparents' house than move apartments every time she quit a job or shacked up with a boyfriend." Then she pauses and looks back to me. "Why would you say that?"

"Say what?" But it's a lie. I know what.

Tess doesn't blink. "Why would you ask me if my mother is dead?"

"I guess because mine is."

Another silence, but not an anvil this time. A wave, a tsunami, whatever's bigger than a fucking tsunami, and it drowns me completely.

It leaves Tess spluttering and desperately trying to catch her breath. "Oh my God," she gasps. "Gideon."

Tsunami is right. That's the right word. Not an anvil, which lands just once, crushes you, and then lets you bleed out in peace. A tsunami, because once it starts, it just crashes over and over and over.

"No, please," I say, and it comes out begging. "I don't want you to—"

"I didn't know, I'm so—"

Sorry. I know. She's sorry, everyone is always sorry and feels terrible and then I feel terrible for making them feel terrible.

"It's fine, I was six." I rush to get out the words, *any* words that will make this stop. "I barely remember anything about it so it's not—you don't have to look at me that way. It's not a big deal."

Tess doesn't say anything. She doesn't call me a liar. But the way her eyes narrow, just a little, I don't think she believes me.

"Really," I say. "It's . . . fine."

She still doesn't say anything. Her eyes keep searching my face. And then she turns her chair so she's facing me head-on. Nothing between us.

"I was six," Tess says slowly. "When I lost my fingers."

I don't know what I should say to that. I hate it when people tell me they're sorry. Maybe she does, too. Maybe she doesn't. So all I say is:

"Oh."

"It's a weird age." Her words are still slow. Deliberate. "To have something really big happen to you."

Then I recoil, because I don't like that. At all. It takes me a second to figure out what I'm feeling, and I think it's . . . offended.

I'm offended for me, because what I lost was a person. An entire whole person. And I'm offended for Tess, because she got *hurt*. She was seriously injured in a permanent way. Nothing happened to me, to my own body. I wasn't the one in the guest room bed, on oxygen, in pain. I was down the hall, playing with dinosaurs.

"It's not the same thing," I tell her.

"Of course not. It's different in a million different ways." She breathes in deep, then out. "But I know what it's like to have your world suddenly change when you're too young to understand it."

Can it work like that? Can people live totally different lives, with experiences the other one hasn't had and can't imagine—but still somehow understand? Even just a little?

It makes me think of a Venn diagram, in math class. Two circles, mostly separate, but with an overlap in the middle. "Two distinct bodies." That's what my teacher called the circles, which I remembered because it felt so true. I was a distinct body, too. My own untouched sphere.

But I'm realizing I missed the point. It wasn't about the distinct bodies. It was about the center.

Just a sliver of shared space, even just the smallest amount. Maybe that can matter.

"It didn't happen to me, though," I say, because I still need Tess to understand that. "It happened to her. Just like your—" I gesture vaguely. "I'm sorry, I don't know what I'm supposed to call—"

"Some people call it a limb difference," she says. "People who were born that way, especially. I go back and forth. Amputation. Finger loss. I don't know." She frowns. "Sometimes 'loss' makes it sound so negative."

That surprises me, because—how could it not be negative? And Tess can read people much better than I can, because she sees it on my face. Not just the surprise. But the question, too.

"Don't misunderstand me, it was traumatic. Beyond traumatic. The hospital, and the surgeries, and then relearning everything, and—it changed my whole life, completely." She pauses. "But that's just it. It changed my *whole life*. I am who I am because of what happened to me."

"Well, but not *just*—"

"Hey, no, that's not special, we're *all* who we are because of what's happened to us. Not *just* because of it, but it's a part. And it can be a big part."

In movies, traits and backstory make a character. I hadn't considered it might be true for real people, too. There are things you were born with, and the things that happen to you. And you wouldn't be yourself—not exactly, anyway—without them.

It doesn't make tragedy less tragic. It doesn't make people getting hurt or people dying before you even really know them any less painful or unfair. It doesn't make any of that okay.

But it does matter.

"Living in my specific body affects how I think about things, how I see the world, who I am in it." Tess shrugs. "And I like who I am."

"I like who you are, too."

Her mouth quirks. "Thank you."

I wish I liked myself as much as Tess does. Or maybe . . . was so certain it was *okay* to like myself. Because a lot of the time, it feels like I'm not supposed to.

"Do you feel like nobody is ever actually going to know you?" I blurt out.

Her eyebrows go up again. "Whoa. Uh . . ."

"I'm sorry. That was a weird question."

"No, it's—"

"But it's better than asking if your mom's dead, right? I'm on an upward swing."

"The question was fine," she says. "You just need to unpack it a little."

I take a deep breath and try again.

"Do you ever feel like no matter how much you tried to explain yourself to somebody—like even if they could see directly inside of you, see all the things that make you *you* . . . ?" I gulp more air in. "They still wouldn't understand you at all."

Tess takes a long moment. "I think it's really hard for people to step outside . . . normal. Their idea of normal. And I think when you have experiences or"—she looks up through her eyelashes at me—"a perspective, maybe, that's outside that idea of normal, it can feel—you can feel—"

"Alienated."

"Yes," she agrees. "That's a good word for it."

This isn't something I talk about. It isn't even something I *think* about, if I can help it, because I never seem to come up with any kind of conclusion. But Tess told me things. Personal things. Difficult things. If I can't do the same, then what kind of a coward am I?

"There's this . . ." I pause. "Gap. A big gap. What's a word for a giant, deep gap?"

She takes her time thinking about it before offering up, "Chasm."

Chasm. Yeah. I like that word. It sounds like what it means. "There's this *chasm* between me and other people. I don't know how to get across it, to them, and I can't get them across to me, either."

"I know what you mean."

I stop short. "You do?"

"Maybe not the exact same way. But I've spent most of my life trying to seem upbeat and hopeful and fine, because that's what people want from me. You feel like you have to compensate. And it creates this distance."

I don't know what that feels like for her. But I do know how distance feels.

"I think it's why my relationships—dating ones, I mean—kind of fizzle out. Because it's fun and easy at first, but the longer it goes the more distance builds and I don't know how to bridge it. Like you said." She throws up her hands. "I don't feel like anyone wants me to be vulnerable, so I'm not, and then it's like, people get mad that I'm not!"

"But you just told me all of that," I say. "Even though you didn't have to. Isn't that . . . vulnerability?"

"Yeah." She looks surprised. "I guess so."

This silence isn't like the horrified beat after I asked if her mom was dead. It's not like the gut-punch moment of realization after I told her mine was.

It's a soft kind of quiet, the kind movies had before they could pair people's voices to their bodies, but you could still tell how they felt, even without the words. It's like a scene quietly shifting, frame to frame, slow enough for you to see it happen. When things change in movies now, it's with explosions and fireballs, gunshots and ear-piercing shouts. But things can still happen, in silence.

Maybe everything can.

"We should finish up." Tess swivels herself back to her computer. "Unless you want to stay here all night."

109

"I'll stay as long as you need me."

Tess raises her eyebrows. I scramble to course correct. Again.

"Not that you need me. You are strong and independent and don't need anybody." I pause again. "Not that you should have to do everything, especially because you do a lot already, and not that it wouldn't be okay if you *did* need—or just *wanted*—" My head feels too light, like I might pass out. "I don't know what I'm saying."

"Don't worry." She smiles. "I get you."

I get you.

Has anyone ever said those words to me, in that order? I think I would remember, if someone had. It would have mattered. So it would have stuck.

I get you, she said.

And God. I think she actually might.

After Tess finishes her last steps—double-checking the front page, making sure each section is in the right order, sending the file to the printer, and then calling the printer to make sure they got it—we grab our stuff and head for the door together.

Tess puts her hand on the knob but then stops. Turns to me. And says:

"I changed my mind."

"About what?"

"The word you used, earlier. Alienated."

"Oh, yeah, well." I shrug. "I'm not as good with words as the rest of you."

"No, you used the word correctly. It's the connotation that annoys me."

"I don't know what you mean."

"It almost puts it back on you. Like it's a state you end up in. Alone on some strange planet, and the only cure is to hide your green skin and assimilate."

"Tess, I . . . still don't know what you mean."

"Other people might make you feel alienated." She swings the door open, then, and holds it there, for me. "But that doesn't make you an alien."

CHAPTER 10

THE NEXT WEEK, I'm on my way to my usual lunch table when Lily collars me outside my math classroom. She's practically levitating with excitement but refuses to say anything until we've ducked behind the portables out by the running track, safely out of anyone's earshot.

"I just got something," she says, holding up a nondescript white envelope. "From the city."

"If you broke into City Hall without letting me come along, I'm going to be so pissed."

"Your lack of self-preservation is legendary," she says. "But sometimes there are legal ways to get what you want. Like a FOIL request."

"A . . . what?"

"Freedom of Information Law." She rips open the envelope. "It's this thing that gives people the right to request government documents or information that are considered a matter of public record. Which includes arrest records."

"You got the arrest records? Finally?"

"Most of them. Some of them got denied; I don't know why." She sits cross-legged on the ground and starts pulling out the papers. "I'll take half, you take half."

The portables offer privacy but absolutely no shade. I'm sweating in the noon sun, and it's making it hard to concentrate. Lily is clearly reading every single word of the file in her lap, but that's just not efficient—at least, not for me. So I do what I know how to do: take in the picture, and look for the pattern.

But as I flick between the reports, I start to panic, because I don't see one.

Same neighborhood? No. All over the place.

Same crime? No. All nonviolent, all property crimes, but there's a difference between committing vandalism and burglary. Not that I've tried either.

Same time of day? No. Day and night, though . . . only during the day on Mondays and Wednesdays, and at night the rest of the time, which doesn't make any sense. Then I see it.

"The name," I blurt out.

Lily looks up from her stack. "What?"

"The name," I repeat, riffling through my stack to double-check. "There's the same name on every one of mine."

"Someone was arrested more than once?"

"Not the perp. The reporter." I point it out to her. "Reporting: O'Hara." Then I throw it down so she can see the next one. "Reporting: O'Hara."

"That's not a reporter," Lily says. "That's a cop." She scoops up her stack and riffles through it. "Oh my God, you're right, he shows up all the time. I only have one without him on it. *One.*"

"The same cop?"

"Same *reporting* officer," Lily says. She slams down report after report. "O'Hara, O'Hara, O'Hara."

"It must be the same cop Luke was talking about," I say. "'Harris, or something.'"

"If he wrote all the reports, he was there, probably the *first* one there, for every one of those arrests." Lily crosses her arms. "Could that really be a coincidence?"

It's not that huge of a police department, so it's possible. But— "If it's a coincidence," I say, "it's a really weird one."

Lily's already typing on her phone. She shakes her head. "None of the reports include his first name, and the department website doesn't list their officers. But still—we have to find him. We have to talk to him."

"What's your cover story?"

She frowns. "What do you mean?"

"You'll have to lie about who you are," I tell her. "Why you want to talk to him. So what's your lie?"

"I can't *lie*," she says. "It's unethical. It goes against every journalistic standard."

"What's that matter? It's not like you're a real reporter."

Lily's eyes go dark. Her mouth tightens. I repeat every word in my head until I figure out which one was wrong, but by the time I do, Lily's already scooped up all the folders and is halfway down the path.

"Wait," I call after her, jogging to catch up.

She doesn't stop. "*Real* reporter. Okay. Cool."

"I didn't mean that."

"Yes, you did."

"I'm sorry I said it, isn't that the same thing?"

She throws her hand up and keeps walking. "No!"

"You're looking at it all the wrong way."

She tosses me a look over her shoulder. "Let me guess, you didn't mean that either."

"No, I did." I step in front of her. "It's an advantage that you aren't a r—" I clear my throat. "That you're not an adult."

"Why?"

"Because he's not going to be scared of you. He doesn't know he *should* be."

Her shoulders loosen. Just a little. "He won't be guarded, you mean."

"He might let things slip, because it won't occur to him you could use that stuff against him."

"So I tell him, what? I'm selling Girl Scout cookies?"

No. Stick to the truth, as close as you can. That's how it's done. "Tell him you're writing an article for the school paper.

That's not a lie, so you won't have misrepresented yourself. But tell him the article's about something stupid, you know, like— 'heroes in our community.'"

She makes a face. "Ugh."

"Yeah, but he'll relax, if it's something that cheesy."

She considers for a moment. Then looks to me. "Do you want to come over after school?"

Lily's house doesn't look the same as I remember, but I didn't expect it to. Not because I forgot. If I try, I can still bring up in my head the pink mailbox with ceramic flowers and vines Lily and I helped paint in second grade, or the blue-green tie-dyed curtains in the front window that reminded me of the pond in Balboa Park, or the multicolored doormat woven out of old T-shirts.

But Lily's house was always a little different each time. Her moms were always swapping something out or making something new, so the house evolved. Like the earth. Or superbacteria.

The mountain of shoes is still beside the door, though.

"Didn't even have to remind you," Lily says, watching me untie my shoelaces.

I kick off my sneakers. "Not everything changes."

I always liked that Lily's moms made you take off your shoes before going inside. It made it feel different from my house. I also liked that they told me from our very first playdate to call them by their first names—Priya and Marzanna. Dad thought that was kind of weird, but he thought they were kind of weird in general. They're both artists—Priya does printmaking and illustration, and Marzanna does "high-concept performance pieces." I was nine before I finally asked Lily what that meant, and she admitted she had absolutely no idea.

"Hey, I'm home," Lily calls out as she shuts the front door behind me. "And I brought you a surprise."

"If it's dessert, you're too late," Priya calls from a room to the left—the kitchen. The layout stuck in my brain, too. "I'm making coconut cake."

I follow Lily into the kitchen, where Priya is standing at the counter, her back to us, mixing something in a bowl.

"Don't worry, he's not the least bit sweet," Lily says. I roll my eyes. Priya turns around, and when she sees us—or really, me—her mouth drops.

"No," Priya gasps, putting down her bowl. "Gideon?"

I can't stop the smile creeping onto my face. "Yeah."

"Yes, I know, he's all grown up—" Lily tries to head her mom off, as if that would ever work.

"Come here," Priya says to me, which I can't really do because she's beside me in a flash, anyway. She reaches up and smooths down my hair, examining it in the same way she used to look at the prints hanging up in her studio. "Oh, good. You still have some of that red."

"Mama, stop *petting* him," Lily says. "He's not a golden retriever."

Priya ignores her but does stop touching my hair. "Gideon, honey. It's been forever. Where have you been hiding?"

I wonder what Lily told them when I suddenly stopped coming over. Did she make it seem like my fault? I doubt she told them the truth.

So what I say to Priya is: "My bedroom, mostly."

She throws back her head and laughs. It's the weirdest thing. People always laugh when I'm being serious and seem to get mad whenever I'm joking.

Priya turns toward an open door to her right—the studio space, with its big windows and sunlight, where Lily liked to choose for hide-and-seek.

"Zanna," she shouts. "Did you hear Gideon is here?"

A moment of silence. Then: "Yes! Hello! Gideon!"

"Hi, Marzanna," I call back.

Priya lowers her voice. "She's under deadline for this huge commission project and completely in the zone, or she'd come out."

"In the zone," Lily repeats, grabbing a mug out of a cabinet. "That just means she's got paint in her hair and hasn't put on a bra."

"How's your dad?" Priya asks me.

"He's fine. He just opened a new restaurant."

"Marzanna saw that. Honey, didn't you see that?"

From the studio: "Yes!"

"What kind of food is it?" Priya asks me.

"Mexican fusion," I say.

And from the studio: "Too expensive for us!"

"Where did the coffeepot go?" Lily gestures with her mug at an empty spot on the counter.

"Mom has it," Priya says.

From the studio: "It's all cold!"

"Of course it is." Lily sighs and tromps through the open door.

"You've grown up so well," Priya says to me. "Your dad must be so proud."

She's trying to be nice. I know she is. It's not her fault it scrapes against my skin like sandpaper.

"That's not the word I would use." I pause. "Or the word he would use."

Her eyes go soft. "He was always tough on you."

That makes me feel prickly, and I don't know why. It's not like I don't think that, too. But hearing someone else say it makes it true in a different kind of way.

And maybe Priya can read that on my face, because she adds: "I only mean—he had high expectations. For you, of you. I know that can be hard."

"No, it's—" I look out the window, into their overgrown garden of weeds and daffodils. "Better than him not having any, I guess."

"Is it?" Lily sweeps back into the kitchen. "Don't be so sure."

"We have plenty of expectations for you," Priya counters. "We *expect* you'll follow your bliss. And if that bliss is taking five APs and ruining your health by staying up until three in the morning—"

"So dramatic." Lily downs the rest of the coffee in one gulp. "Last night was barely one a.m."

Priya holds up her hands in surrender.

"Anyway," Lily says. "Gideon and I have a project we need to work on, so—"

"I didn't know you were in any of the same classes."

We're not. Lily's stacked her schedule with APs and Honors, and I'm in the classes Presidio calls "Regular Track." They should have named it the "Please Just Pass This Bullshit So You Can Graduate Track," but I guess that wouldn't have sounded encouraging.

"It's for the paper," Lily explains.

Priya turns to me. "You're on the paper?"

"I just started this semester. It was Lily's idea."

"That's great!"

Lily's already edging toward the door. "Yep, super great, so we're just going to go—"

"Really," Priya says, "I'm so glad you two are connecting again. I know, I know, people grow up, they make new friends, but it's nice to see you together." She ruffles my hair. "It's nice to see *you*, period."

"Ugh, Mom needs to get you a puppy, already," Lily tells Priya, pulling me by the sleeve toward her room.

And from the studio: "No dogs!"

Lily sits down at her desk and flips open her laptop. I stand in the open doorway, not sure what to do.

Lily never liked anyone sitting on her bed. She had a very specific way of arranging her collection of extremely creepy porcelain dolls that came from her grandmother in Poland every year, and she didn't want you messing them up.

"What's wrong?" Lily asks. "It just looks so different?"

The dolls and ponies and pastel bedsheets are gone, but this room is still Lily's.

"I wasn't going to sit on your bed, because you always had a thing about it, but the rocking chair you used to have is gone. And you're already sitting in the desk chair. So I was weighing my options."

She's quiet for a moment. "You really do remember everything."

"Yeah."

"Sometimes I wish you didn't." She looks away. "You can sit on the bed. It's okay."

I sit down. Lily brings up her browser and starts typing.

"Okay. Officer O'Hara, San Miguel." She presses Enter and scrolls for a while. "Here we go. An article about the policemen's benefit dinner, last year. He's quoted talking about 'really feeling the community's support.'"

"Does it have his first name?"

"Better. It calls him Officer Hank O'Hara, thirty-one, of San Miguel." She nods. "Which is helpful."

"To know he's thirty-one?"

"To know he actually *lives* in San Miguel. Plenty of cops don't live where they work."

I guess that makes sense. Hard to imagine someone living in La Jolla or Del Mar on a cop's salary, but rich people call 911, too.

"Hank O'Hara, San Miguel . . ." She clicks on something, then jerks back in surprise. "Oh . . . my God."

"What is it?" I look over her shoulder. "Rap sheet?"

She turns the screen so I can see better. "Dating profile."

HANK (M, 32)

6'1 because I guess that matters (if you're shallow)

Here for a good time, not a long time

Being with me is like playing an N64: there's no problem that can't be fixed by blowing it

"Ew," says Lily.

"What's an N64?" I ask.

"No clue."

She scrolls down to the selfies. And oh. The selfies.

"Does he not own a single shirt?" I ask.

"Does he not have a single friend to take a photo *for* him?" Lily wonders.

Not every mystery is solvable. Or important.

"Okay, we know he's kind of a tool, but that doesn't help find his address." She x-es out of the tab and scrolls through the search results again. "Nothing." She types some more. "I paid for a premium subscription. Hank O'Hara should bring up *something*—"

"But it wouldn't be under Hank," I realize. She looks over at me. "That's not his legal name. He might go by that, even at work, but his deed or lease wouldn't be under his nickname."

"What is Hank short for?"

"Hankrick." She says nothing. "Hankbert." Her eyes bore into me. "I'm kidding. Henry."

She types it in, shaking her head. "It's only one fewer letter, what kind of a nickname is that?"

"I don't know, blame the English."

"Yeah, my ancestors sure did." Then she makes a small, triumphant noise. "*There* we go! Henry F. O'Hara, 3047 Linda Lane."

"I can't believe you found that so fast," I say.

"The internet is magic."

I shrug. "I don't use it all that much."

"Someday, Gideon," she says, jotting something down in her notebook, "you're going to realize the world didn't stop in 1942."

"Unfortunately."

She stops writing. Looks up at me. Tilts her head. "Maybe for *you*."

"Well . . . yeah," I say, sensing a trap. "Because I like—"

"I know you like the clothes and the movies," she says. "But that was not a great era for a lot of people. Like, as a brown girl with two moms, not a time period I'd want to step into. Personally."

When she says it like that, I sound like a privileged dick. And I obviously know she's not wrong about the forties. Even I can see how sexist noir is, a lot of the time. At best, the genre glosses over racism and bigotry, which is its own kind of problem. At worst, you've got Charlton Heston caking on brown makeup to play Detective Miguel Vargas in *Touch of Evil*, while all the *actual* Mexican actors get cast as criminally stupid gangsters.

I watched that movie exactly once and was glad when it was over. But most of the time, I don't think about it. And I guess it's because most of the time . . . I don't have to.

"You're right," I tell Lily. "That's a really good point."

She looks startled. "Wow."

"You don't think it's a good point?"

"I know it is," she says. "I've just never heard you admit that someone else might be right."

When she says it like *that*, I sound like a privileged, know-it-all dick.

She types O'Hara's address into her phone. "Let's go."

★ ★ ★

Officer O'Hara's house is appropriately average for a guy we know nothing about. And infuriatingly nondescript for a guy we *need* to know more about. Ranch style, wraparound fenced porch, built in the 1960s like everything else in this city, which tells me nothing except that he doesn't have the money or the desire to renovate. Which really tells me nothing at all.

I don't know anything about cars—not modern ones, anyway—but the one in his driveway seems just as average as anything else. Lily catches me looking at it.

"He must be around," she reasons, and I nod. He's single. No need for two cars.

Lily knocks on the door. And then again, a moment later. But nobody appears.

"Either he's freaked out by your trench coat or he's not home." Lily turns around and steps off his doormat. "But his car's here."

And then my mistake dawns on me. "Not his squad car."

"We'll have to come back, I guess," Lily says. "What a waste of gas."

She's looking at this all wrong, again. What an opportunity.

While Lily steps back up to the door to knock again, something to the left of the door catches my eye.

"Lily. Look at this." I point to underneath the mailbox.

"Footprints?" she says.

"Muddy ones. It rained last night, and early this morning."

Dad's jacket was still hanging up to dry in the bathroom when I left for school, and the sidewalk was still damp as I walked. It's the kind of thing you notice only when you live in a place that sees only forty rainy days a year.

"They lead up to the mailbox and then right back down the stairs. But not to the door." I kneel down to look closer. "Who would go only to the mailbox but not the door?"

"The mail carrier," she says. Like it's obvious.

"You don't know that."

"Have you ever heard of Occam's razor?"

"No, I use the store-brand ones."

"What?" She shakes her head. "It's a problem-solving principle. It says the simplest explanation is usually the right one."

"And if the shoe print was completely flat, no indentations or pattern, what would Oxman say?"

"*Occam.*"

"He'd say no mail carrier would wear a shoe without any tread. So the simplest explanation is . . . it was someone else."

I throw open the mailbox and start pawing through it. A catalog, a takeout menu, and . . . bills. Lots of bills.

"This one's from a debt collection agency," I tell Lily, turning it over in my hand. Nothing on the front that would be helpful. No "Past Due" or "Final Notice" or "Your Credit Is Fucked, Dude."

"Put it back," she orders me. "That's a federal offense!"

"Only if I open it." As Lily tries to peer in the front window, I hold the envelope up to the light, but they've thought of that—you can't see through. What are the odds this is the only notice he's gotten? Low. Even Oxman and his razor would agree.

It's not collection day, so it's no surprise his bins aren't there. Glancing over the porch railing, I see both of them—green and brown—behind a little wooden fence that must lead to his backyard. I hop over the railing, not nearly as gracefully as I'd hoped. That's one advantage movies have when it comes to action: trained stunt doubles.

The little wooden gate isn't locked, only bolted from the inside, so I snake my hand through one of the slats and unlock it.

"Where'd you go?" Lily calls from the porch.

I'd tell her I'm down here, but I don't want to call attention to it. Instead, I open up his green bin and start rummaging through for anything useful.

Plastic takeout box, deli container, Come Again Soon happy-face bag—he eats out a lot, probably can't cook, not that I should judge, I also can't cook.

One-half of a bill, torn through the center—keeping that for now.

I tuck it under my arm and go back to sifting through.

Beer can, another beer can, another beer can, a water bottle—so occasionally he hydrates—another beer can.

Another ripped bill, not the same font as the first—

Lily leans over the porch railing. "Oh my God, are you going through his trash?"

"No." That would be gross. "It's recycling."

"Gideon!"

"What?"

"What do you mean, *what*?"

When I unfold the first ripped bill, my eyes snag on numbers at the bottom of the page.

lance was $6,972.45

lance is $0.00

"Balance," that's clearly the word that got cut off. Balance. Was and is. High and then nothing. Huh. I unfold the second ripped bill. Different font, different-color logo at the top of the page.

Dear Mr. O'Hara

In consideration of payments received
hereby releases and discharges the abo
will be notified the debt has been satis

Different letters mean different companies—agencies? Whoever handles debts. Different debts, too. Not from just one maxed-out credit card, but two sources, maybe a third, if the letter from his mailbox is any indication.

"What did you find?" Lily asks. "Anything?"

"He's in debt. Like, a lot of debt." But—no, that's not exactly

128

right. "He *was* in debt," I correct myself. "But now he's in a lot less. All at once. Really quickly."

I don't think that's how debt works, unless you have a millionaire grandpa who dies or a lotto ticket that wins.

"So he's got more money than he used to." Lily takes in the view of his house. "Not that you'd know it."

"It's not a coincidence," I decide. "Him being the reporting officer. He's getting something for it."

Lily nods. "Come on, let's go before someone sees us."

The unopened letter is still in my hoodie pocket. I hand it to Lily over the porch railing. "Can you put this back?"

The heels of her boots tap on the wooden porch, then slide to a sudden stop. The mailbox shuts with a clang—and a short gasp from Lily.

"Gideon," she says, softer this time, which is good. And more urgent, which might be good or might be bad. "Get up here."

The fastest way is back over the porch railing, but that's also the noisiest, so I go through the gate. That requires less upper-body strength, which is a bonus.

Lily's standing by the open mailbox, something small and white in her hand.

"Look what I found," she says, holding it out—a note. Tiny and folded and carefully taped.

"Where was it?"

"On the side of his mailbox. Taped to it." She starts to peel the tape, then stops. "I don't know, maybe it's nothing."

I glance around. Maybe it is, maybe it isn't. But either way, we've overstayed our welcome here.

"Drive a few blocks," I say, "then we'll open it."

"I wonder how long it's been there," I say as Lily drives. "The note."

Lily thinks about this. "You said it rained last night."

"Yeah, and it was misting this morning. That's how the footprint got there. The mud."

Lily thinks for another moment. Then she says: "The note was on the side of the mailbox. And the porch isn't covered. Wouldn't it have gotten wet?"

I turn the note over in my hands. She's right—not only isn't the paper wet, it's never *been* wet. No wrinkles or running ink. I nod. "Somebody put it here today."

We stop in the parking lot of a strip mall to read the note. At least here, we know some lady from the HOA won't be spying on us through binoculars.

Careful not to damage the paper, I rip the tape and open the note.

← ↑ 2mrw ☽ 🏴 🐟

And underneath, in an almost illegible scrawl:

USUAL TIME

"What the hell?" Lily says. "It's a cartoon."

No, it isn't. "It's code. It only has to make sense to whoever sent it, and whoever got it."

"O'Hara."

"Right."

"Then how are we supposed to figure out what it means?"

An arrow left, then an arrow up. No. Not left. *Back*.

"Backup." I point to the arrows. No mystery there—someone wants O'Hara for protection. Who better to hire than a cop who needs cash?

"Tomorrow," Lily reasons through the next part. "Night. Tomorrow night."

The gun is self-explanatory. But . . . fish?

"There's an arrow," I point out. "So maybe you're supposed to read the last two together. Gunfish? Is that . . . a thing?"

"The arrow's not just pointing at the gun," Lily says slowly. "It's pointing at—"

She starts typing on her phone, thumbs moving a mile a minute, then pumps her fist. "I knew it. *Trigger*fish, it's a whole species. See?" She holds up the screen so I can see a picture.

"It looks like an angry pancake."

"I hope you don't eat pancakes that have fins."

"So, okay, a triggerfish," I say. "But what the hell does that mean? How does that tell O'Hara where to go?"

"Maybe the aquarium," Lily suggests.

"That's so far."

"It's a straight shot on the Fifty-two."

"Yeah, all the way to La *Jolla*," I say. "Maybe it's a seafood place. Like it's on the menu somewhere, and that's where they meet."

"We can't look up every menu in Greater San Diego."

We don't have to. I stick the note in one pocket, pull my phone out of the other, and dial.

"Hey," Dad says in that strained, too-close-to-the-mic way that tells me he's got the phone nestled in between his ear and shoulder. "I'm about to start. I've only got a second."

"Does any place in San Miguel make triggerfish?"

"What?"

"Like as food, does anywhere make it?"

"You can't eat triggerfish," Dad says. "It's poisonous."

"Oh." I look over at Lily and shake my head no. "Okay, thanks anyw—"

"Is someone trying to get you to buy them alcohol?"

My jaw drops. "What? No!"

"Because that isn't even on the market yet."

"Dad, what are you talking about?"

"Triggerfish is a beer," Dad says. "Or will be a beer, when they finish that brewery. It's already taken years." He pauses. "No one's asking you to buy them alcohol?"

"Why would they do that? I look like I'm twelve."

"Well. Good." He pauses. "Then . . . why did you ask?"

"Huh?"

"About triggerfish."

"Oh. Um." I scramble for an answer. "Trivia contest. At school."

He pauses for longer. "Do you understand this is cheating?"

"There's no prize."

"Maybe the prize is your own integrity."

"God, I'll leave the question blank, all right?"

"What question?" Lily whispers.

"You don't have to use that tone," Dad says.

"Sorry for the tone thank you for the help bye!"

I hang up. Lily shakes her head. "How does he put up with you 24/7?"

"Badly," I say. "Triggerfish is a beer. That's what he said, in between lecturing me. They're building a brewery somewhere around here."

Lily sits with that for a moment. "And that's where O'Hara's supposed to meet . . . this person."

"Someone who couldn't call him. Or email him. Or even leave a straightforward note."

"They don't want anyone surprising them."

It's more than that. "They don't want to leave tracks."

"So they have to leave notes that can be destroyed, and meet at places that aren't populated. Like a brewery that hasn't opened."

"A construction site, it sounds like."

"But . . . when? What time?"

The usual time. Which helps us not at all. "Sometime between sunset and sunrise."

Lily makes a frustrated noise. "That's too big of a gap. We

133

can't stake out a construction site all night; even *my* parents would freak out."

"What time does construction have to stop?" I ask her. "Like, according to the city, when do you *have* to stop drilling and stuff, for the day?"

She types on her phone. "Eight p.m."

"So we figure after that. Or maybe a little earlier, since tomorrow's a Friday. Everyone goes home earlier on a Friday, right?"

Lily gasps sharply. "Not everyone." She shoves her phone in my hands and rummages in the back seat for her folder of arrest records. "I'm going to read you dates; you tell me which ones landed on a Friday."

We sift through them rapid-fire, until Lily's left with a handful of records. "The earliest arrest O'Hara ever made on a Friday was ten p.m. The latest was three a.m., the next day. He must work overnight on Fridays."

"Sometime between eight p.m. and ten p.m.," I say slowly. "That's his only window."

Lily folds the note back up and sticks it in her center console.

If nothing else, we'll figure out who O'Hara was supposed to meet. We'll know who's been paying off his debt and who might be feeding him the people he's been arresting.

She stares at a spot in the distance for a while. Buckles her seat belt. Starts the car. "I'll pick you up tomorrow at seven forty-five."

It isn't until I'm in bed that night, inches away from sleep, that I realize—we never put the note back.

CHAPTER 11

LILY PULLS UP to my house at seven forty-five on the dot. I'm already on the curb, dressed in what she would call "normal" clothes—jeans and a dark hoodie. My trench coat and hat are inside. Crashing a biker bar and snooping around O'Hara's house were one thing. Infiltrating a secret meetup at night is another. Better to have clothes that blend.

My phone is also inside, which is probably paranoid of me, because I don't think Dad has used the tracking app more than twice since he put it on when I was in sixth grade. Once last year, because I wasn't picking up the phone after he locked himself out, and once in seventh grade, when he dragged me to a harvest festival out near Julian and I got "lost" in the corn maze.

When I climb in the car, Lily's not dressed like she usually is, either. No sundresses or pleated skirts or shoes with bows, but a black T-shirt, black sneakers, and black pants. I didn't know she owned this much black. I didn't know she owned *pants*.

The drive goes by in silence. Lily doesn't put on the radio or try to talk, and I don't ask her to. It isn't until we drive past a sign that reads, "Triggerfish Brewery—Coming Soon!" and pull into the desolate, weed-ridden parking lot, that Lily says anything at all.

"There aren't any cars." She cranes her head to take in the full view. "Maybe it wasn't the brewery. Maybe we read it wrong."

Or maybe whoever was supposed to meet O'Hara bailed when he didn't show up. Which is entirely our fault.

I open the car door. "Only one way to find out."

"No lights are on," Lily adds as we walk across the empty lot. "Gideon . . . there's nobody here."

The way she says it puts my teeth on edge. Like there's no point in even exploring. As if investigation works the same as online research, where you input a question and get an answer. Detectives don't get to be right without being a little wrong first.

"So we take a look, leave, and try Officer O'Hara again tomorrow," I say while she shines her phone light toward the door just ahead of us in the darkness. "No harm done."

This is more like it, I think as we approach the front of the building. It's dark, and quiet, and a little eerie. It feels just like a movie.

EXT. BREWERY—NIGHT
GIDEON and LILY stand in the rubble and dirt
outside the half-built brewery. Behind them, a

backhoe sits idle. In front of them is a large
metal front door, surrounded by a plywood wall,
posters plastered across it advertising movies
and politicians and a comedy show headlined by
someone named Mo. The door itself is
crisscrossed with yellow tape. Police tape.

Except . . . it doesn't look at all like it does in movies. I mean,
it's yellow and black and all that, but whoever put it up didn't
do a good job. There are still giant gaps, definitely big enough
for someone to sneak through.

"Come on," I say to Lily. "Let's go inside."

She looks worried. "Through the police tape?"

"We'll duck under."

"What if it's there for a reason?"

"It probably is. To keep out squatters. Same with the security
alarm."

"Security alarm?"

I point out the sign next to the door: "Protected by Argos
Security." And when I go for the doorknob, Lily grabs for my
arm.

"You'll set it off!"

"The door's already a little open—see?"

Lily bends down to look closer, to where I'm pointing at the
hinge, not all the way shut. "If it's already open . . ." She pauses.
"And the alarm isn't going off . . ."

"Then there's no alarm at all. It's just for show."

"Or it's been turned off," she says. "By someone inside."

I stop mid-doorknob turn, because she's right. I hadn't considered that possibility.

"Okay," I agree. "So—quietly."

The door eases open without a creak, much less an alarm sounding. When Lily and I cautiously step inside, it's pitch-black and dead silent. Not even a drip from a faucet or a rat scuttling across the floor.

"I think I feel a light switch," she whispers. "Should I . . . ?"

"Yeah. There's nobody here."

INT. BREWERY—NIGHT
The lights flick on one by one, illuminating the
empty, cavernous brewery floor. Everything is
covered in a layer of gray dust, as though
construction has been paused for weeks. Possibly
months. With the endless stretch of cold concrete
below, and the metal catwalk high above, this
doesn't feel like a building. It feels like a
shell. Or maybe . . . a skeleton.

I shake my head, because I have to focus. Look for what's wrong, I remind myself. What isn't right?

But it all seems pretty normal—the ropes and the wrinkled blue tarps on the windows, the big worktable in the center and the chairs around it, one of them overturned—

Wait. An overturned chair?

I rush over to it. It's tipped all the way on its side, a foot away from the rest of the chairs. It didn't just fall over with the breeze, someone knocked it over and didn't put it back. A workman? Maybe. Or—

"Lily. Look at the table." Lily steps over and looks where I'm pointing—several large smears in the dust. "See that?"

"Yeah." She bends down closer. "But what's it—?"

I try to picture what would make that kind of mark. "Someone touched the table. Or put something on it, at least. They cut through the dust."

"All the way through." I can see the gears in her head turning. "And no more dust has had time to settle."

"Somebody *was* here."

"Recently," Lily adds. I nod. She frowns. "We weren't wrong about the location. But we were wrong about the time."

I hate to admit it, but it looks like she's right.

"Maybe they left something else," I say. "Some clue, about who they are."

So we both start looking around—her more than me, since her phone light is better than my pocket flashlight, which keeps blinking out.

"This is creeping me out," she says with a strong shake of her head. "Let's go."

"Now?"

"There's no one here. There's nothing to see."

That's the problem with most people. They think if they don't see something immediately, it must not exist. One glance and you're done. As if the world is all fluorescent lighting. As if it doesn't have shadows.

"Just give me a minute," I tell her. "One minute, sixty seconds, you can count."

I start off toward the back of the building, where we haven't even looked yet. Lily rushes after me. "I'm not letting you go *alone!*"

If my life were a noir—and this is the closest it's ever felt to one—this would be a tracking shot.

INT. BREWERY—NIGHT

SHOOTING over GIDEON'S shoulder, then pulling
back behind LILY as she trails him. They stumble
past pallets of wood and pyramids of paint, only
flickering overhead lights and Lily's cell phone
illuminating a path.

When I stop suddenly in my tracks, Lily crashes into me, catching herself with her hands on my shoulders.

"Jesus," she says. "Why'd you—?"

"Do you see that?" I grab for her hand and point it in the direction I mean. "There. In the corner."

"A shadow," she says. "It's dark."

As if shadows are just voids. As if nothing could hide there.

"No, Lily, there's something there."

"Boxes. There's boxes everywhere."

That's an assumption. It's not a *bad* assumption, but it is an assumption. And that isn't the same as fact.

"Shine your light," I tell her.

Slowly, shakily, Lily holds it up.

Something—someone—is crumpled in the corner.

Lily gasps, short and sharp. "Oh my God. Is that a—"

Person? "I think so."

"But is he—"

Alive? "I don't know."

"We have to get out of here," she says. "Come on, we have to get out of here *right now.*"

"We can't just leave."

"Yes, we can," she insists. I guess when it comes to fight or flight, she's solidly on the side of flight. "I remember where the door is."

This isn't a movie. This is real. It doesn't feel fun anymore. It only feels scary. But I still have a job to do.

"No, we need to see."

"What?"

I start walking forward. "I need to see."

"Gideon!" She grabs for me but catches air, because I'm already out of reach. "Stop, don't—"

"Hey," I call out, not to her, but to the person. "Are you okay?"

"Are you *crazy?*" she yells, not to the person, but to me.

I'm fumbling for the penlight in my pocket, but I can't get my fingers around it. They're too numb, even though it isn't cold.

Finally, I latch on to the light, pull it out, and shine it on the figure just a few feet away from me. When I see it—when I see what I see—my feet skid to a halt. Lily notices.

"Why'd you stop?" she asks. "Did he move?"

"No." I turn back around to her. "Kind of hard to do that when you're dead."

Lily claps her hand to her mouth and stifles a—shriek? scream? Some kind of appropriate sound. I feel oddly calm. And somehow, that's even scarier.

"Holy shit," I hear her say under her breath. Then repeat, again. And again. "Holy shit, holy shit, *holy*—"

But then I don't hear anything else. Not because she's stopped, necessarily, but because I'm choosing not to. I know she's going to make me leave in a minute, maybe less, and I need to remember what's happening. What exists in this moment, in this space, around me. And the dead man. What *is.*

Black hair. Brown eyes. Open. Wide open.

On his back. Pool of dark blood around his head.

Tall, but not very. Thin, but not extremely. Not old, but not young.

Clothes, his clothes—T-shirt, jeans, jacket it's too hot for, must be for style—all perfect, like they were designed for him. Made for him. Altered to fit exactly.

Jacket sleeve rolled up—no, pushed up, bunched up. Only on the left. Just above the elbow. Just an inch higher than the strip of rubber, tied tight around the arm, digging into the skin.

Something is wrong. Other than the body several feet away from me. That is obviously wrong. But there's something else. It's almost like it doesn't feel real. I know it is real, because I can feel my heart pounding in my chest and the dampness of the floor through a hole in my shoe and a creeping kind of terror, too.

But this isn't *right*. None of this makes sense.

"Lily," I say, hating how my voice shakes, "something is really, really wrong, here—"

When I turn around, my creeping terror instantly transitions into full-blown horror. She's dialing her phone.

"Wh-who are you calling?"

She doesn't look up. "911!"

My stomach drops into my shoes. Forgetting the dead guy entirely, I run back over to her, snatch the phone out of her hands, and end the call. "Why would you do that?"

"Why wouldn't I?" Lily whisper-screams at me. "There's a dead body!"

"You don't call the *cops*!"

"I do when there's a corpse!"

"But not from your own phone, never from your own—"

"What, from yours?"

"No, from a pay phone!"

"A pay—" She stares at me for a long, long moment. "What *decade* do you live in?!"

"When you call from your own phone, they can trace you," I try to explain. "They'll know you called; you'll have to tell them what you were doing here."

"So I'll tell them! We were investigating the crime wave; we came here—"

I take both of her shoulders, and she's too surprised to object. "No. *No.* We were not investigating anything. Okay? Tell them something else, anything else. We were walking, we were looking for your lost cat, we were going to make out in the alley—"

"Ew, Gideon!"

"It's a fake story, Lily, get a grip!"

She's starting to breathe faster. Too fast. Her eyes dart wildly around the room. "What do we do now?"

Even if we're gone by the time the squad car pulls up, they'll trace Lily's phone. Maybe show up at her house, which might be worse. We're screwed either way. Might as well get what I need.

"We get a closer look," I tell her.

"At what?"

I glance back over my shoulder. "At him."

She gapes at me. "*Why* would we do *that*?"

"He's a clue."

"He's a person!"

"He was a person," I say. "Now he's . . . evidence."

She puts her hand over her eyes. "Jesus Christ, evidence of *what*?!"

"I don't know yet, that's why I have to look for clues—"

"Clues! Oh my God, this is not part of our—this has nothing to do with us!"

Another assumption. Or maybe just a hopeful wish. But I don't think it's the truth.

"Just—" I hold out my hands, already backing away. "Stay there."

"No, Gideon, do *not*—"

I'm already shutting out the noise again.

In film noir, they never show you what's happening inside the detective's head. Maybe he'll get a pensive look in his eyes, but mostly he's stone-faced and stoic as he examines a body or pokes around a trashed hotel room. But for me, it's like my brain stem branches in a thousand directions at once, grasping at a thousand tiny details, because you don't know what's going to matter, what's going to be important when you come back to the real world. You have to scoop it all up before it all scatters and falls, like sand in a sieve.

Diamond stud in his left ear.

Short hairs on his black suede jacket—white? Yellow. Light yellow.

The jacket—brand? No. No logo. Dirt on the front, right sleeve tugged down, wrist with a—

Wait.

I can't quite see it, but I don't know, I won't know unless . . .

Unless I touch the body.

I need gloves. I should have gloves. They never have them in movies, but they didn't have DNA technology in 1941, either. I wrap the end of my hoodie sleeve around my hand and slowly, gingerly, reach toward the body. If he's cold, I can't feel it from under the fabric. It makes my skin crawl all the same.

This is nuts. Why am I doing this, I shouldn't be doing this, but I have to see.

I nudge his sleeve up farther, and there it is. Just like I thought.

A wide strip of pale skin all around his wrist, standing out bright against the rest of his arm, with a perfect oval in the center.

I drop his arm like it's on fire and inch back, a couple of feet away. I try to keep going, try to keep pulling the details, but it's harder and harder.

Hair is shorter there—

Smear of ink on his hand, his right hand—no, that's my right, his left—

But if it's on his left hand, then—

None of this makes sense, none of this is right.

Faintly, from what seems like miles in the distance, someone is calling my name. I don't listen. I look without blinking at the dead guy in front of me. *Black hair. Brown eyes. Open. Wide open.*

It isn't until a hand grabs me by the collar and yanks me to my feet that the sound comes back. A rush of faraway traffic noise and Lily talking fast to someone, stumbling over her words, and the thump of my own heartbeat as I stare up at the man who's got my shirt collar in a vise. A man who is wearing a blue uniform and a gold badge and who is definitely, *definitely* a cop.

Maybe he thinks I'll run—as if I'm capable of running on legs that feel like cooked spaghetti—because he instantly transfers his hand from my collar to my upper arm and holds on.

"The hell is wrong with you?" he shouts, his grip so tight on my arm it makes me wince. "Didn't you hear me say to turn around?"

My mouth is sandpaper. My brain is mush. "I—"

When I look at the body again, his eyes follow, too, down into the shadow. And when he sees what I see, his fingers loosen, just a notch.

The cop shakes his head and says: "Oh, *fuck*."

My thoughts exactly.

CHAPTER 12

LAW & ORDER lied to me.

They make it seem like when you're the person who stumbles on a dead body, the detectives bring you space blankets and hot cocoa and tell a nonspeaking extra in a police uniform to give you a ride home.

It's more like being tossed around like a football. The first officer on the scene radios down to his partner and basically shoves us out of the room. His partner intercepts and has us sit on the curb outside like *we're* the suspects but doesn't ask us anything. Just talks on his own radio, keeping us firmly in sight.

When he finally decides to acknowledge our presence, it's to accuse us of petty larceny.

"Turn out your pockets, please," Cop #2 says to me, then holds out a hand toward Lily. "And I'll take your purse."

"I'm sorry, you think we're thieves?" Lily asks as she hands it over.

"You'd be pretty bad thieves to have left money in his wallet, but . . ." He shrugs. "Due diligence."

Lily tenses up when he pulls out her investigation notebook, but he doesn't even flip through it, just tosses it back in her bag.

I turn out the pockets of my jeans, and he seems supremely disappointed there's nothing but lint and a balled-up gum wrapper.

"I don't suppose you can ID him," he says to us.

"The dead guy?" I guess.

"Have you seen him before? Know his name?"

"We found him like that," I say. "Never seen him before."

"We've never even been here before," Lily scrambles to add. "Ever. I told the other officer, we were just taking a walk, and then—"

But he's already on his radio.

"Hey," he says into it. "No, they don't know him. Didn't take anything off him either." He pauses. "Yeah, exactly, just dumb kids."

Lily looks relieved to hear him say that, but I'm not. What a *dick*.

"You thought we'd taken his cards."

He doesn't even look at me. "Hm?"

"He had a wallet. I saw the outline in his pocket, and also, you said he did. But you don't know his name."

That makes him look up, irritated. "Neither do you."

"That means you didn't find any credit cards in his wallet.

You didn't find *anything* in his wallet with his name on it. Not a driver's license, not a business card, nothing. And if *I* were a cop, that would make me think someone didn't *want* him to be identified. But what do I know? I'm just a dumb kid."

Cop #2 picks up his radio, turning his body away from us.

"Ellicot to Central," he says. "What's the ETA for our backup at the brewery?" He waits a moment as the dispatcher talks. "No, not dangerous. Just . . ." He throws a glance in my direction. "Extremely annoying."

"This is the worst time to be showing off," Lily hisses at me.

"I'm not." I mean, I am a little bit, but that's not my primary objective. "I'm trying to help."

"How about help yourself," she says. "Help *me*. Stop talking."

Eventually, another squad car arrives, and the two backup cops go inside the brewery. Cop #2 unlocks his own squad car and opens the door to the back seat.

"Okay, you two," he says. "Go on in the back."

"Did you want to ask us where we live, first?" I say to him. "Or is it more fun to guess?"

Lily kicks at my leg.

"Don't," she whispers.

"This was a fucked-up night," I say at a regular volume. "I'm tired and cold and want to go home."

"Officer," Lily says, "maybe I could call my mom? To come get us?"

"You can tell her to meet you at the station."

Lily looks a little sick, but she climbs in the back. I don't follow her.

"Are you going to get in," he asks me, "or am I going to put you in?"

I get in.

The second we walk through the station-house door, they separate me and Lily. At first, I think it's because they want to question us separately, to see if our stories match. But it quickly becomes clear that they're a lot less concerned I'm a suspect and a lot more concerned with letting my parents know I was trespassing on private property after city curfew.

The desk cop I'm assigned to has a badge that reads "McBride," but with the impressive mustache he's got, I internally rename him Officer McBeardFace. I think there was a cop with a mustache the last time I ended up here, but I can't remember if it was him. All the adults kind of blended together. When he sits me in a chair next to his desk, I do the quickest scan I possibly can. Just to know who I'm dealing with.

Coffee mug from Bear Mountain—skis in the winter, so athletic and at least a little disposable income.

Framed medal—actually, framed medals, plural: one has a sneaker with wings, another a mountain, another with the number 26.2.

He sees my eyes moving around but picks the wrong reason why.

"You're not going to try and run, right?"

I look back up at him. "Do you only do marathons, or short distances, too?"

"Uh." He blinks. "I also do halves."

Better not risk it. "Then no."

Just then, one of the frosted-glass doors to my left bursts open, and three people emerge from the office: a cop, a woman in regular clothes, and a man who is so red-faced and jolly looking that if you replaced the badly fitting suit and the even worse comb-over, you could cast him as Santa Claus.

All the adults blended together . . . except for him.

The woman—blond, skirt suit, glasses—trails behind him, clutching a stack of folders to her chest.

"Sir," she says, reaching out for his arm, but trips a little on her heels. "The mayor has called twice; we really need to—"

But Police Chief Thompson doesn't even look like he hears her.

"What a bombshell, huh?" he's saying to the cop next to him—God, how many could this bullshit city possibly *have*—who nods in agreement. "Just wait until fuckin' Willets hears about this one. He's going to go on public access and say I put the needle in the guy's arm myself."

Willets—Fred Willets. Araceli said he and the chief can't stand each other, and it looks like she was right.

"It would be good to get in front of it," the blond woman says. "Don't give him time to build a narrative—"

"That Patrick Bateman–looking prick couldn't pull a narrative out of his ass."

The cop who came in with the chief spots Officer McBeardFace and breaks away for a second, waving him over. McBeardFace indicates me with a tilt of his head. His friend gestures again, insistently.

"Don't move," Officer McBeardFace orders me. I hold up my hands as if to say, *Fine.*

Whatever they want to talk about must not be something I'm supposed to hear. Which means I've definitely got to hear it.

I pick at a loose thread in my jeans, trying to seem as though I'm totally uninterested in the conversation happening just a couple of feet from me. I can't look up, which means I can catch only about half the words. But I fill in my best guesses as they go.

"Did—hear—?" *Did you hear about the dead guy. Something like that. What else could be so important?*

"—?"

"Vin—son." *The name. Probably a last name. Starting with V and ending in -son.*

Then, loud enough for me to hear, Officer McBeardFace says: "No shit." *He's surprised. It's somebody he knows—or knows of.*

I look slowly at them, banking on the fact that they're wrapped up enough in their conversation not to notice me listening. Which turns out to be correct.

"I thought it was a John Doe," Officer McBeardFace says.

His friend shakes his head. "Crawford ID'd him when he got

there as backup. He's picked him up before."

"Crawford doesn't do OC."

"Not for that. Intoxication, possession." Just then, he glances over at me. I look away quickly. But not quickly enough. "I'll catch you up later."

The main door bangs open, and a cop comes stalking in the door, but if it weren't for the uniform you would have thought he'd just broken out of jail himself, the way his eyes keep darting around and his Adam's apple jumps in his throat.

Even with a shirt on, I recognize him: Officer O'Hara.

"Hank!" the chief says, holding out his arms like he's going to go for a hug. "Did you hear? You missed all the action."

"Yeah," Officer O'Hara says. "I, uh, heard."

"The mayor is on your office line," the blond woman interrupts. "For the *third time*."

"Oh, God," the chief groans.

"No," she deadpans. "Just the mayor."

The chief blinks. Laughs. Claps her on the shoulder so hard it shakes her glasses. Then he waddles off down the hallway. Before the woman turns to follow him, she shoots O'Hara a cold stare, and he looks away quick, like he's embarrassed. I think about all those shirtless selfies.

"Are they together?"

Officer McBeardface looks up. "Who?"

"Officer O'Hara and the lady with the glasses and heels."

He looks over just in time to see her disappear into the

frosted-glass office with the police chief. "Phoebe? Jesus, no, they can't stand each other."

Yep. Stood her up on a date, for sure.

"I thought Ellicot brought you in."

"Who?" I ask before remembering the name Cop #2 used over his radio. Ellicot. "Yeah, he did."

"Then how do you know O'Hara?"

That was stupid. Think, I order myself. Think faster. "He came to my school to do an assembly on the dangers of, uh, weed and pills and . . ." I can't think of a third thing. "Tranquilizers."

"God," Officer McBeardface says, "no wonder he's so miserable lately." He pauses. "No offense to your classmates."

"None taken."

"Okay." He picks up the phone. "Let's call your parents."

CHAPTER 13

I TELL OFFICER McBeardFace I'm happy to give a statement right now, and no, I don't need a parent present because I'm an adult. I tell the second officer who comes over to try his luck the same thing. By the time they take me into the deputy chief's office, I've got my story on lock.

"I understand you're refusing to give us your parents' number?" he asks me.

"I'm not a minor."

"Kid," he says. "Come on."

"Really," I insist. "I'm not."

"Do you have any proof of that? Like . . . a driver's license, for instance?"

Okay. Time for a new tactic.

"Am I under arrest, Deputy Chief"—I check his name tag—"Garcia?"

You don't have to stay if you're not under arrest. But I guess that might be different if you're a kid. Which I'm still not copping to.

"You could be, you know," he says. Which means I'm not. "You *were* trespassing."

"The door was unlocked."

"Breaking and entering would be a different charge."

"Well—if I'm not under arrest, then why can't I go home?"

"I'm trying to send you home," he says. *"With a parent."*

I say nothing.

"Listen." Garcia puts both hands on the table. "You've reached the end of the line, here. Give me someone to call for you, or you can hang out in *there* until either you change your mind, or someone reports you missing."

He gestures out the window with his chin. I turn around in my seat and consider the single holding cell in the corner. On the one hand, I won't have to talk to anyone, and I might get to spot Officer O'Hara again. On the other hand . . . it's a cage. A very literal, steel-bars-and-locked-door kind of cage.

"So. What's it going to be?"

I swallow. "He's going to kill me."

"Who, your dad?" he asks. I nod. "You broke city curfew to hang out in a half-built brewery and then contaminated a crime scene. He *should* kill you."

"He won't even pick up," I try to explain. "He's a chef, it's dinner service, his phone's off—"

"What restaurant? I'll call the hostess."

Before I can come up with some lie for why *that* won't work, the door bursts open.

"Garcia, what the hell's taking you?" The police chief swaggers inside. "I could use you with Phoebe, she's about to give me a migraine—"

Garcia nods toward me. "Just finishing up with a witness."

I keep my eyes on the desk and my head turned away from the door, because the only way this night could possibly get worse is if . . .

"Well, no shit," the chief says, and the door frame squeaks as he leans on it. "Boy Detective."

. . . he recognizes me.

"I—" Garcia looks across at me, then up at the chief. "What?"

"Yeah, I guess you hadn't started yet, had you? It was a few years ago," the chief says to Garcia. Then to me: "So what dumbass thing did you do now?"

My face burns. "Nothing."

"He found the body," Garcia clarifies. "Him and a friend."

"Oh, Garcia, you've got to watch out for this one. You know how at the academy they teach you about serial killers wanting to insert themselves into the investigation?" He spreads his hands out wide. "They've got nothing on this kid."

"I'm not a serial killer," I tell Garcia.

"Good to know," he replies.

"Serial pain in the ass, more like it," the chief says to Garcia. "First time I ever heard of this kid, it was because he wouldn't stop harassing the 911 operator. He was like eight—"

"Ten." I was short for my age, but still ten.

"He kept going on and on about how there had been a robbery. Eventually the operator girl flagged the number. But what do you know, not four hours later we get the call from the neighbors. Some expensive diamond set."

"Sapphires."

"So we go over and talk to him, and he's got the whole case figured out. Knew who the perp was—clocked that the perp *was* a perp—and told us exactly how to track him down. Easiest bag of my entire career. Weirdest little kid you've seen in your entire life."

I want to correct that, too, but I don't know how.

"Anyway, we thought it would make a cute PR thing—so we bring the kid in, do this whole faux award ceremony, let someone from Channel Five come and film. I put on my dress blues and personally pinned the little medal on him." He grins at me. "Remember?"

As if I'd forget the best day of my life. Not even *this* day, which has to be one of my all-time worst, could make me forget that.

"And you'd think that would be the end, right?" he's asking Garcia. "He gets his award, he gets on TV, everyone goes aw, and the world keeps turning. But not for Boy Detective, here."

He's not really going to do this, he's not really going to tell this part of the story—is he?

"Maybe two years later, we start hearing from him again. Only this time, it's not about a necklace, it's about some teacher at the high school."

It's official: this is the third-worst day of my entire life and now he's really, *really* going to make me relive the second.

"So Boy Detective somehow got it in his head that the photography teacher at Presidio was selling fake IDs to some of his students—"

I didn't *get it in my head.* Everybody had heard that rumor, even at my middle school. I was just the only one who decided to investigate.

"And, you know, we told him we'd check it out"—he looks down at me—"which we did, by the way, though there was plainly nothing going on and nothing to see. But he kept calling, and calling and just would not let it go."

I thought if I could replicate that first real case—do it all over again, but bigger and better this time—everything would go back the way it was. My agency would have clients again, Lily would be my friend again, people would take me seriously again.

But the longer the chief tells this story, the more I'm realizing the truth I refused to see before: they never took me seriously at all.

"And again, you'd think that would be it. He'd get the hint, move on. But what Boy Detective did—" He stops, like he's just realizing I'm still in the room. "Do you want to tell it?"

I've changed my mind. This is the second-worst day of my

life, and it's not even over yet.

The chief misreads whatever murderous expression is on my face. "No? All right. Well, not getting the support he was hoping for, I guess, he goes down to the high school one weekend and tries to climb through a classroom window and go looking for evidence. And then—I shit you not—he got stuck."

Through the office window, I see Lily walk past the rows of desks, both of Priya's arms wrapped protectively around her as they make a beeline for the Exit sign. Lily doesn't see me. She isn't looking.

"Some neighbor calls it in, so we show up with the fire department, and then one of the news channels shows up, because they'd heard the scanner and thought it was a *real* break-in, and it got maybe ten seconds on the news that night."

They never said my name or showed my face. It didn't matter. All it took was one parent hearing the report about a kid in a trench coat and a fedora and the whole seventh grade knew. It spread like wildfire. Or syphilis.

I'd been so upset over being ignored, I hadn't considered it might be worse to be laughed at instead. But I could handle that.

What I couldn't take was being pitied.

"It was a shit show," the chief says. "I guess I can't be surprised that wasn't the end of it. Trouble just finds you, doesn't it, Boy Detective?"

"That's not my name," I say, biting off each word.

"Finally." Garcia sighs. "So what is it?"

"It's a color. Brown?" The chief snaps his fingers. "No. Green."

Action heroes might fight to the death and cowboys might go out guns blazing, but this isn't that kind of movie. Detectives know how to accept defeat. I look Garcia right in the eyes.

"My name is Gideon Green and the restaurant you're looking for is called Verde."

The drive from Verde to the police station should take fifteen minutes, minimum. Dad makes it there in nine.

"Hi," he says as he bursts through the door, "I'm George Green, I got a call, I'm looking for—" When he spots me, his shoulders drop, and he sighs for two full seconds. "Him."

I've seen him pull all-nighters perfecting a new menu item and drag himself home after a Mother's Day lunch/dinner service combo. But I've never seen him look more exhausted than he does right now.

Deputy Chief Garcia gestures to the chair next to me. "Come in, Mr. Green."

Dad walks over, but he doesn't sit right away. He touches my head, then seems to scan my whole body. I don't know what he's looking for, exactly, but at least he isn't yelling yet.

"Are you okay?" he asks me, low and serious.

"I'm okay."

"Are you sure?"

There might be a bruise on my arm courtesy of Officer

Friendly, but it doesn't seem worth mentioning. "Yeah, Dad, I'm fine."

He nods and then finally sits down next to me.

"Thank you for coming down," Garcia starts off.

"Of course."

"I'm sorry to have to pull you away from work. Your son said you're a chef?"

"Chef/owner, yeah," Dad says. "I just opened a new place, Verde."

"It's a clever name," Chief Garcia says. "Mexican food?"

"Mexican fusion."

I wait to see if Dad will drop his favorite canned line here, which is that—with a Mexican mom and a white dad—he is *also* a result of Mexican fusion. He doesn't.

Garcia spreads his hands on the tabletop. "So here's the situation."

By the time Garcia is wrapping up his story with *give a statement* and *not charging him, but*, I can feel Dad's eyes burning a hole in my skull. I stare at my hands. It's the same basic theory as surviving a bear attack. No sudden movements, climb a tree if it's available, and pray to the god of your choosing.

"Gideon, what on earth would possess you?" Dad demands.

There's no answer I can give that would make this situation better. If I told the truth, they'd freak out, drag Lily into it again, and ruin the investigation. If I lie, they'll think I'm—what did Ellicot say? *Just a dumb kid.*

164

Maybe it's better, sometimes, to be underestimated. Even if it hurts your pride.

"I don't know," I say, and it comes out a whine. "We were bored."

"We?"

"I didn't mention—he was with a girl," Garcia says.

Dad's eyebrows shoot up. He turns back to me. "A girl, what girl?"

"Not a *girl* girl," I say, feeling my face get hot. "It was just Lily."

This only seems to confuse Dad more. "Lily? How did you talk her into this?"

Telling the truth about that would require telling the truth about a lot more things, so I look down at my shoes and shrug.

"You were *bored*," Dad repeats. "Of all the stupid things! I can't believe you."

You shouldn't believe me, I think. I'm lying my ass off.

Garcia, maybe sensing how close Dad is to flipping his shit, leans across the desk and catches my eye.

"I'm very sorry you stumbled on this accident," he says to me. "I hope that will convince you not to go wandering around construction sites in the future."

For a split second, the condescension prickles, but then—an *accident*?

I thought he knew.

"It wasn't an accident," I say.

That throws him for a loop, which throws *me* for a loop. He really doesn't know. "Yes, it was," he says, recovering fast. "That area has been a site of several overdoses and the deceased was known to use. We found a bag with paraphernalia on the catwalk, not to mention the tourniquet on his arm—"

"Okay," I agree, because I don't know the dead guy. I'll take his word for it. "But this wasn't an accident."

"What are you talking about," Dad says, low and urgent. Less of a question, more of a desperate plea for me to shut up.

"It was murder," I say simply. "He was murdered."

For a moment, they both stare at me in silence. Then Garcia sighs deeply. "He fell from the catwalk. It would be very easy to do, in his altered state. You didn't see a murder."

"Why would you even *say* that?" Dad asks.

"Mr. Green, it's all right," Garcia assures him. "This is a perfectly normal response to seeing something traumatic."

"I'm not saying it because I'm traumatized. I'm saying it because it was murder."

"Stop," Dad says to me.

Garcia clears his throat. "I'm sure you'd like to get out of here and deal with all of this privately."

"Yes. Thank you," Dad says to him.

"But—"

Dad cuts me off. *"No."*

"We'll need him to give a statement about what he saw," Garcia says. "And we're going to have to fingerprint him, to exclude any prints he left at the scene."

Dad looks grim but nods. "Of course."

"But once that's done, you can take him home." He looks to both of us. "Any questions?"

Dad shakes his head no.

"Yes," I say.

"Gideon," Dad warns.

"Will my fingerprints go into the national database or just a state one?"

"*Gideon!*"

Garcia looks baffled. "Are you . . . planning on committing crimes in the future?"

"I guess if I did, I'd wear gloves— Ow!" I rub at the spot on my ribs where Dad just elbowed me.

"I don't even know how to respond to that," says Garcia.

Dad raises both hands in defeat. "Welcome to my world."

CHAPTER 14

AFTER THE FINGERPRINTING and one last lecture from Garcia about staying off private property, Dad is allowed to take me home.

He doesn't say a word until we get on the freeway. And even then, it's only two of them.

"Start explaining."

"Explain what?"

The look he gives me is pure murder. And I would know. I just saw one. "Yourself! Obviously!"

"The deputy chief already told you everything—"

"Not everything," Dad says. "You called me today to ask about triggerfish—which no one cooks—and then five hours later you get picked up by the cops *at* Triggerfish Brewery?"

I was really hoping he hadn't remembered that. But good memories run in the family.

"How do you explain that?" he asks.

". . . Coincidence?"

He clenches his jaw. "Do you think I'm an idiot?"

"No." I pause. "Because you're not supposed to call people that."

"You're lying to me."

"No, you really aren't supposed to."

"About tonight!"

It feels kind of snake-eats-tail to lie about lying, but what choice do I have? "I'm not."

"Of course you are. I don't know why, and I don't know how you can just sit there and lie to my face, but you're doing it."

"I heard that it was cool, inside the brewery," I say, really wishing I'd thought of a better story ahead of time. "Other people at school have gone inside, when it was dark, and explored and stuff. And I thought you might know about it, a little, because it's the same industry, but I didn't want *you* to know *I* knew, and—"

"So you pretended not to know what it was?" The way he looks at me, I think he's—somehow—buying this. He's also—definitely—questioning my intelligence.

"Yeah. I guess you could say I was . . . fishing." I laugh, a little. He glares. A lot. "Do you get it? Because it's Triggerf—"

"You are unbelievable," he says. "Do you have any idea what my father would have done to me if he'd had to come pick me up at a police station?"

"Driven you into the desert and left you there?" He clenches

169

the steering wheel tighter. "Or . . . did you not want me to guess?"

"No, I did not want you to *guess* the answer to a *rhetorical question*."

Questions have answers. That's the entire point of them. Rhetorical questions are stupid.

Dad shakes his head. "You wouldn't have survived a week with that man."

That's what a detective would call an untestable theory, since my grandfather died before I was born. I'm not sure I would have met him anyway—Dad and I might not get along great, but he and *his* dad were much, much worse. In a violent way, I think, though Dad never comes right out and says that. But he hints at it, when he's really pissed at me. Like right now. That I'm lucky to be his kid and not my grandfather's.

And yeah, of course I'm glad that's never been Dad's style. But the expectation I should be *grateful* for it—that feels messed up.

"The sneaking out is one thing," Dad says. I'm not sure it counts as *sneaking* out if I was the only one home. I decide not to argue this. "You're sixteen, that's normal. Not acceptable. Normal. But then—" And here his voice gets louder. "Then you go and disturb a *crime* scene, because . . . why? You like detective movies and you think that makes you one?"

I wince. If he knew what we were actually doing there, he wouldn't say that. If he actually knew how much I'd done, he'd take me seriously.

"You promised," he reminds me. "Do you remember? The *last* time I picked you up from that police station, you promised me you were done with the detective thing."

"I was!" Then I scramble to add, "I . . . am—I retired!"

"But you weren't done. It just *morphed*. First the movies, the clothes, now running around breaking into places. And for the record, it is *absurd* that you call yourself retired—"

"What else should I call it? I had clients. I solved cases."

"You also got detained," he says, "at twelve years old."

"One time!" I pause. "Well, one time until now—"

"It wasn't just that. It was also the calls from other parents wondering why you were digging through their trash looking for 'evidence.' It was your elementary school art teacher suggesting therapy because all you'd draw were men with fedoras and guns. Your middle school principal telling me you'd refused to take off the trench coat for PE, because 'Philip Marlowe could run just fine.'"

And doesn't it always come back to that? Isn't it *always* about *all* the ways I've managed to embarrass him?

"But nothing comes close to tonight," he says. "What could come close to touching a dead body?"

"I used my sleeve!"

"To touch a dead body!"

"It's not like it's the first one I've seen." I regret it the second I spit it out. Dad doesn't say anything, just swallows so hard I can hear it. The air in the car contracts, and both of us silently suffocate.

Say something, I want to yell at him. Or beg him. They're so different, I can't understand how I could want both. *Say anything. Just once in ten years, say anything at all.*

He doesn't, though. Not then, not for another full minute, until we're about to take our exit home.

"I don't understand why you can't let that part of your life go."

At first, I think he's talking about her, and I open my mouth to say: *What* part? *The part where I had two parents?* But then he adds: "There's more to life than a game you played as a kid."

It wasn't ever a game, to me. It definitely isn't now, after what I saw tonight.

"That's the last time I felt like anyone took me seriously," I say. *Including you,* I don't say.

"You want to be taken seriously, but you have no clue what the consequences of that might be."

"What do you mean?"

"I mean there's a flipside to being taken seriously, Gideon," he says, "and that is being seen as a threat."

I shake my head. "I don't—"

"You should be down-on-your-knees thankful the cop who found you tonight didn't take you seriously. That the deputy chief let you walk right out of that station—you have *cousins* who would never be that lucky."

"Lucky—?"

"Yes!" he insists before I can get another word in. "You are *lucky* those people looked at you and only saw a stupid, harmless kid. Because if they'd seen something different . . ."

He swallows again, so hard it looks painful.

"Do you have any idea how bad this could have been?" His voice is quieter now, but just as sharp. "Do you get that you could have ended up arrested, or hurt, or—" He takes a deep, shaking breath. "And do you care, even a little bit, about what it was like for me to get that call?"

"I know," I mumble, "it was dinner service."

"Dinner service—" he repeats, incredulous. "I mean how it *felt!*"

I thought he was just mad—mad that I made him leave the restaurant, mad that I embarrassed him. But maybe the anger hasn't crowded everything else out. Maybe there's still room for another feeling I can't quite place, and I wait for him to tell me what it is.

He doesn't. He just keeps driving in silence until we pull up at the house. When I go for the door, though, he stops me.

"Wait."

I screw my eyes shut. What else could he possibly have left to yell at me about?

He opens his mouth. Closes it. And when he opens it again, what comes out is: "Are you sure you're okay?"

"Yeah," I say, surprised.

"I mean . . ." He rubs the back of his neck. "Do you want to talk about it?"

"Which part?"

"The . . . seeing the—what you saw."

"Oh," I say. "No."

He nods and looks away, so I assume that means I'm dismissed. But the second I try for the door again, he says: "I didn't realize you remembered."

I know what he means. I ask anyway.

"Remembered what?"

"The funeral. Hers."

I want to say: *My own mother's funeral?* And I want to ask: *How could you think I wouldn't remember the worst day of my entire life?* But all I say is:

"Yeah. I actually remember it pretty well."

"Oh."

I wait for him to say: *I do too.* And I wait for him to ask: *Do you want to talk about that?*

He doesn't. Instead, he clears his throat and says:

"You won't always. It'll fade, the older you get. You'll see."

I want to ask: *Is that supposed to make me feel better?* And I want to say: *What if I don't want to forget?* But before I can, he adds:

"Who knows, maybe someday you'll even forget tonight." He shakes his head and laughs, but like it isn't funny at all. "Maybe *I* will."

174

I think about the way he looked at me when he walked into Garcia's office, how the first thing he did was ask if I was okay. And then ask again. Just to make sure. I think about the hostess coming into his kitchen, to tell him his only child—his only real family at all—had been picked up by the police. I think—really think—about how that must have felt.

"Dad . . ." I hesitate. "Are . . . you okay?"

"I'm fine. I'm just—" He looks up and doesn't blink. "God, Gideon, you scared the shit out of me tonight."

No amount of yelling could make me feel worse than that.

"I'm sorry," I say. And I really am, for that part. "I didn't mean t—"

He cuts me off with a wave of his hand. "Don't."

"Don't what?"

"Do not," he says, "tell me that you *didn't mean to.*"

"It's true!"

"But it doesn't matter." I frown. He sighs. "Just . . . go to bed."

CHAPTER 15

THERE ARE SOME mornings where it feels like you fell asleep only ten seconds ago, but already, your alarm's blaring to wake you up again.

This morning would be like that, except it's Saturday, so I don't have an alarm set. What actually wakes me up is my phone ringing, with Lily on the other line.

"Are you awake?" she asks. "I didn't want to call too early."

I look at the clock on my bedside table. Eight a.m. Does Lily understand what a weekend is for?

"I'm awake." I rub my eyes. "Now."

"What happened after we got split up? My moms asked if they could take you home, too, but the officer said no."

"I put off calling my dad. For a while."

"Oh, God."

"No, it's good. I saw some stuff. Useful stuff."

I tell her about Officer O'Hara and how freaked out he

seemed. And the police chief, who didn't seem nearly freaked out *enough.*

"This is getting so complicated," Lily says. "It's like the more we learn, the less I understand. Tess *totally* knows there's something I'm not telling her, and if we can't nail down this story when it comes time to decide editor in chief—"

"We'll figure it out," I promise her, trying to sound more confident than I am. Someone has to be. "Can you do some background research on the chief? Do you still have your computer and everything?"

"Uh, yeah. Why wouldn't I?"

"I thought maybe they'd take it. Or your phone."

"My moms? Have you met them? Priya keeps asking if I need to process my feelings about seeing a corpse, and Zanna just wants to tell me about all the protests she's been arrested at."

"We didn't get arrested."

"Tell her, not me."

"Yeah, and tell my dad, he's acting like I killed the guy myself."

"So I take it he *is* mad."

Dad decides to make his entrance then, swinging open my door without knocking. Which is new.

He nods his head at my phone. "Who is that?"

"Lily."

"Give it to me," he says, hand outstretched.

"Why?"

"What's going on?" Lily asks me.

"This isn't a discussion," Dad says to me.

"Not a discussion, apparently," I say to Lily.

That's when Dad reaches over and just takes it.

"At least let me say goodbye!" I protest.

He ignores me. Hits speakerphone. Holds it up.

"Hey there, Lily," he says.

"Oh, um. Hi, Mr. Green."

"Listen, I just want to apologize on my son's behalf for getting you mixed up in this."

"Oh my God," I say, burying my face in my hands. *"Dad."*

"Mr. Green, it really wasn't like that."

He doesn't seem to hear her or me. "And to let you know Gideon won't be available for the rest of the day. Maybe the year. I haven't decided yet. Say hi to your mothers for me."

"Uh, okay, but—"

He hangs up the phone and sticks it in his own pocket.

"That was so embarrassing," I tell him.

"I don't think you want to throw stones about what's embarrassing."

That metaphor always confuses me. Nobody should be throwing stones, even if their house *isn't* glass. And who lives in a glass house, anyway? Other than plants.

"Can I have my phone back?" I ask hopefully. Maybe he only wanted to talk to Lily.

"I'm going to hold on to it for now."

A month ago that wouldn't have bothered me. Which is

probably why he's never taken it. Lily and I have work to do, though, so I need it.

"But if you take it away," I say, trying to appeal to practicality, "how will you track my every move?"

"I don't have to. You're going to be right where I can watch you, all day."

Huh? It's Saturday, he has a brunch service in two hours—

Oh no.

"Clearly, I can't trust you to stay home by yourself, so you're coming to Verde with me. You can spend the afternoon doing side work."

"Side work" is restaurant-speak for the bullshit chores no one wants to do. Rolling silverware, filling up ketchup dispensers, wiping down tables after a party leaves. It sucks even when it isn't punishment. I've done it before.

"This is child labor," I tell him, and the eye roll I get back is massive.

"*Pobrecito.*" I wonder if he's ever said that nonsarcastically. I wonder if *anyone* has ever used that word nonsarcastically. "Get dressed. You're not going to make me late."

In the car, halfway to Verde, I decide to try out a new defense strategy. I'm not asking for full immunity. Just a commutation of my sentence.

"Dad, I know you're mad at me—"

"Glad you picked up on that."

"But this is an overreaction."

"No, it's a logical consequence *of* your actions. If I can't trust that you're safe when I leave you alone, then you can't be left alone."

"You know," I point out, "you were the one who told me to get out of the house."

"I didn't mean you should go wandering around a construction site at night!"

"Maybe you should have been more specific."

He blinks. Then turns. And the look he gives me makes me shrink all the way down in my seat.

"You are," he tells me, "on the *thinnest* of ice."

I drop my eyes to my shoes and fold my arms across my chest. I should shut up. I know I should shut up. But I have more questions.

"So, what, you're going to drag me to the restaurant every weekend?"

"No," he says. "I'm going to drag you there every day."

My stomach drops. "What do you mean, *every day*?"

"I mean, when I go to work in the afternoon, you come with me. You can do your homework in the back office."

Detectives don't panic, so I'm definitely not panicking right now. It's just that my heart is beating too fast and my lungs are contracting, or whatever. How am I going to help Lily if I'm locked in his office? And wait, forget the investigation, what about—

"What about the paper?"

"I . . ." He sighs. "I don't think I'm comfortable with that."

"What?"

"Maybe in a few weeks, if I feel like you've made an effort—"

I don't care how thin the ice is. I would rather drown.

"You can't do that!"

"Excuse me?"

Excuse me is code for *You better rephrase that*, but I don't care. I meant those words exactly. "I *said*, you can't *do* that."

"Who do you think is in charge here?" Dad says. "Me or you?"

"I have a job at the paper. People depend on me. You can't just make me quit—"

"We'll talk about this later," he says, cutting me off. I hadn't even noticed, but we've pulled into the staff parking behind Verde.

The second we walk in the door, Dad's general manager is at his shoulder. Every time I've met him, Mario has been in some stage of calming Dad the hell down, which I appreciate as a person who can only wind my dad up more.

"So we have a small issue," Mario says.

Dad rubs his temples. "Oh, God."

"I said small, cálmate."

Dad does not, in any way, do that. "Just tell me, what?"

"Sarah is a no-call no-show."

"Christ, again?"

"I keep calling her phone, but it goes to voice mail."

"Well, then leave one, telling her she's fired."

"And in the meantime?" Mario nods his head over at the lone waiter tying on his apron behind the bar. "I only have Josh. He can cover most of the tables, but I don't think all, so—"

"Gideon will take them."

Mario and I look at each other, then at Dad, and say in unison: "What?"

"Give Josh all the tables he can handle and put Gideon on any he can't."

"He hasn't been trained—" Mario says.

Dad looks at the clock. "You've got an hour, give him a crash course. It's not rocket science."

"Dad." I am dangerously close to begging. "No."

"I was younger than you when I took my first order. You're fully capable."

Is that supposed to be comforting? Or is it an accusation? Like: *I could do this at fourteen, so if you can't, there must be something wrong with you.*

He takes me by the arm and leans down a little, like he's about to impart some kind of wisdom. Or an ancient prophecy. One about human sacrifice.

"It's easy," he says, and I hate how excited he sounds by the prospect of dragging me into yet another thing he loves that I'm not cut out for at all. "Smile when you walk up to the table. Be polite, even if they aren't. Write legibly. Understood?"

I glare at him. He waits.

"And then *you* say . . . ?"

"This is a terrible idea."

"Nope." He shakes his head. "Try again."

Through gritted teeth, I say: "Yes, Chef."

Mario does his best—gets me a spare uniform button-down and an apron, goes over everything on the blessedly limited brunch menu, and watches me struggle to learn how a corkscrew works— but we both know this is a disaster in the making. He waits as long as he can to give me a table, but eventually the brunch rush is in full swing, and he doesn't have a choice.

If my life were a noir, there would be a full-on montage here. Noir doesn't have montages as a rule, but there would be no other way to convey the rapid-fire chaos. It would be like:

INT. RESTAURANT, DAY—MONTAGE

QUICK CUTS:

—Gideon fights with the POS machine, which stands for point of service but should really stand for piece of shit.

—Gideon gets flagged down by Table 7 (even though it's not his table) for a side of ranch.

—The woman at Table 6 makes Gideon check three times that there are no nuts in the gazpacho, even though there are never nuts in gazpacho.

—Women at Table 3 ask about their drinks and Gideon says they're almost ready even though he totally forgot to put them in.

—More ranch is scooped into a tiny ceramic ramekin for Table 7, who should face criminal charges for what they're doing to a perfectly good omelet.

"Table 6 needs you," Josh, the other waiter, whispers to me as we pass each other. "They look like you pissed in their cereal."

"Nobody ordered cereal."

He shakes his head and keeps walking.

When I get over there, the lady at Table 6 looks at me like I've run over her dog, reversed the car and backed over it, then sped away yelling, *"I will kill again!"*

"Is everything all right?" I ask her.

"My soup is cold."

I laugh. She doesn't. I realize it isn't a joke.

"I mean, yeah," I say. "It's gazpacho."

"I don't care what it's called, it's *cold*."

"But it's supposed to be c—"

"It's completely unacceptable for you to make soup this cold," she says.

"I didn't cook it."

That only seems to make her angrier. "Just take it back."

I grab the bowl and stomp back to the kitchen.

"She said the soup is cold," I say, setting the bowl back on the pass counter.

Dad's sous-chef stares at me. "We only have gazpacho."

"I know."

He groans. Takes the bowl. And sticks it right in the microwave above his head. I must look horrified, because then he adds: "Customer is always right. Even when they're fucking stupid."

"Yeah," I agree, "and can you believe she got mad at *me*?"

Dad, who was walking by, suddenly stops midmotion. "Why did she get mad at you?"

"I told her gazpacho is supposed to be cold, and she said not *that* cold, and I was like, 'Look, I didn't cook it—'"

"Gideon, Jesus Christ," he snaps. Then calls over his shoulder, "Héctor—" What follows is Spanglish so fast and furious I can only pick out the words "on the fly" at the end.

As Hector assembles the plate of meat and cheese rapid-fire, Dad turns back to me. "Now you'll go out there, tell them the platter's on the house, and then you apologize. Got it?"

"To *her*? She's a jerk!"

"Doesn't matter." He nods his head at the pass, where the bowl and the platter are both now waiting. *"Go."*

The gazpacho's so hot now, the bowl burns my hands, but I don't even care. I'm too pissed. He wants me to be nice to them, and for what? For *his* ego, for *his* restaurant, the thing he actually cares about. Screw this. Screw him.

"Your soup." I set it down in front of her. "The crudo platter is on the house." I set that down, too. "We so very deeply regret your pain."

After dropping off the boiling gazpacho, I pass by the women at Table 3 and a snippet of their conversation snags my attention.

"I keep telling Andy not to invest in this food-and-beverage kind of stuff," the woman in blue leggings is telling her friends. "It's too unpredictable. Look at that brewery, it's been almost two years and even Fred Willets's money couldn't get it off the ground."

I stop dead in my tracks.

"Did you say Fred Willets?" I blurt out.

Blue Leggings raises her eyebrows. "Um. Yes?"

"Fred Willets owns Triggerfish Brewery?"

"He owns a large share—" She looks around at her friends. "I'm sorry, did you need to ask us something?"

There's an empty chair next to her at the four-top, so I sit right down. "How do you know he's an owner?"

Blue Leggings moves her chair ever so slightly away from me. "My husband invested, too, so . . ."

"Is he involved in the construction? Like would he have keys to the site?"

Black Leggings clears her throat. "Sweetie, maybe you could get us some . . . tea?" she suggests to me. "Like . . . iced tea?"

"Yeah," Blue Leggings agrees. "Iced tea would be so great." She smiles at me, all teeth. "If you could . . . *go* and get that?"

I probably shouldn't have sat at their table.

"Yeah," I say, hopping up. "Sure. I'll bring that right away."

But I don't. Instead, I walk straight out of the dining room, skirting quietly past the kitchen, and into Dad's office in the very back, where I dig my phone out of his desk drawer.

"Hi," Lily says, sounding confused. "Didn't your dad take your phone?"

"Don't worry about it."

"Maybe you could chill out for like a *day* before pissing him off again—"

I cut right to the chase: "Fred Willets owns the brewery."

"What?"

"Triggerfish. He owns it. Or—he partially invested in it, I guess."

There's a long pause. Finally, Lily half whispers: "That's weird."

"I know."

"No, it's weirder than you know," she says. "Remember Luke telling us about tagging that business? It's closed now, but I looked it up way back when I was first investigating, and Willets owned *that*, too."

"Araceli said he owns a bunch of stuff around town, didn't she? It could be a coincidence."

"Could be." Another long pause. "I'll see what I can find."

Fred Willets put money in Triggerfish, I think after we've hung up and I finally grab the pitcher of iced tea. Maybe it wasn't random, the location. Maybe someone picked it because they had access.

Or maybe someone picked it to ruin the business before it ever got off the ground.

The woman from Table 6 snaps her fingers to flag me down again. I glance back at Table 3, but they just look relieved to have me gone. The iced tea can wait.

"Would you like the check?" I ask her hopefully.

"I will have the churros for dessert," she says, not even looking at me.

"No."

That makes her look up. "Excuse me?"

"No, you won't have the churros for dessert."

"Because you're out?"

"Because they have walnuts," I say. She just stares at me. "Which are a kind of nut. Which you are allergic to."

She waves me off. "It's fine, I can have a little bit."

I wonder how much trouble I'd get in if I just flipped over her table right now.

"Then you're not allergic," I grind out.

"I asked for the churros." She sticks her menu up in my face. "Not your opinion."

I know I'm about to do something stupid, something I'm

really going to regret, but I'm too mad to care.

"It's not an opinion. It's a fact. If you can eat nuts, then you don't have a nut allergy, which is weird, because you definitely said you were—and I'm quoting—'deathly allergic to nuts.' So if *I* were to call you a *liar*," I say, way too loud, but still not caring, "*that* would be a fact, too."

The whole restaurant is so quiet you could hear a pin drop. If anyone brought pins to a restaurant, which they wouldn't.

The lady at Table 6 interlaces her fingers.

"You'd better go get your manager."

Mario spends forever soothing the woman at Table 6. If I wasn't so relieved to be rescued, I'd almost be mad at how good he is at it—nodding solemnly as she rants about how awful I am, speaking to her in a tone so calm and empathetic you'd almost think he agreed with her.

But of course he doesn't. It wasn't my fault. Still, he shakes his head when he walks up to me, after brunch service is over and the last table has finally left.

"Well . . ." He clears his throat. "Your first shift could have gone better."

"Yeah. I know."

"I've had people spill hot soup, drop knives, break wine bottles." He shakes his head, walking toward the kitchen. "But I don't think I've ever had to comp all the tables on someone's first shift."

Waiting alone in the empty dining room feels a lot like when I was little and would break something. The crash, and then the silence. Knowing what's about to happen was going to be bad, and trying very hard to convince myself I didn't deserve it.

At least the suspense is short-lived. I can hear Dad shout from inside the kitchen. I could probably hear him from the next county over.

"He said *what?*"

I wince.

Dad stalks out the swinging kitchen door and into the dining room. I take a large step to the left, strategically putting the hostess stand in between us.

"Come here." He crooks his finger at me. I stay where I am. "Do you not see my lips moving? *Come. Here.*"

I inch forward, slowly, until I'm more or less in front of him, and he more or less looks like he wants to knock me to the floor.

"What the hell is the matter with you?"

My throat is all sawdust. "I—"

"What were you thinking, talking to a guest like that? Did you think it was funny, did you think you sounded *clever?*"

"All I did was tell that lady—"

"All you did was run your mouth."

We're gathering an audience. The line cooks are looking at Dad, not me, which is merciful. He must notice he's being watched, though, because he pauses. Does he wish he hadn't started in on me like this, in front of everyone?

He glances around. Takes a deep breath. And launches right back in.

"You just go around saying whatever pops into your head. Doesn't matter who you're talking to! It could be me, it could be a customer, it could be the *cop* who's *detaining you*, you don't care!"

The back of my neck goes hot when he brings up the police. As if that's something I want the whole kitchen to know about.

"Dad, I didn't mean to—"

"No, you never mean to! It's never your fault, is it?"

I've heard this before. It's nothing new. But there's a difference between getting yelled at in the privacy of your own home and having to stand in the center of a room while a bunch of strangers watch your dad tell you exactly how much of a screwup he thinks you are.

"What is your future going to look like, if you can't keep your mouth shut when you need to, and you won't listen to a word anybody else says?"

He wants me to just shut up? Fine. I bite the inside of my cheek, fold my arms across my chest, and don't answer him.

"No, come on, tell me," he says. "Tell me exactly what you think you'll be able to do with your life."

"Well," I say, as all the anger and embarrassment rises in my chest and spills out of my mouth, "I guess if all else fails, I could go work in some kitchen!"

Oh shit.

Too far. Way too far.

For a second, nobody moves. Nobody even breathes. Or at least I don't.

But then Dad is stripping off his apron to the floor and closing the space between us fast, and I'm scrambling to remember where the emergency exit is.

I take a stumbling step back, right into the sharp edge of Table 6. I put one hand back on it to steady myself.

It isn't until we're nearly toe-to-toe that Dad stops. He glares. I gulp.

"Now you listen to me," he says, pointing a finger so close to my face I flinch. "I take a lot of shit from you, a lot more than I should, but what I'm *not* going to do is stand here and let you disrespect all the people who work for me."

My clammy hand slips on the table edge. I grip tighter. It hurts.

"This isn't some kitchen, this is *my* kitchen and *my* business and the thing that puts food on *your* fucking plate, kid, so you better watch what you say. Do you understand?"

Behind Dad, the staff is still watching, totally silent, expressions unreadable. Do they feel bad for me? Or do they think I was asking for this?

"That was a question," Dad says, snapping my attention back to him. "It has an answer."

Oh, this one's not rhetorical? I almost snap back. But since I don't want to die today, I close my eyes and say, very quietly: "Yes."

He shifts his weight back. I take a breath. But he's not done.

"How you can stand there and put down not just what I do, but what everyone here does, everyone who tried to help you today—it's beyond me."

But that's not what I meant, I'm on the verge of saying. *I didn't mean to make anyone feel that way.* It has to matter, at least a little, that I didn't mean to. Doesn't it?

Maybe it does. And maybe it just matters way, way more . . . that I did it.

"You couldn't do any of their jobs on your best day. Your very best."

The whole scene swims and blurs, like someone's smeared Vaseline over a camera lens. Not because I'm about to cry, in front of all these people, in front of the dad I'm never going to be good enough for. I'm not. I won't.

"I know you think you're too good for this, Gideon, but here's the truth and you better believe me when I say it: you aren't anywhere good *enough.*"

Maybe if I duck my head quickly enough, no one will be able to tell. Maybe the blurry and now slightly wet floor beneath me will open up and swallow me whole. A person can dream.

Either Dad decides he's gone far enough, or he got exactly where he wanted to be. He turns away.

"Go wait by the car."

CHAPTER 16

DAD MUST DECIDE the negatives of having me at the restaurant far outweigh the positives, because he doesn't take me with him on Sunday. He also barely speaks to me, and I'm happy to return the favor. When I wake up Monday morning, on the kitchen table is my phone and a note.

Went to Verde. Will be back by 2 PM. Come home immediately after school.

Even in writing he's trying to use as few words as possible. Not a great sign. And neither is the Post-it on my phone that says, "Tracking stays on."

I can't find Lily anywhere at lunch, so I ditch my food and duck behind the portables to call her.

"You aren't at school," I say when she picks up.

"I decided seeing a body was deserving of a sick day."

Fair. "Did you get to look into them more? O'Hara? And the police chief?"

"I—" There's dead air on the line for a second. "I'm not sure if we should."

"Should what?"

"Keep going with this."

She can't be serious. Just when it's getting real, just when we've proven she was right all along about the crime wave—no one's ever been murdered over a clerical error—*now* she wants to pull back?

"You want to stop? We can't stop."

"Friday really freaked me out, you know?"

"Yeah, Lily, I totally get it, but—"

"We saw a dead person. And I know it was just a horrible accident, and you were really the one who saw the body, not me, but we're going into these situations we aren't prepared for at all—"

We can't leave it like this. She wasn't the one who had to sit through the police chief recounting *her* biggest fuckup in excruciating detail. He's told that story before, I can tell, and I can't let his new punch line be Friday night and my dad dragging me out of the station. Again.

The next time he tells that story, there's going to be a different ending.

"So maybe it's for the best," Lily says. "That we take a break."

"But it wasn't an accident," I blurt out before she can completely talk herself out of this.

There's a rustling sound, like she's suddenly sitting up straight.

"What are you talking about?"

"It wasn't an accident and it wasn't a coincidence we found that body. We just didn't stumble on a tragedy—I mean, it's tragic, someone's dead, but—whoever O'Hara was supposed to meet did that."

For a few seconds, it's so quiet I wonder if the call dropped. Then Lily stammers out: "Are—are you saying somebody *killed him*?"

"Not *somebody*," I say. "Whoever wrote the note."

"Oh my God." She breathes out, deep. "Oh my—"

"There's more. Whoever that guy was, the guy we found, who died—he mattered."

"Jesus, of course he mattered!"

"No, I mean, the police knew him. Or . . . knew of him." I give her a rundown of the conversation between the two cops. "What do you think an OC task force is?"

"Orange County?" she suggests. "Maybe the dead guy was from there."

"That's a far drive."

"Then I don't know."

"His last name is—was—something ending in -*son*. Like Vinson, or Venison, or something."

"Venison is deer meat."

"I said, 'or something!'" I wait a beat. "Can you look into that, too? Who he might be?"

Lily sighs into the phone. "Gideon . . ."

"We can't stop now. The cops don't even think it was a murder."

And that's when I realize—as much as I want the chief and everyone else to see they're wrong about me and always have been, there's another part to this, a way more important part that isn't about me at all.

"A man died," I say, "and he's not going to get justice. Unless . . ."

"Unless we, two teenagers, try to solve it?"

I take a beat. "When you put it like that, it does sound like a pretty bad idea."

"Absolutely terrible," she agrees.

"You're going to do it, though, right?"

"I'll . . ." She sighs. "Do some research."

That's not a yes. But it's not a no. So I'll take it.

The next time I hear from Lily, it's sixth period, I'm sitting through a lecture on exponents, and she's lucky I'm awake enough to feel my phone vibrate in my pocket. Rushing to put it on silent before my teacher hears, I hold my phone under my desk to see what she's sent me.

First is a text.

Is this him?

Second is a picture.

And there, staring back at me, is a dead man. *The* dead man, or what he looked like in life, anyway. Broad shoulders and slicked-back hair, the same diamond stud in his left ear, and—

The watch.

On his wrist, facing the camera. Clearly showing it off. Clearly proud of it. The watch I knew was missing from the body. *I knew it.*

I text Lily back as discreetly as I can.

yeah that's definitely him

who is he?

Her next message is two links. The first sends me to a funeral home website. There's the same picture of the dead man at the top of the screen. And below it, an obit.

MARCO L. VINCE

Marco L. Vince, beloved son and brother,
passed away unexpectedly . . .

It's short, only a few sentences, and I'm too excited that I was right about the watch to do anything more than skim it.

Valued member of Vince Enterprises LTD. Survived by his
sisters, Jasmine and Alexis; his mother, Roberta; and his
father, Paul. Visitation at Holy Redeemer Catholic Church.

I was right about the watch, but I completely misheard those two desk cops at the police station. They didn't say *Vinson* or

Venison. They said he was *Vince's son.*

I stop reading there and text Lily again:

**It's his dad, they were talking about his dad, he must be the
one who matters**

Did you even LOOK at the second link?

I tap the next link, and this one sends me to a newspaper
article with the headline "Local Mogul's Son Found Dead in
Apparent Overdose."

The article's way too long to read, though, so I text Lily again.

Im in math rn, summarize
Please

Paul Vince is a businessman
Well
"Businessman"

?

In theory he runs a chain of discount furniture stores
**In reality, they're a front for money laundering and a lot of weird
shady stuff**
He's been written up and investigated in SD a bunch, and even

**been arrested a couple times, but nobody's really been able
to pin anything on him.**

Nothing that sticks

And he's been moving his territory into San Miguel

One of his stores just opened, not far from the brewery

Money laundering, shady business stuff—the cops didn't mean
Orange County when they talked about the OC task force. They
meant organized crime.

Any connection to the bar?

Can't find one

Class drags on, but if I wasn't paying attention before, now
it's like I'm not even on the same planet. My mind is in overdrive,
piecing together the new facts.

Here's what I know:

The dead man has a name.

He's the son of a shady businessman, if not one himself. And
that means he's the son of somebody with enemies, if he doesn't
have any of his own.

No one thinks his death was a murder—not the cops, not the
media, not even his family.

But no, I realize. I don't *know* that last part. I'm only assuming it. Just because the cops told a reporter it was a drug-related

accident, just because that reporter wrote the story that way, and just because Marco's own obit reads like he went peacefully in his sleep . . . that doesn't mean no one thinks it was murder.

It just means someone needs it to seem that way.

Two class periods later, school is over, but I'm still wrapped up in how Marco L. Vince ended up dead on the floor of Triggerfish Brewery—and why. So wrapped up, in fact, that when I walk out of my classroom and down the hall, looking for a good place to call Lily, I don't notice Tess until I nearly collide head-on with her.

"Hey," she says. Then frowns. "Where are you going?"

"Um—"

"*Herald* office is that way, dude." She points over my shoulder.

Shit. Right. Not only do I have to quit the paper, I have to quit at the start of a Late Night week. Everyone's going to love that. Especially Tess.

"I was looking for Lily," I lie.

"Oh, she called out sick." She grabs my arm, lightly, and turns me around. "Glad I could save you the trouble."

We're the first ones in the office, and Tess immediately goes to turn on her favorite computer. Knowing I'll never get a smaller audience than this, I take a deep breath and prepare to quit one of the only things I've ever liked.

"Tess—"

She turns around. "Yeah?"

"I can't do the paper anymore."

"What?"

"I'm sorry—"

"Look, I know copy editor isn't the best job in the world," she says, abandoning the computer and walking back over to me. "But please don't bail."

"I'm not bailing—"

"Well, good. We'd miss you too much."

I have to quit. I'm supposed to be telling her I'm quitting. But now that all seems secondary.

"Would you?" I ask.

"Of course."

"No, I mean . . ." I hesitate. "Would *you*?"

Then *she* hesitates. Because I think she knows what I'm asking. "Yeah," she says softly. "I would."

"Oh," I say, and my voice is just as soft. "Okay."

"Is that really enough to make you stay?" She takes a step closer to me. "That . . . I want you to?"

"Yes," I say without hesitation.

I've never seen Tess flustered. But the way she sucks her breath in here and can't seem to figure out what to do with her hands, I think she might be.

"Well—I mean . . ." She settles for folding her arms and smiling. "Great. If it means you'll stay."

"It's not that I don't want to stay. I'm not allowed to."

She wrinkles her nose. "What do you mean?"

"So. In a series of events that weren't my fault at all—"

"Oh, God. What did you do?"

"Nothing! It was just a wrong-place, very wrong-time kind of thing, and my dad completely overreacted and now I'm not allowed to be anywhere out of his line of vision."

She's quiet for a moment. Then she asks: "Do you really want to stay? Or do you just not want to hurt my feelings by quitting?"

"No," I promise her, "I do want to be here, for every Late Night, every dinner. I want to be here for—"

If this were a movie, the last word would be: *you*. But this is real life, and I am a coward.

"I want to be here for everything," I finish. And it takes saying it out loud to realize—it's true.

I want to be here because Tess is here, but I want to be here because *I'm* here, too.

That doesn't make any sense. Or maybe it does.

When I'm here, I'm not going through the motions of a school day. I'm not biding my time, counting down the minutes and hours until I get to be somewhere different. I'm not a shadow in the corner, watching everybody else pass me by.

When I'm here, in this room, I *feel* like I'm here.

"It's my dad who has the problem," I say, "and I've tried to explain to him I can't leave, it's not fair, but he's being so unreasonable—"

"Call him."

I take a step back. "What?"

203

"If you call, will he pick up?" she asks. I nod. "Then call him."

"And what am I supposed to say?"

"Tell him . . ." She pauses. "Tell him Ms. Flueger wants to talk to him."

I look around. "She's not here yet."

"He doesn't know that." Tess smiles. "Call him."

I try the home phone first, since he's probably still there. He picks up on the second ring. I expect him to start interrogating me about why I haven't started walking home yet, but he doesn't.

"Do you need me to pick you up?"

"No." Then I hesitate. Out of the corner of my eye, Tess gives me a thumbs-up. "Um—Ms. Flueger wants to talk to you."

"Who?"

"The staff adviser. For the paper." I look at Tess again. She makes a "keep going" gesture. "You know, that thing you told me I had to quit. . . ."

He sighs. "Right, yeah. Put her on."

When I hand Tess the phone, she draws her back up totally straight, flips her hair over her shoulder in a very un-Tess-like way, and drops into a voice that's slow and smooth and disconcertingly adult.

"Hi," she says, drawing out the word. "Is this Gideon's dad?"

Dad must confirm he is—it's a relief to know he hasn't disowned me yet—because she keeps going. "It's so nice to meet you, Mr. Green. First, I've got to tell you what a wonderful job you've done with Gideon. He is just the sweetest kid."

Stop, I mouth at her. She winks.

"No, not any trouble at all," she says after a pause. "Honestly, he's been a great addition to the newspaper, and we would be so sad to see him go. I wonder if there's anything I can do to change your mind."

Tess pauses for a moment while Dad talks. "Yes, he did mention something about—" She stops again, much longer this time. Then her eyebrows shoot up, and she turns to look at me. "The police? *Really.*"

I bury my face in my hands.

"Well, I completely understand why you'd be concerned." She waits a beat. "No, of course. But this is a perfectly safe place for him to be. I'm always here supervising."

I guess that's not technically a lie.

"And you know, a lot of parents like their kids on the paper because of college apps, and yes, it's wonderful for their résumés, but . . ." Tess lowers her head a little. And her voice a little, too. "I think it's more important than that. For your son."

My breath catches, then. Because when she says that, it isn't in her Ms. Flueger voice. It's in her own.

"Correct me if I'm wrong, but it seems like maybe Gideon spent a lot of time alone before. In his own head. Feeling like he didn't really have a place, maybe. Somewhere he belonged." And she fixes her eyes on mine. Because when she asks that, she's not asking Dad. She's asking me.

I nod, slowly. Tess smiles, sadly.

"Everyone on the paper is very close," Tess says, back to Dad. "It's . . . a family. In a way. And I think it's been good for Gideon to be a part of it. I think he would lose something if he had to leave."

What is it about hearing someone say what you've already thought that makes it real? Is it that I didn't have the words, so I'm grateful she found them for me? I think it's more. Tess knows how I feel, even though I've never told her. She didn't guess. She's not a psychic. She didn't decode it. She's not a detective.

She just knew. Because she recognized it. She knew, because she'd felt it, too.

"I promise you, if he's here, he's safe, and"—she smirks at me, barely able to contain her laughter—"definitely not in a holding cell."

I am never going to live this down.

"Yes," she says in response to something Dad asked. "I won't let him out of my sight."

Tess hands me back the phone, then retreats to a far table to pretend like she's not listening.

"She seems nice," Dad says to me.

"Yeah, she is."

"And she really seems to like you."

My face goes hot, and I turn away so Tess can't see it. "I guess so."

He's quiet for a moment, like he doesn't know where to go from here. "Gideon, about Saturday."

God, are we really going to rehash this? Wasn't it enough for him to yell at me in front of his entire staff? But then he takes a breath and says: "I'm sorry."

And then I have to sit down.

"Um—" I manage to get out, but nothing else before he jumps in again.

"I was angry, and frustrated, and especially after the night before, it was the last straw—" He pauses. "But I shouldn't have done that. I shouldn't have talked to you like that. Especially in front of everyone."

As a rule, my dad does not apologize. I never thought that was some huge flaw—noir detectives don't apologize much either, and they do way worse things than Dad ever has. But it made me feel like I couldn't apologize either, or he'd win. But maybe it isn't a competition. Or shouldn't be. Maybe it's a give-and-take. Or should be.

"I'm sorry I was a terrible waiter," I say.

"I don't think it's your calling." He pauses. "Is this?"

"Is what?"

"Your teacher seemed to think I'd be doing you a real dis-service, making you quit. That this was good for you. Important for you."

"Yeah, she's right," I say, glancing over at Tess. She lifts her eyes up to meet mine. Smiles. "She's pretty much right about everything, so . . ."

Tess mouths the word *Aw* and makes a heart shape with her

hands. Which makes my heart jump. And my throat close up.

"Okay," Dad says, snapping me out of it.

"Really?"

"Yeah." But he sighs the word, like he's still not sure. "Look. Here's the deal I'm going to make you. Keep your phone with you and the tracking activated. When I check, I want to see your location either on school grounds or at home. You do that, and we're good. Got it?"

"Got it."

"If not, you're going to be back at Verde rolling silverware until your fingers fall off."

It's always nice to be able to roll my eyes when he can't see. "Okay."

"I'll see you later. Have a good time."

I hang up and stick my phone back in my pocket. Tess looks so pleased with herself that if I didn't want to kiss her for talking Dad into this—actually if I didn't want to kiss her in general—it might be annoying.

"Sounds like it worked," she says.

"Tess," I tell her, "you're the greatest person I've ever met."

It's the truth, but I don't think she knows. Because she only laughs. "You need to get out more."

She says that, but I bet *she's* never been kicked out of a dive bar. Or broken into a construction site. Or sat in the back of a cop car.

"I've been trying," I say.

She tilts her head. "Can I ask you a question?"

"Yes. You can even ask me another one."

That makes her laugh again. "Where's your favorite place in the world?"

Not Doc Holliday's or Triggerfish and definitely not the San Miguel police station.

"My bedroom."

Tess makes a face. "God, is it really?"

I almost say yes. Because it's been true for so long. But instead I say: "No. Not really."

She shrugs, like, *Then, where?* It takes me a minute to realize the answer because it's so far from what's been true for so long. I always thought of true things as unchangeable. If the answer changed, it was because you hadn't figured it out before, but the right answer had always been right. You just hadn't known it.

But now, I think . . . it's more complicated than that.

"Here," I tell her. Simply. Truthfully. "This is my favorite place."

Her expression shifts. Is it pitying? Or just softer? I can't tell.

I sit down on the table next to her. Not too close. But not so far. "Where's your favorite place in the world?"

She doesn't hesitate. "Pacific Beach."

"Oh, yeah," I say. "I've driven by. It looks nice."

Tess's mouth drops. "You've never *been?*"

"My dad's not really a beach person and then I wasn't either, so—"

"Let's go," she says in a rush of pure excitement that makes me think of a little kid at the Disneyland gates. "You have to go."

"Right now?"

"No, not right now, on a weekend. But you should see it, we should go."

We?

"You and me, you mean?" I say. "Together?"

"Only if you want to."

"I do."

"Okay, then," she says. "I can't this weekend, but maybe the next Saturday?"

"Cool," I say. "It's a da—" But then I stop. Because the word I was about to say was "date." And I don't know if it's a date. I also don't know what to do with my hands, and I don't know why they feel so sweaty.

She looks confused. "It's a . . . day?"

I double down. "Yes." And when she still looks confused, I double down harder. "Like, an event. A thing. It'll be a . . . day."

"Uh-huh."

"Only if you want it to be," I add quickly. Then just as quickly realize that made no sense.

She lifts an eyebrow. "I do want it to be a day, yes."

I try to swallow, but my mouth feels like it's filled with cotton balls, so instead I cough out the word: "Cool."

"Mostly because the beach is closed at night."

"Right."

"But first . . . you have to tell me something."

My heart is pounding. My stomach is churning. It would probably be bad for the future of this not-date if I threw up all over the table.

"Yeah," I say. "Anything."

Tess leans back on her hands and smiles. "How'd you end up in that police station, Gideon Green?"

CHAPTER 17

"YOU DID *WHAT?*" Lily shouts at me when I stop her outside the
Herald room the next day.

"It's not a big deal."

"Do I get a say in that? Whether it's a big deal?"

I knew she'd be mad, but I figured it was better she hear it
from me than Tess. Maybe that was the wrong move.

"Lily—"

"No, I don't, because you went behind my back."

"I didn't have a choice! I'd already told her about the whole
police incident—"

"Sure." Lily nods. "Of course. Totally something you should
go around talking about."

"It wasn't my fault!"

"Yeah, it never is."

"God, you sound just like my dad."

"Maybe that should tell you someth—" She stops. Shakes her

head. "The point is you told Tess without bothering to ask me first. And why? Just to get in her pants?"

I can feel my face getting hot. "No."

"No, that's not *just* why?"

It gets even hotter. "I don't want to . . . get in her pants."

"You are such a liar."

"I'm not!"

There are multiple reasons why I'm not. First, I don't see the logical connection between me telling Tess that Lily and I were engaged in a covert investigation and Tess deciding she and I should have sex. Second, Tess wears shorts a lot more often than she wears pants.

"Are you under the misguided impression that you're subtle, Gideon? Like, at any point in your life, have you had anything *other* than the subtlety of a sledgehammer?"

"I have no idea what that means."

"It means you've never been able to hide how you feel. That includes this crush."

Crush is for rom-coms. The movies I watch call it passion, infatuation, *love*. And most of the time, it ends in betrayal or death. Or both. In noir, loving somebody destroys you more often than it saves you. I still haven't figured out if that's true in the real world, too.

"It's not a crush."

"But if both of you want to do this whole cutesy denial thing, fine. It's nauseating, but whatever."

"Both, what do you mean *both*—?"

"What you *can't* do is start spilling information that isn't yours to tell."

I don't know what to say to that, so I just stare at her, helplessly. She sighs and seems to soften, a bit.

"You should have asked me," she says.

"I know."

"I had my reasons for not wanting to tell anyone yet."

"I'm sorry."

"So what did Tess say?"

Then suddenly, a voice: "Feel free to ask me yourself."

Lily squeaks with surprise, and we both turn around to see Tess leaning in the open doorway.

"How long have you been standing there?" I ask her, trying and failing not to sound as panicked as I feel.

Tess raises her eyebrows. "Like two seconds. Why?"

"No reason." Her eyebrows go higher. I look away.

Lily takes over. "So." She folds her arms. "I assume you're going to tell us to stop?"

"No."

Lily's arms drop. "Really?"

"Look, I'm not going to pretend I'm thrilled," Tess says, then looks from me to Lily and back again. "I mean, you guys do realize you've already broken like . . . several laws?"

"But, bright side: we've only been caught once," I point out.

"Oh yeah," Tess deadpans, "your lawyer's going to love that defense."

"It's not the first time the *Herald* has pushed boundaries," Lily says. "Right?"

"A controversial op-ed isn't the same as a dead body."

"A murdered body," I correct her.

"A murdered body." Tess pauses. "I want to trust you, Lily. But you're taking serious risks, which means so am I, and that's the part that bothers me. You made me take risks I didn't agree to."

"So you *do* want us to stop."

"No." She sighs. "Journalism is weird that way. All the most famous exposés, the greatest works of investigative writing, were born from decisions that no rational person would make. Like, holy shit, Nellie Bly, *don't* get yourself trapped in a nineteenth-century insane asylum! Yeah, Woodward and Bernstein, probably not the safest idea to take down the president of the United States with the help of a secret informant who named himself after a porn movie."

"What?" I ask.

Lily closes her eyes. "Tess, Deep Throat didn't name *himself* Deep Throat—"

"My point is: stories, really good stories, don't come from just sitting around. I know that. And even if what you're doing to get that story is risky and scary and—just going to mention it again—*illegal* . . ." She shakes her head. "At least you've got precedent. But before I agree to this risk, to backing you up if this all goes to shit, I want to know: Is there something here?"

"Yes," Lily says. "I—*we*—don't know exactly what, but there's definitely something here."

Tess holds up her hands. "That's all I needed." Then she adds what I think is real hurt: "That's *all* you needed to tell me."

Lily looks down at the floor. "I thought you'd be mad."

"Because you didn't take no for an answer?" Tess asks. "If there's really something here, I'm glad you trusted your instincts. And it's good to see you stick to your guns."

Lily bristles. "What, like, 'for once'?"

Then it's Tess who looks like she's got her hackles up. "That's not what I said."

I raise my hand. "I don't understand what's happening."

That seems to snap them both out of it. "What's happening is we have an investigation to get back to, but—" Lily says to me, then looks to Tess. "We need your help."

"Name it," Tess says.

"I know it's a Late Night, but you know what Gideon and I really need?"

"I'm almost afraid to ask."

"An hour, maybe two, where you cover for us."

"What?" Tess and I say in unison.

"We'll be back by dinner." Lily's already got her keys in her hand. "But I know where we need to go next."

★ ★ ★

216

Lily lays out her whole plan, rapid-fire, on our walk to the parking lot, and I have to admit it's not bad. It isn't until we're in her car that I realize I've forgotten about something.

"Shit. What do I do with my phone?"

"Your phone?" she asks.

"Yeah, it's my dad's new thing, since the whole police incident. My tracking has to be on, and if he looks, he has to see me at school or at home. Nowhere else."

"Okay," Lily says. "We'll drop the phone at your house, it's on the way. And I'll set it up so any calls get forwarded to my phone."

"You can do that?"

"In about five minutes. I used to do it all the time for Mia, when she wanted to hang out with her boyfriend without her parents knowing."

True to her word, Lily spends only four minutes and thirty-two seconds setting up the forwarding. It takes her another five minutes to change into the outfit she had hidden in her backpack—a button-down shirt, a pencil skirt, and heels. Business casual, not femme fatale. It freaks me out how adult she can look, just by changing her clothes. If I put on a suit, it looks like I'm attending my own First Communion.

I leave my phone in my desk, and Lily and I start the drive to Vince Discount Furniture Warehouse.

"Their website is pretty bare bones," Lily says. "Because duh, it's a front. But Marco Vince was listed as the manager."

"And managers have offices," I add. The idea that we should go looking at his office was mine. All Lily wanted to do was ask around about him.

"We have to be prepared that the police might have searched it, already—"

"Why would they? They think it's an overdose."

"—or that his family came to take his belongings. But at the very least, we can get a better sense of him. And that's valuable."

I'll settle for valuable, but exciting would be a whole lot better.

There's only one other car parked in the lot when we get there. Lily gestures at it triumphantly. "See? I told you it would be totally empty. No reviews online, good or bad—no one actually shops here." She puts the car in park. "Thank God they put photos on their Yelp page, or I'd have no idea about the layout."

The layout is important, and so is the order we go inside—Lily first. I stand beside the big front windows, casually trying to look like I'm waiting for a ride or something. Inside the store, the lone sales guy is by the register, looking bored. Lily walks in, staring at her phone as though something important is on the screen. There's no chime or bell when she opens the door—which is a relief, or none of this would work.

I watch as Lily wanders aimlessly into a far corner of the store, then looks around, frowning. As if lost.

The sales guy, noticing, goes over, and Lily turns quickly to face him, making sure his back stays to the door. That's my cue—I push open the door as quietly as I can and creep toward the front desk, keeping my eyes on them as I go.

"I'm here for an interview with Mr. Vince," Lily's saying to him.

That catches him off guard. As expected. "What?"

"At four p.m." She looks down at her phone as if she's checking. "We set it up a couple weeks ago, and I tried emailing to confirm a couple days ago, but he didn't get back to me, so—" She gives a little shrug and a big smile. "Here I am."

"Oh my God," he says, looking up at the ceiling. "I don't know how to tell you this, but, um. He . . . died."

"He *died*?"

"Last week."

I'm at the desk now.

"Oh my gosh. How horrible. Was it—?" She glances around the room. "It wasn't . . . here?"

"No, no," he says. "Mr. Vince—the other Mr. Vince, Marco's dad, sent someone to tell us about it, but didn't . . . You know. Give detail."

"I didn't realize it was a family business."

"Yeah," he scoffs. "That's the only reason Marco was manager." Then quickly backtracks. "Shit, I'm sorry. That sounds so—he just wasn't super smart or anything. Or even . . . together? Like I'm shocked you even managed to set up an appointment with him, you know?"

Lily nods. "Well, maybe I could get Mr. Vince's number? Or

email? Set up another time with him? I'm really interested in the position."

"Look, I know this isn't my business, but you seem really nice, and . . ." He shakes his head. Drops his voice lower. "You don't want to work here."

"Why not?"

"It's totally toxic, for one thing. Maybe it won't be so bad now, but the two Vinces had such a fucked-up relationship." He jerks his thumb over his shoulder, and I nearly hit the floor. But he doesn't turn around, only gestures in the direction of a door marked "Staff Only." "He hasn't even come in to clean out Marco's office."

Bingo. Keys in my hand, I creep around the back of the desk and edge along the far wall, the ottomans and sleeper couches making the world's comfiest obstacle course.

"And I don't know if you were hoping to work on commission, or what, but—" I ease the "Staff Only" door open. The sales guy drops his voice again, even lower. "Nobody really sells anything."

Lily's voice is all confused innocence. "I don't understand."

"That's probably for the best."

"Well," Lily says as I shut the door silently behind me. "Thank you. I appreciate it."

Whatever he says back is muffled by the door, and I can't pay attention to the end of the conversation, anyway—I have a different job.

When I spot his name above the office closest to the door, I heave a sigh of relief. This might be easier than I thought. But when I go to open it, my heart sinks.

Fuck. *Fuck*, I think as I shove the useless set of keys I just stole into my pocket. His office door isn't locked with a key. It's locked with a *code*.

It doesn't look that different from the lock on Dad's office at Verde, and that's a four-digit code. Dad's password is his birthday—month and year. I don't know Marco Vince's birthday.

If my life were a noir, I would think back to everything I knew about him, and some small detail, some strange quirk or interest of his, would lead me directly to the answer. But this isn't a noir, and all I know about him is that he wasn't that bright.

I take a deep breath and give it my best, stupidest guess.

1-2-3-4.

It clicks open.

Thank God for stupid guesses.

INT. MANAGER'S OFFICE—DAY

It's a total mess—papers piled so high on the desk its color is a mystery, dust bunnies colonizing the corners, and what might have once been a sandwich congealing on top of a stack of boxes. GIDEON riffles through the mountain of

221

papers, but, finding nothing of interest, quickly abandons it.

CUT TO: Gideon pulling open the top drawer of the desk. Pens and empty cigarette cartons and a battered, red Bic lighter.

CUT TO: The next drawer down. Empty.

CUT TO: The bottom drawer, which SNAPS as it opens. Nothing inside but a balled-up fleece blanket—

I pull back. That's weird. It's boiling in here. What would he need a blanket for? Then I notice the broken Scotch tape—half on the side of the drawer, half on the side of the frame, now split cleanly in two. That's what snapped when I opened it.

God, it's such an amateur trick. Taping the side of a drawer, or the top of a door, so you can tell if someone's opened it. Such an amateur trick, but I walked right into it. If Marco were still around, I'd be in trouble, but instead, I now know something valuable is in this drawer.

When I toss aside the blanket, there's a single thick accordion folder beneath.

My heart is beating fast as I open it, to reveal . . . well. Everything.

There are screenshots of text messages, printed-out emails, photos of men I recognize—Jackel, Pyro, Officer O'Hara—and lots more who I don't. Notes, too, in shorthand, like:

11/17 PV met PO @ 13:45 for xchange

PV must be Paul Vince, the older Vince, and PO—police officer. O'Hara, for sure.

There are pages and pages like this, and I don't have time to read them all, or even most of them. The rest of the plan is simple: I find what I can in five minutes, go out through the back door, and meet Lily around the corner by the frozen yogurt place. I've already been in here too long. It's all going to have to come with me. I shove the whole folder underneath my arm, extricate myself from the mess of the desk, and step out of the office and into the hallway.

And that's when I start to panic. Because there *isn't* a back door.

I don't have my phone, so I can't call Lily or text her. How am I going to get out without the sales guy seeing me? I could make a break for it, but judging by my performance in the hundred-meter dash in PE, that's not a great option.

Lily was sure there was a back door, but there isn't. There's only a long hallway, empty except for a single bucket and a mop. I tilt my head up toward the ceiling, hoping against hope and any rationality for a skylight or something, but there's only cobwebs and a smoke detector in the far corner.

A smoke detector.

I can work with that.

I dash back into the office and grab a piece of paper off the desk and his lighter from the top drawer. Then, as quietly as I can, I push his wheelie chair out into the hallway. It wobbles and spins and I climb up on it, but I manage to balance myself enough to stand all the way up.

I flick on the lighter. Light one corner of the paper on fire. Hold it up toward the smoke detector. And wait.

The second the piercing, eardrum-shattering alarm starts blaring, I jump down, toss the singed paper in the bucket, and wheel myself back on the chair into Marco's office, closing the door behind me. Only moments later, the sales guy throws open the door to the hallway, cursing as he rushes toward the blaring sound. I peek out to see him dragging a ladder in from one of the other rooms. As soon as his back is to me, I launch myself out of Marco's office, out of the open hallway door, and out of the store itself, dropping the keys back on the desk on my way.

In a parking lot a few miles from the furniture store we just sped away from like it actually *was* on fire, Lily stares at the folder in her lap.

"So what does it tell us, this—I don't even know what you'd call it."

If this were a noir, they'd call it a dossier. So I will, too. "A dossier."

She flicks through it as if she hasn't just read everything. Twice. "What do we know that we didn't before?"

I pull out the shots of Jackel and Pyro first. "We know Vince Senior was responsible for them getting arrested." Next, I fish out the printed email exchange between him and Charlie Kirk, bartender and apparent owner of Doc Holliday's, arranging to pay off all the bar's many and expensive fines. "We know Charlie the bartender gave the two of them up, in exchange for payment. Maybe more than the health department fines, but at least that."

Lily nods, rifling through some other photos of men I don't recognize. "And these guys, they're all on my list of arrests. All petty stuff, all did a little time—"

"So they were sacrifices, just like Jackel and Pyro. Charlie the bartender sacrificed his criminal patrons in exchange for keeping his bar open."

"But I checked everyone on my list," Lily insists. "None of these men had any connection to Doc Holliday's."

"Maybe it's not just Charlie that Paul Vince is working with. Maybe—" I pause. "He's just the only one we know about."

As Lily drives us back to school, I keep talking through it, piece by piece. It always helps to say things out loud.

"The notes in here about meeting with the PO, the picture of O'Hara—that only makes it more solid. Charlie gave them up, told O'Hara exactly when and where to pick them up, and Vince paid them both. That's how O'Hara cleared all his debt, too."

"But . . . why?" Lily wrinkles her nose. "What benefit does Vince get from any of this?"

That's the part I still can't figure out. "I don't know."

"And why have this information where someone could find it?" Lily continues. "Paul Vince has never had a serious charge stick. He's smarter than this."

I think about the code on Marco's office door. "But his son isn't. Wasn't."

"His dad never would have let him keep this information in hard copy." Then it dawns on her. "His dad *didn't*. Marco stole it."

"I think his dad was keeping him out," I say. "Keeping him busy at the bullshit furniture-store front. Maybe because of his drug problems, maybe something else, I don't know. And maybe Marco was resentful. He's the only son, you'd think he'd be the heir, but he wasn't. He was shoved off to the side, and maybe he didn't like it." I know I wouldn't. "Maybe he wanted in."

"So it was leverage."

I consider that. "Or blackmail."

Lily's phone rings. "Probably Tess, wondering where we are," she says, reaching over to press the car's bluetooth button. "Hello?"

There's a pause on the other line. Then, a voice that makes my stomach drop right into my shoes: "Who is this?"

Lily frowns. I swat at her arm and, when she glances over, mouth: *It's my dad.*

"Oh!" she says. "Sorry, Mr. Green, it's Lily."

226

"Hi, Lily," he says, sounding confused. "Where's my son?"

Bathroom, I mouth at her. She wrinkles her nose. "Um. Math room?"

I throw up my hands.

"Math room?" Dad repeats.

"Yeah, well, um, he and I are working at the *Herald* and he just stepped away for a minute for . . . math tutoring."

Gently, soundlessly, I bang my head against the dashboard.

There's another, longer pause. "But—wait, my phone says he's at home, not at school."

That makes me sit up straight again. Shit. *Shit.*

"Did I say at the *Herald*?" Lily's voice is about an octave higher. "I meant we're working on a *Herald* article, together, but at your house, so—"

I mime slicing my hand across my throat and mouth, *Stop, stop.* She does. Then I take a breath and launch in.

"Hi, Dad," I say, trying to sound casual. "What's up?"

"Hi," he replies. "Why did Lily pick up? And she said you were in the math room—"

"No, we're at the house, it's a—" I grope wildly for a good explanation. "This virtual tutoring thing Mr. Baker does. The Math Room. I was asking him a couple questions and I left my phone on the kitchen island and asked Lily to get it."

"Oh," Dad says. "Is she . . . doing okay?" I glance over at Lily. She looks offended. "Seemed kind of out of it."

She's fine, just bad at improv, I think. "Yeah, I know." Then

227

drop my voice, as if I don't want her to hear. "She's been pretty stressed out. Did I tell you she's in eight APs?"

Lily rolls her eyes.

"Wow. No. I can see why she'd be stressed."

"Yeah, aren't you glad I'm not in any?" I ask.

I can practically hear him shake his head through the phone. "Uh-huh."

"You're welcome."

"Go back to math tutoring," he says. "I'll see you later."

When Dad hangs up, Lily switches off the bluetooth and glares at me. "Eight APs?"

"Exactly. You're stretched too thin."

"We only have seven class periods."

"You're taking one independently," I suggest. "Ancient Greek."

"Not an AP course."

"Mesoamerican history."

"Also not an AP course."

"Macroeconomics."

"Ugh." She pulls into the school parking lot. "I am taking macro."

CHAPTER 18

THAT NEXT MONDAY, Dad meets me outside the house when I get home from school. That's enough to clue me in that something is wrong—he should be getting ready for work, but he's still in his regular clothes. The thing that *really* clues me in, though, is the look on his face. A tight kind of panic, like he's freaked out but trying to hold it together in front of me.

"What's wrong?"

"When you go inside," he says slowly, "you will see Deputy Chief Garcia at the kitchen table."

My backpack drops from my hand. "What?"

"He says he needs to talk to you, and it's just a casual conversation, but . . ." Dad glances back toward the house. "Gideon. Do I need to get you a lawyer?"

There's too many reasons he could be there—did they find out I set off the alarm at the furniture store? Or that Lily's been investigating Marco Vince's death like the murder it was? Hell, maybe

I'm about to be cited for drinking underage at Doc Holliday's.

Or maybe . . . it's about the murder itself.

"Do you actually think I killed somebody?"

"Of course not."

"When you caught a mouse in the kitchen I made you drive it to Mission Trails Park and release it in a field."

"I remember."

"I didn't kill anybody."

"I know," he says. "But is there any chance you might have seen something that's going to get you in trouble? Is there anything you aren't telling me?"

I shake my head. He breathes out. Though it's not exactly a sigh of relief.

"Okay. Let's go talk to him."

Dad sits me across the table from Garcia and stands behind me. Normally, I'd be annoyed at how close he's hovering, but not now.

"I need to go over the statement you made about finding the body at the construction site," Garcia says. "All right?"

"Sure," I say. "What changed?"

"Changed?"

"Something changed, or you wouldn't be talking to me again. Either you found something new, or someone told you something new. So . . ." I shrug. "What changed?"

"We're reinterviewing everyone based on the coroner's report."

"You only just got it?" In movies, it happens so fast.

"San Miguel doesn't have its own coroner. The body had to be sent downtown, and there's a backlog." He pauses. "It was ruled a suspicious death."

Oh.

"You know he was murdered," I say, and I'm trying not to sound excited about it, because . . . well, murder. But— "I was right. Now you know I was right, that it was murder."

"I didn't say that. I said it was a suspicious—"

"Because he didn't overdose and then fall."

"He did fall," Garcia says. "His injuries are consistent with a fall from the catwalk."

"But not because he was high."

"The tox screen didn't indicate that, no."

"Then what?"

Garcia looks over my head at Dad. Sighs. Focuses back on me.

"We have forensic indications—at the scene and on the body— that give us reason to believe somebody else was there when he fell. And that person either watched him fall and then let him die, quite slowly." Garcia pauses. "Or they helped him fall."

My stomach flips. Throat closes up. And the image of Marco— blood around his head, eyes wide open—swims to the front of my mind so suddenly and strongly I barely see Garcia anymore.

Does it make it more real, to have someone say I was right? Or . . . was there a part of me, buried down deep, that didn't *want* to be right?

"But I think you knew that already," Garcia says, and the

231

image vanishes—but not the unease. "Didn't you?"

I jerk back so suddenly Dad puts his hand on my shoulder. "No, I only knew someone had killed him, I didn't know *how*—"

"I'm here today," Garcia says, leaning across the table, "because I need to know what you saw. And I need to know it now."

"I didn't see anything. I told you, Lily told you, we found him like that, and there was nobody else around; we didn't see any—"

"Then why would you say it was a murder?"

"His watch was gone."

Garcia's eyebrows shoot up. "What watch?"

"Exactly."

"Gideon . . ." Dad squeezes my shoulder. "Just spit it out."

"He had a tan line on his right wrist," I say. "Also, the hair wasn't as long there, because something used to rub against it. Like a watch. And I think it was pretty big."

That starts a quick, relentless volley back and forth, where I've barely finished answering before he's throwing me the next question. It's the kind of thing you might find in a screenplay . . . or a trial transcript.

GARCIA

Wouldn't that prove robbery, not murder?

ME

That's what I thought, until the cop asked
me if I knew his name. Which means they

didn't. So no ID, no credit cards, but he
had money in his wallet and a diamond
earring. Why would someone take everything
with his name on it but leave the money?
Because it wasn't about money at all. They
wanted to hide who he was.

                    GARCIA

Why take the watch?

                      ME

Maybe it was engraved. I don't know.

                    GARCIA

You saw the tourniquet on his arm. Correct?

                      ME

Yes.

                    GARCIA

But you didn't think he'd overdosed? You
didn't even think he'd been high?

                      ME

No.

                    GARCIA

Why?

ME

Maybe I did at first. But only at first.
When I played the scene back in my mind and
looked at all the details, they weren't
right.

GARCIA

What do you mean?

ME

The tourniquet was tied tight. In a knot,
like the way it is at the doctor if you have
to give blood. How could he have done that
himself? And then there was the tan line.

GARCIA

What about the tan line?

ME

It was on his right hand, which means he
wore his watch on his right hand. And his
left hand had a big smear on the side. I
think pen ink, probably.

GARCIA

And . . . ?

ME

That means he was left-handed.

                        GARCIA

How could you possibly know that?

                          ME

I am, too. And when we write stuff, because
it's left to right across a page, we smear
the words.

                        GARCIA

And what does it matter? That he was left-
handed.

                          ME

The tourniquet was tied on his left arm.
Who shoots up with their nondominant hand?

"What would you know about shooting up?" Dad cuts in,
breaking the volley.

"You saw all of that," Garcia says. "In just a couple minutes.
In the dark."

"No," I say. "I had a flashlight."

"I guess I'm wondering how likely it is that you came to be
there," he says mildly. "And then how likely it is that you'd be
able to correctly guess the cause of death with very little to go
on. My own officers didn't come to the conclusion you did."

                          235

Well, yeah, because they knew what they were looking for. A drug hangout spot means an overdose, or an accident caused by one. A dead addict means no need to look twice. They saw what they expected to see, because they'd seen it so many times before. I didn't know enough to make any assumptions.

I don't say that to Garcia. Besides, he isn't done with his monologue.

"So now I have to decide what is more likely. That you really are some kind of savant who just *happened* to stumble onto *another* crime scene. Or . . . that you know more than you are telling me." He pauses. "Which do you think is more likely?"

"That sort of depends." I look up at him. "What's a savant?"

"You know what, I think we're done." Dad's voice sounds tight, but he doesn't hesitate with his words. "Gideon has told you what he knows. And I'm sure you can appreciate that this is very hard for him to talk about."

"What do you mean, it's—" I start to say. Dad glares at me. "Um. Deeply traumatizing."

"Obviously," Garcia agrees. He looks to Dad. "Thank you for your time. I'll let you know if another conversation is needed." He places a small card down on the table in front of me. "If you remember anything else, Gideon, this is my card."

I don't take it. "Okay."

"And do me a favor." Garcia gets to his feet. "From now on, keep yourself out of this case."

CHAPTER 19

WE DON'T HAVE school that Friday because of a teacher development day, so it's a rare opportunity for me to see what Dad does while I'm at school. The answer, it turns out, is he wakes up late, eats breakfast, and then spends hours on his laptop at the kitchen table, probably going over numbers for Verde.

I wish I hadn't procrastinated so long. I should have asked him earlier, when he was more relaxed, because anything on his laptop is bound to amp him up, and I need him in the best mood possible.

But I've run out of time. Tomorrow is Saturday, and Tess is expecting me at Pacific Beach.

This could be fine, I try to convince myself. *Maybe he'll say yes.* It's been two weeks since the whole police incident and the Verde incident, which is only two incidents in an entire adolescence. Right? There's room for negotiation, at least.

"Hey, Dad?"

He doesn't look up from his laptop. "Hm?"

"Can I . . . go somewhere, tomorrow?"

His eyes don't move from the screen. "No."

So much for negotiation. "Oh, come on."

"Did you really think that was in the cards after your behavior lately?"

"I thought you might at least ask *where* I wanted to go."

"Okay, I'll bite." He closes the laptop and gestures at me. "Where?"

"The beach."

He frowns. "No, seriously, where?"

"I am serious. The beach. Pacific Beach."

"You know, it's hard for me to say yes to something that's clearly a lie."

"I'm not lying!" He still looks skeptical. "What do you want to do, take me back to the police station, have them strap me to a lie detector machine?"

"Cool it."

"I'm not lying to you."

"You don't even like the beach."

"I know," I say, wanting this so badly that I blurt it out without thinking, "but she does."

"She?"

"Um—"

"You mean Lily?"

"No," I say. "Her name is . . . Tess."

Slowly, Dad reaches over and pulls out the chair next to him.

I stare at him. He gestures to it. This feels like a trap, but what choice do I have? I sit down.

"Who's Tess?" he asks lightly.

"She's the editor in chief of the paper. Tess Espinoza. She's a year ahead of me, so we've never had classes together, but we're, um. Friends."

"Is that why you wanted to stay so badly? On the paper?"

"It might be . . . part of it," I admit.

"Tell me about her."

"What about her?"

"Well. What's she like?"

This is making my skin itch. It shouldn't be this hard to talk to my dad. But I haven't done it in so long—shared something like this with him—that it feels awkward and uncomfortable.

But if this is what I have to do to see Tess tomorrow, I'll do it. I'd do just about anything for her outside of murder or arson, and I could be persuaded on the arson.

"She's so smart," I say, because it's the very first thing that comes to mind. "Way smarter than me, and you'd think I wouldn't like that, right? Because I always want to be right; you say it all the time. But I *like* that she's quicker than me. And knows all these things I don't." I take a breath. "She's really funny, too, but not in a mean way. Not ever like she's trying to hurt somebody. I don't think she could hurt somebody. It's what makes her really good at being editor in chief, I think. That she wants to do the best she can, for everyone."

Dad smiles. "She sounds great."

"And she's pretty, too," I rush to add. "Not that it matters, not that it's the most important thing. I know it isn't the most important thing, that she's pretty. But she is."

"Are you two . . . ?" Dad pauses. "Dating?"

"No," I say quickly. "No, we haven't even . . ." I shrug. "I don't see that happening."

Dad is quiet for a moment. "Do you want it to?"

And then it's me who's quiet. Because I don't know how to answer that. *Yes, I want that.* But—

"I don't want to want things," I blurt out.

He looks confused. "What do you mean?"

"I don't think I'm the kind of person who gets to have that," I say, slowly. Carefully. "So I don't want to want it. If it won't happen."

"But what makes you think that?" Dad presses me. "What makes you think you won't—?"

"I'm a lot," I say. Underneath the table, I'm digging my nails into my palm. "You know? To deal with, to be around, and I just don't . . ." How can I explain this to someone like him? How can I tell him the way I feel, without making it sound like he made me feel it? Even if maybe . . . he did?

"I just don't see it happening," I finish.

Dad doesn't say anything for a while. He just looks at me, and I can't read his expression. Is he sad? Or confused? Or . . . hurt, somehow?

240

"You should go," he says finally. "You *can* go, I mean. On Saturday."

I breathe a sigh of relief. "Thanks." Pushing back the chair, I get up. "I'll keep my phone on the whole time—"

"What are you bringing?"

"Bringing?"

"To the date."

"It's not a date."

"You should take something anyway. What food does she like?"

The only thing I know she likes for sure is In-N-Out fries, animal style. "I don't know."

Dad's already out of his seat and pacing the kitchen. "You're on the beach, so something you can eat with your hands. Something that doesn't need a cooler. . . ."

"Dad, no, you don't have to make anyth—"

He's already in the cabinet, dragging out a huge bag of flour. "Let's do marranitos."

Just hearing him say the word makes me feel seven years old again. We used to make them all the time when I was younger and he was less busy. I loved those cookies—not just for the sugar and the ginger taste, but the shape they came in. Little pigs, with curly tails.

I wonder if it makes him feel seven again, too. In his tiny childhood kitchen in Bakersfield, rolling out dough with his mom.

"Go find the cookie cutter," he orders me. "It's by the Tupperware, somewhere."

Dad begins laying out the sugar, butter, and flour on the kitchen island for his mise en place, which is just restaurant speak for getting your shit together before you begin. It's one more way Dad and I aren't the same—I always wanted to dive right in, headfirst.

As he hands me a stick of soft butter to unpeel from its wrapper, he says: "I didn't ever think I'd get married."

I stop midpeel. "Really?"

It can't be for the same reasons as me—Dad has always been able to get along with people. No way he could have opened two restaurants otherwise.

"I was barely older than you when I left home," he says, turning to the cabinet where he keeps all his bowls. "It made me pretty independent. I didn't need anybody, I thought. I knew I could get through life just fine on my own, so . . ." He shrugs. "I assumed that's what I'd do."

You can't build a case on assumptions. It seems like you shouldn't build a life that way, either.

"That's how people think, when they're young." He glances at me out of the corner of his eye. "In absolutes."

Why does he do that? Say *people* when what he really means is *you, specifically.*

"That's so condescending."

He gives me a look. "Gideon."

"If you're young, you can't possibly know anything?"

"When you're young," he says, "you can't imagine all the

possibilities that are open to you. It's not a dig, kiddo; you just haven't been alive long enough to experience them. That's all."

"So what changed your mind?"

He sucks in air through his teeth, so deep his shoulders hitch.

"Your mom."

Oh.

"Because she wanted to get married?" I ask. It's usually the girl, isn't it, who wants to get married first? That's how it is in movies.

"Because I did. The second I met her, I didn't want to be alone anymore." He smiles, like there's something playing in his head. "How could I, when—well. It was your mom. You know?"

That cuts deeper than any of the knives on the block by the sink. Burns at me hotter than the stove top Dad is lighting to melt the butter. How could he say that? Worse, how could he possibly *believe* it?

"I don't know anything about Mom," I snap at him before I can stop myself.

He takes a step back from the counter. A small one. "Of course you do."

I can't stand it when he does that. Brush off something I've said about my own life with total certainty. *Of course.*

"No." I look him in the eyes. "I don't."

Dad busies himself with unstacking the mixing bowls. "You know she was a teacher. You know she was from Redding, up in the mountains. You know she moved down here to go to

243

SDSU." He swallows. "You know she loved you."

What I remember most is feeling warm. Not inside—or not *just* inside. I don't ever remember her wearing long sleeves, so her arms were always bare when she hugged me. Or held me. And they were always warm.

Her face is so fuzzy in my memories. That feels like the part I should remember, but it isn't. I remember her skin. Soft, and freckled, and warm.

"That isn't the same," I tell Dad. "It's not the same as knowing *her*."

"She had a best friend. Jane. Do you remember Jane? She was really tall, short hair? Weird glasses."

"Uh, maybe?"

"I think I still have her number." He turns toward his room, like he's found an escape route. "She'd be able to . . . you know."

"Talk?"

"Yeah."

He bends down to turn the oven on.

"Why can't you?"

He straightens up. Turns around. Blinks at me. "What?"

"Why can't you?" I repeat. "Why can't *you* ever talk about her?"

Dad is quiet for a very long time. I'm almost about to ask again, when he takes a deep breath, lets it out, and says:

"I thought it would be easier."

"What do you mean, easier?"

"Just what I said. I thought it would be easier not to talk about it, constantly. Easier not to . . . dwell on it."

"Yeah?" I ask. "Easier for who?"

"For you," he says, and it's sharp and hurt. "Not me. *You.*"

"Me?"

"You were so young when it happened, you barely even remembered—I thought it would be easier on you."

"It wasn't," I say. "Isn't."

"I didn't want you to miss her more than you had to. More . . . clearly than you had to."

He wanted to protect me from something he couldn't. He tried, but there's no protecting anybody from tragedy, just like there's no stopping them in the first place. That's what makes them tragedies.

Dad didn't want me to miss the person I'd lost. All I did was grieve a ghost instead.

"She was my mom. I was always going to miss her."

For a minute, the only sound is the occasional crack of the oven as it heats up.

"I'm sorry," Dad says finally, looking down at his hands. "I'm just . . . sorry."

Is he sorry for never talking about her? I wonder. Or is he sorry that I had to grow up without a mom at all? And then I think . . . maybe it isn't *or.* Maybe it's *and.*

I square my shoulders, take a breath, and ask what I've wanted to since I was six years old: "Can you tell me something about her?"

"I . . ." He looks shell-shocked by the question. "I don't know what you're looking for."

"Stories."

"Stories?" he repeats.

"Yeah, because I know facts. I know where she was born, and where she worked, but I don't have any stories."

Facts always mattered to me—when I was a detective and when I wasn't one, too. Maybe that's why I was okay, for years, only having those facts and nothing more. But it's like Tess told me: facts don't exist on their own. They're told to us, by people, and every sentence and word in a story is a choice. The way a person tells a story can show you—for better or worse—how they really feel. I want to hear a story about my mom. And I want to hear the way my dad tells it.

Facts matter. They're the truth, and that matters. But I'm starting to think stories matter just as much.

Dad puts both hands on the countertop and stares down at the flecked pattern like he could disappear into it.

"She had red hair."

"That's only another fact."

"Gideon, just—" He holds up a hand. "This is hard. Okay?" I nod. And wait. And listen.

"That was the thing I noticed first," Dad continues. "I was working in this little place downtown. It was a pass-through kitchen, so from where I was on the line, I could see some of the patrons. And there was this girl who would come in every

Wednesday, with this amazing red hair."

It *was* amazing. I remember that. It's like a lock clicks open at the back of my brain. It's like a box gets taken out of storage, off the very back shelf, and unwrapped. Her hair was long, and it would spiral down by my face when she held me in her lap. I would grab for one of the curls—not to pull it, but just to rub it between my fingers. It felt softer than anything.

"She only ever got coffee," Dad continues. "And she always sat alone, with a textbook. So I started sending the waitress out with a different pastry each time. She never turned it down. And then I nearly got fired, because I couldn't stop looking at her. I was screwing the whole kitchen up. At that point, I figured— better make this worth it. So I asked her out.

"She didn't have much family—wasn't close to them, anyway, and I was the same. We thought we'd make a family together. The kind neither of us got to have. And . . . we did. For a few years, a few perfect years, we did.

"She liked food—all food, any cuisine—but didn't know much about it. The first time I took her to a sushi place, she put the whole clump of wasabi in her mouth at once. I felt horrible, but she just laughed, even with tears streaming down her face.

"I only knew her for eight years. Eight years and two months from the day I met her until the day she died."

It almost knocks me over. Eight years. Dad has known me for twice as long as he knew her. And she's been gone longer than he was ever with her.

Dad misreads the look on my face. "Too much?" he asks gently. I shake my head. It wasn't too much. Not at all. It was honest.

I feel like I need to do that, too, now. Tell him something, so he knows what he told me wasn't too much. So that maybe he'll do it again, one day. It's not a trade, exactly. More like . . . a gift. Honesty. But not just any kind of honesty. The kind that hurts. Vulnerability.

"In my head, it was like this . . . wall," I say. His eyes snap up, like he wasn't expecting me to speak. "Her being gone. Whenever I would start to think about it, I would imagine a brick wall that I could build higher and higher, however high I needed to. To keep it"—I make a vague pushing kind of gesture—"away. I guess."

Dad nods. "For me, it's like a box. It's there, it's safe, all those . . ." He takes a breath. "Memories. I can take them out, if I want. Sometimes. But mostly they just stay there. Locked away."

"Is that what you're supposed to do? To deal with something like this?"

Dad shakes his head. "I have no idea what you're supposed to do."

I always thought he knew what he was doing. Even if I thought the choices he made were wrong, or unfair, I figured at least he was certain. But he wasn't. Isn't.

"You said you used to think of it like a brick wall," Dad says suddenly. "Does that mean you don't? Anymore?"

I guess I did use past tense. *Was.* I'm not sure it's right. If this were an article I was copy editing, I might have circled that *was*. Drawn a question mark beside it.

"I told Tess about Mom," I admit. "I didn't have to, but I did. I think that's why I said that."

"Special people in your life can do that, sometimes," Dad says. "They can break through you. Like that."

The way he says it, it's not a platitude, to use a word Tess would like. It's something he knows. Because he's had it happen, too.

"Can I have another story?"

He takes a sharp breath in through his nose. "I—"

"Please, just . . . one more." God, I sound like a kid. I *feel* like a kid, the kid I actually was, begging him to read one more book before I had to go to sleep. And he always would—I'd sort of forgotten. But he'd always give in, at least once. One more book. One more story.

Maybe he remembers that, too. Because he looks down at the countertop and says:

"One year, right after we'd first gotten married, Grandma Felicitas sent us this Easter card. And it was . . . horrific."

"Because of Jesus on the cross or whatever?" We don't see my grandma that often, but I remember going to her house in Bakersfield when I was little and being terrified of the gigantic crucifix she kept on the wall.

"No," Dad says. "It was this bunny."

"A bunny?"

"A *demon* bunny. I don't know what was wrong with the artist, but this rabbit looked like it wanted to eat your *soul*. I immediately tossed it in the recycling. But your mom . . ." He grins. "Fished it out when I wasn't looking.

"The next morning, when I opened up the bathroom cabinet for my toothpaste, there was the bunny card taped to the inside mirror. I nearly had a heart attack. A week later, I went to get something from the pantry, *boom*, Demon Bunny staring down from the top shelf. I peel back the covers at night, Demon Bunny's taken my side of the bed. And the whole time, your mom is just sitting there with this angelic little smile on her face."

"Why didn't you just throw it out?"

"Oh, I *did*," he says. "She'd made *copies*."

I burst out laughing, and then he does, too. I can't remember the last time that's happened. Both of us, laughing at something together.

"I couldn't even pretend to be mad about it. I just laughed and told her I loved her. And then like always . . ." He stops for a second. "She sang it back to me."

Sang it? "She made it into a song?"

"She used a song," he says. "Her favorite one. By Irving Berlin. It's called 'Always.'"

"I don't know it."

"Yeah, well, it's pretty old. From the thirties, or sometime around then. She was so funny—that's the only kind of music she liked, old musicals, that big band stuff, you know."

I do know. She might not have watched the movies I love, but—it's close. It feels so close. *She* feels so—

"Mom liked old music?" I ask, and my eyes sting and Dad goes all blurry. "Stuff from the thirties and forties, she liked that whole . . . time?"

Dad takes a sharp breath in, like he's realizing it, too. "Yeah. She did."

And I stand there, stunned to silence by the possibility that somehow, a part of me held on to a part of her. That somehow, we could have our own shared sliver of space.

"Do you have it?" I look toward the living room, where Dad keeps his old CDs stacked by the TV. "The song. Her song."

Dad takes his phone out of his pocket and types on it for a while. Then he lays it down on the counter, turns the volume up all the way, and hesitates for only a second before pressing play.

At first, there's only a violin, sliding through high notes. Then a man's deep, rich voice, singing slow:

I'll be loving you, always

With a love that's true, always

I can't decide whether the melody is happy or sad. It'll sound sweet and light for a moment, then the next note will dip. Is he wistful? Resigned? Content?

I think about the man who wrote it, and I want to understand what he meant, what he felt, what he wanted me to feel, nearly a century after he wrote it and a decade after my mom sang it.

Happy or sad. Joy or pain. Tragedy or love story. Then I think—what if there's no *or*? What if there's only *and*?

Tragedy and love story. It's both. It's all of them. It's . . . everything.

And I'm supposed to feel it. That everything.

Days may not be fair, always

That's when I'll be there, always

I wonder if there's going to be a day, years later, when I try to tell someone about what's happening right now. This afternoon, this moment. With every breath, every note I hear for the very first time, I wonder if I'm living inside a story.

I lock the details in, the way I know how to.

Rain streaming down the window. The smell of marranitos rising in the oven. And Dad humming along.

Not for just an hour

Not for just a day

Not for just a year

But always

CHAPTER 20

THE SOUNDS OF the morning news float in from the kitchen.
Dad likes having the background noise as he starts his day. Which
is just another way we're totally unalike. What's the point of
having something on if you aren't going to pay attention to it?

I try to block it out, because it's never anything interesting—
oh look, it's going to be sunny and warm all week, what a
surprise—but then I hear the voice.

"This is nothing but a political ploy," someone's saying, loud
and brash and almost bored. "It's completely transparent."

I've heard that voice before. I know I have.

I rush into the kitchen, and on the TV screen is Police Chief
Thompson on the steps of the station house, with his assistant
behind him and a swarm of mics and recorders stuck in his face.

I turn up the volume.

"Are you concerned about the possibility of a vote of no
confidence?" someone off-screen asks.

The chief's eyes travel down to a note card in his hands.

"Any vote of no confidence would be nothing more than a political attack on the San Miguel Police Department, spearheaded by a council member intent only on self-aggr—" He stutters. Stops. Frowns at the card. Grins back up at the reporters as if this is all one big joke. "Sorry. My assistant's handwriting. Chicken scratch."

Behind him, his assistant turns so red she's nearly purple. God, what an asshole.

"Spearheaded by a council member intent only on *self-aggrandizing*," the chief works out, "to benefit his own mayoral campaign. Such a vote would only symbolize the way the police department is hampered by bureaucracy and would in no way change my commitment to protecting and serving the people of this great city." He ducks his head and begins to walk out of frame. "Thank you."

"Are you actually watching that?" I turn around. Dad is standing by the sink, coffee cup in hand. I hadn't even noticed him.

"What's a vote of no confidence?" I ask.

Dad shakes his head. "I'm not sure, exactly. He's become pretty unpopular over the last couple years, so it may just mean they want him out."

Lily will know. And if she doesn't, she'll figure it out, quicker than either Dad or I could. I dig my phone out of my pocket and text her:

254

Police chief was just on TV, something about a vote of no confidence

City council is part of it too, I think Willets is gunning for the Chief

Do you think it's connected?

"Is that . . . Tess?" Dad asks, trying and very much failing to seem casual.

I stick it back in my pocket. "Yeah."

"You said you were meeting her at eleven?" I nod. "I'll have to drop you off a little early, so I can get back to Verde in time."

"That's fine," I say. "Thanks for driving me there."

"Of course," he says, starting to smile. "It's exciting."

I wish he wouldn't say stuff like that—it only makes me more nervous. "It's not a date."

He holds his hands up in surrender. "Okay, it's not a date." Then he nods at the kitchen island, where I just now notice is a foil-wrapped plate tied up with—to my complete horror—green birthday present ribbon in an enormous bow.

Oh my God, I think.

"Oh my God," I say.

He frowns. "I thought I did an okay job."

"She's going to think I'm a serial killer!"

"Because you made her something?"

"But it's *not* me doing it, because that's not something I would do, it's just what *you* would do!"

Dad stops. Straightens up. And looks at me with such obvious hurt in his eyes, it makes me take a step back.

"I'm trying," he says. "Okay?"

And shaking his head, he walks out of the kitchen.

I stand there, alone, knowing I said the wrong thing—again—but not sure exactly why. Wasn't it true? It is what he would do. It isn't what I would do. I don't get it.

But . . . it hurt his feelings. Clearly. I don't understand why, but maybe it doesn't matter, that I don't get it. I can't control that part. And I can't unsay what hurt him, either.

At ten a.m., when Dad gets into the driver's seat and sees the plate of cookies—ribbon and all—sitting on my lap, he doesn't say anything. But he smiles as he starts the car.

Tess is a little late to meet me, which is fine. It means I get to pick out the best spot on the beach—the best in my opinion, anyway. Far enough from the water that there's no chance of a sudden wave drenching your towel, far enough from the boardwalk and pier that you don't have to be bothered by tourists, and close enough to a "Watch for Riptides" sign that I can text Tess with a clear marker of how to find me.

Tess waves when she spots me, across the beach. She's got on shorts and a T-shirt, so maybe she doesn't want to get in the water after all, which would be totally fine with me.

"Hey," she says with a grin, and to my surprise plops right down on my towel. "Sorry I'm late."

"Oh, no, it's okay."

Tess unzips her backpack and pulls out her own, clearly well-used beach towel. She lays it out and moves over. Then she twists around, squinting in the direction of the boardwalk. "Wonder if the snack shack is open yet."

Well, I'm not going to get a better opening than that. "Do you like marranitos?"

"Hell, yes," she says. "But I don't think they have them at the snack shack."

I reach over and plant the plate of cookies in between us. "My dad made some and basically forced me to take them, so . . ."

Her face breaks into a smile. "Really? That's so sweet of him to do."

"It's no big deal," I say, unwrapping the foil. "He's a chef. It's his job."

"Food is love, you ingrate." She takes a bite out of the marranito. Tail first. Just like I would. "Haven't you ever heard that?"

She's joking about the ingrate part—I think. But the rest of it . . . Of course I've heard that food is love. But food is also stress, and money, and worry, in my house. It's everything, all parts, good and bad.

As Tess munches on her marranito, mine stays in my hand. I'm too busy chewing over her words to eat anything real. I'm too busy replaying the conversation in the kitchen. Maybe Dad wasn't trying to be pushy. He was anyway, but maybe he didn't mean to be. It's possible. To be a good detective, you have to be able to consider the possibilities. Even if they don't make sense to you right away.

I'm trying, he said, and I didn't know what he meant. I barely even thought about it. What was he trying to do? Share something with me? Connect with me?

Food is love, Tess said, and maybe that's the glaring clue I didn't see.

Could shoving a plate of cookies in someone's arms be a way to say you love them, if those exact words don't come easy and never have?

Maybe.

Just then, a multicolored beach ball bounces next to us. Tess reaches over to scoop it up. When the owner—a boy who's maybe ten—runs over to claim it, she holds it out with both hands.

He takes it from her but doesn't leave. Instead, he frowns and asks:

"What's wrong with your hand?"

And just in case she wasn't clear on which one he meant, the boy points, with a jabbing finger, at her left hand.

It's none of your business, you little asshole, I think, but as always, Tess is quicker.

"My fingers? They got bitten off by a shark." She gestures at the ocean in front of us. "On this very beach."

As always, Tess is quicker and bolder and more surprising by the second.

"A shark?" he asks.

"Yeah, right over there, by that white buoy."

The boy takes a cautious step away from the water. "There aren't sharks here."

"Not since I've become a one-woman shark-killing machine," Tess agrees. "You're welcome."

He stares at her, wide-eyed. She smiles, almost angelically.

"But I still haven't killed the one that got me. So I come down here on the right kind of days—sunny, lots of people out, those are the days they like—and I wait. I know he'll be back. Maybe it's today."

The kid stares at her for another moment, takes a look at the water, then turns tail and runs back in the direction he came.

"God*damn*, Captain Quint," I say.

She puts her sunglasses back on. "I'm assuming that's *Jaws*?"

"It is."

"Never seen it."

"What a backstory. Do you just keep that in your pocket for any nosy little kid who asks?"

"No." Tess laughs. "If they're really little and just curious, I tell them the truth. I save the urban legends for the people who are old enough to know better."

"It must be hard, though," I say. "To have to talk about it all the time."

She shrugs. "It's fine."

"Is it actually?"

"You think I'm lying to you?" Tess says, her eyebrows poking up from behind her sunglasses.

"No, I just think there's—" And then I have to pause, because I'm working this out as I'm saying it. "There's an in-between. Just because something isn't a lie doesn't mean it's absolutely true, either. You know?"

Tess is quiet for a moment. "The parents are always way more embarrassed than I am. They're always jerking the kid away and whisper-yelling about being polite, which—I get it. I do. But I don't want a little kid to, like, *associate* me and my body with getting in trouble. That's the part that isn't fine. I'd rather they ask. I'd rather be able to give them an answer."

I nod, because that makes total sense to me. It's hard enough to feel different—*be* different—without people acting like it's something shameful, something that has to be pointedly ignored. "I could understand that."

"It's nice," she says abruptly. "It throws me for a loop sometimes, but—it's nice."

"What is?"

"That you care so much about what's true. And that when you ask for the truth . . . you actually want to hear it."

"Doesn't everybody?"

She shakes her head. "No."

Has anyone ever liked me the way Tess does? Not in spite of all the things that make me different, but . . . because of them?

"I'm hot." She starts to tie her hair back. "Come on, let's go in."

"You go ahead," I say. "I'll be fine here."

"Can't you swim?"

I was born in Southern California, Land of a Thousand Swimming Pools. "Yeah, I can swim."

"So, come with me."

Tess stands up and without hesitation or self-consciousness strips her T-shirt over her head, revealing the sky-blue bikini top underneath. Sleek and practical, the kind of thing you'd need to ride a wave. Simple and unadorned and the single most amazing article of clothing I've ever seen in my life.

Barbara Stanwyck's perfectly set blond curls have nothing on the windblown brown waves escaping from Tess's ponytail. Mary Astor's bashful gaze and red lipstick pale in comparison with Tess's piercing brown eyes and her wide, ChapStick grin. Ava Gardner vamping in her sleekest black dress could never be as beautiful as Tess in her swimsuit and cutoff shorts.

"Wa—" I stutter. Clear my throat. Try again. "Was that supposed to be like . . . bribery?"

Tess smirks. "Why, did it work?"

And then I don't know what to say at all.

This is good, right? The way she's talking to me, the way she looks at me—she likes me. I think. Maybe. It's a possibility, and you have to consider the possibilities. Even if they scare you.

261

"Maybe," I say, desperately willing my voice not to crack.

"Well." She cocks her head. "Are you planning on going in with your shirt on, or . . . ?"

Who gets scared of a girl liking them but not a dead body? What kind of a person is freaked out *not* by sneaking into a biker bar but by the tiny possibility that a somewhat unclothed girl might actually want to see them somewhat unclothed, too?

What the hell is wrong with me?

My shirt comes off with a lot more fumbling than Tess's did, and then I'm just sitting there. No trench coat. No hat. None of the things that kept everyone at arm's length and kept me safe. Safe . . . and alone.

I'm not alone, now. Tess is standing in front of me, holding out her hand. And I'm just sitting there, working up the courage to take it.

"Come on," she says, reaching out even closer. When I grab her hand, it's so warm I could melt.

Once I'm on my feet, she lets go, which is a relief—any longer and she would have noticed how much my palms are sweating. She turns and walks to the water without waiting for me, which is a relief, too—side by side, she'd notice how fast I'm breathing.

At first, I hang behind her, keeping a careful distance. I need to pull myself together, and besides, a little distance is good. Isn't it? It is.

Distance keeps you safe. Distance keeps people from hurting

you, from leaving when they can't understand you . . . or from leaving at all.

That's logical. It's right. But God—it's not what I *want*.

I want to run up and put my arm around her waist. I want to feel her warm hand in mine, again, and not just for a moment. I want to kiss her, if she wants it, too.

You can't do any of that from a distance, no matter how much safer it might be.

And I realize—so suddenly and strongly it nearly knocks the air out of my lungs—I don't want that distance anymore.

Tess turns around then, just as she steps into the water. And when she smiles, it's like a dam breaks, or a wall crumbles, or maybe it's just a rope that snaps. But I run, and keep going until I'm standing right beside her. Under the same sun, feeling the same wind and the same freezing cold waves against my ankles.

I let her lead as we wade in, but I stay close. I try to keep up. I try not to stare at her, too—the way the light hits her hair and her arms shine in the water—but it doesn't work, and eventually, she notices.

"You act like you've never seen a girl in a bikini before, dude," she says.

"I have," I say as the water climbs higher, lapping around my waist. "But not like—" I clear my throat. "Not like you."

She laughs. "Are you saying I'm not like other girls?"

"You are like other girls," I tell her, a line from a noir floating back to me. "Only . . . more so."

When she laughs again, it's the most magical sound I've ever heard.

Tess swimming is like nothing I've ever seen. It's not that she's fast, though she is, or graceful, though she's that, too. When we reach a break in the waves and she flips onto her back to float, she looks . . . like she's home. We all have the things—or the people—that open us up, and the ocean must be hers.

The movies I love are filled with shadows. It might have started that way because film noir had small budgets, and a cheap set looks better under dim lights than bright ones. But it became a fixture, a trope, something people came to expect. Renaissance painters called it "chiaroscuro": the contrast between light and darkness. Sunlight piercing through a detective's venetian blinds. Black shadows hiding a woman's face, except for a band of brightness across her eyes. A man in a trench coat stepping out of an alleyway and into a streetlamp's glare.

When I thought about my own life, it felt like that. That I existed mostly in shadow—invisible and obscured and unknowable—with only brief moments in the light. And I liked it that way, I thought. It's easier to stand in shadow than in light. You can hide better.

In the middle of the ocean, there are no shadows. There is only the heat beating down from above, sparkling on the water, and light, so much light, everywhere. It warms my skin. Makes spots dance in my eyes. And Tess—

God. It makes her glow.

Suddenly, she slides off her back and swims up to me, so close I can smell the salt in her hair and see each bead of water on her eyelashes.

"Can you stand?"

"What?"

"Can you stand?" she repeats, laughing. "You know. With your feet?"

Cautiously, I stretch my legs out under the water, until I can feel my toes sweep the sand below. When I set my feet down, the water's only halfway up my chest. "Yeah. Why?"

"Because it makes it way easier to do this."

One of Tess's hands is on my shoulder, and then the other is on the back of my neck, and her lips are pressing into mine, salt water and sweetness all jumbled up together.

It takes my brain a moment to catch up, and by the time I can find the words—*Tess is kissing me, I am kissing Tess*—my arms are already wrapped around her waist, pulling her even closer, so there's not even a sliver of distance between us.

Life is meant to be both, I know. Shadows and sunshine. Tragedies and triumphs. Good and bad in everything, everywhere, and everyone.

But in this moment, and the next, and the next, even with my eyes closed—

All I can see is light.

CHAPTER 21

THE NEXT WEEK after the beach moves like molasses. On the one hand, I keep feeling like we should be doing something else, we should be pursuing our next lead. But as Lily helpfully reminds me, we don't *have* a next lead. The dossier tells us what's going on, but it doesn't tell us where to go next. It doesn't tell us who's ultimately in charge.

"We know Paul Vince is paying off people—" Lily reasons.

"Like Charlie the bartender at Doc Holliday's."

"Yeah, and a few other sketchy places around town, to set up some low-level criminals."

"And then he's feeding that info to O'Hara and paying him to make the arrests."

Lily flips through the pages "But *why*? What does he get out of this?"

"Less competition, maybe?"

"What possible competition could someone like Luke

Dobson be to Paul Vince? It doesn't make sense. No, somebody else must have a stake in this," Lily insists. "Don't forget. Cui bono?"

On the other hand, it's nice to be able to spend time with Tess. Even if it's just at Late Night, and even though we haven't told anybody yet. She thinks Ryan and Noah would become totally unbearable if they knew, and I feel the same about Lily. We will, eventually. When we have to. But for now, it's nice to have something that's private. Something only the two of us get to share.

So that's why I freak out a little, when Lily pulls me aside at lunch that next Monday and says: "So I feel like it's important for us to tell each other these things—"

"We weren't hiding it," I blurt out. "It just happened."

She stares at me. "What are you talking about?"

"Nothing." I clear my throat. "What are *you* talking about?"

"I'm going to go to a city council meeting today," she says.

"Oh. Why?"

"According to the agenda, they're going to talk about the no-confidence vote. I figured there might be a clue in that. Somewhere. So I convinced Araceli I'd go instead."

"It's a good idea. What time should I get there?"

She grimaces. "Two of us from the *Herald* might look weird. Araceli always goes alone. But the meetings are streamed; you can watch it live."

So that's what I'm doing with my afternoon: sitting on my

bed, letting Asta chew on my fingers, and watching the most mind-numbingly boring thing I've ever subjected my TV to.

Whoever's working the camera is pretty amateur, and the lighting's god-awful, but it's not like city council livestreams are directed by Fritz Lang, so they're never going to meet my personal cinematic standards. At least the angle isn't bad—I can just spot Lily's neat, high ponytail and the back of her crisply ironed pink blouse.

"The vote concerning the San Miguel Police Department and Chief Thompson will take place two weeks from today," a tired-looking councilwoman is saying.

"I don't think a delay is necessary or useful," Fred Willets counters. "If the city council doesn't have confidence in Chief Thompson, that won't change in two weeks."

The woman looks more exhausted with every second he speaks. "Councilman Willets will remember that a two-week public notice *is required by procedure* and not being utilized to annoy him personally."

Fred Willets gives her a dark look but says nothing else on the subject.

"If the vote is so passed," she continues, "the council will then proceed with a referral for the termination of Chief Thompson."

Lily hadn't mentioned that part. Maybe she didn't know—if they give the chief a vote of no confidence, it isn't just symbolic. He'll be fired.

The head councilwoman straightens her stack of papers. "Let's move on to the next item of business."

Fred Willets raises his hand. "I have a point of procedure—"

But I don't even hear him. Because with his arm raised, his left arm, I catch a glimpse of a gold watch, peeking out from underneath his button-down shirt, that almost looks like—

No.

No.

I rush Asta back into his habitat, scramble to find my phone, and pull up the very first photo Lily sent me of Marco Vince. The headshot where he's showing off his watch, his *gold watch*, his clearly prized possession that whoever killed him knew to take. That whoever killed him *did* take.

I study the watch face, the linked bracelet chain, every nook and cranny and possible identifying marker I can. Then I rewind what I just watched and carefully freeze on the moment Fred Willets's watch pokes out. It's only a second.

But it's enough.

They're identical.

My head spins. Stomach twists. Lungs contract.

Steadying myself on my bedpost, I force my brain to work. Think. Solve.

Fred Willets has Marco Vince's watch. He is wearing Marco Vince's watch.

He knows who killed him, or he did it himself.

But why would he do that, why except—

He was the one partnering with Paul Vince. Paul Vince wants to expand his empire into San Miguel, and Fred Willets wants to be mayor.

Cui bono? Who benefits?

He benefits.

Who benefits from a soaring crime rate in a small city? Who gets to take a bizarre, astronomical rise in crime and use it as a campaign launchpad?

He does.

Who benefits from the kinds of crimes getting committed? No assaults, no violence, nothing that would make people panic or sell their homes. Smaller things. Vandalism, theft, arson—

No deaths. No mayhem. Just enough to make people scared, enough to make them want someone strong leading them, someone who could stop their cars getting broken into or their businesses tagged.

But then—O'Hara. Why O'Hara? Willets hates the police chief; he hates the cops.

He hates the cops. But he needs the cops.

The chief could never see what was right under his nose. Not when I was ten and not now, when Willets has been playing him like a fiddle. Someone has to be arrested so the crime can be public, so the sentencing can make the paper, so Willets can quote the article in his next speech. Tess was right, she's always right: stories matter. He found a way to create the one he needed.

It's like my brain and body have split. While the gears in my mind have been grinding and turning, connecting the dots, my hands have been on autopilot. Grabbing my shoes, getting them on my feet, finding my house keys. I'm picking up my phone when my brain finally catches up and reminds my body that I need to leave it here, at home. The tracking is still on, and I don't need Dad knowing where I'm going next.

City Hall.

My legs ache and my lungs are on fire from sprinting a mile from my house to the city center, but I barely care, because I'm coming to the peak, to the end, to the very best part of it all.

This is the crowning moment of detective stories, which are not the same thing as noirs, though they can intersect: when the detective gathers everyone together, suspects and allies and police alike, and unmasks the killer. When he lays out exactly how the crime was perpetrated and how close the criminal was to getting away with it. How they *would* have gotten off scot-free, except they underestimated the detective. That was their fatal flaw. It always is.

On the steps of City Hall, I take three seconds and three seconds only to wipe any visible sweat off my forehead and get my breathing under control. In and out. In and out. In and out. If I want to get in that room—and I have to get in that room—I've got to be inconspicuous. I've got to be a blur in the background, before I can turn on the spotlight.

So I stand tall—but not too tall—and walk quickly—but not too quickly—in the doors, through the metal detector, right by the bored security guard engrossed in his bag of chips, and down the hall, past the signs showing me the way to the city council meeting room.

My life might not be a noir, but today, I get to be my own version of Nick Charles, clever and funny and *right*. I get to be the person who breaks the case wide open, in front of everyone.

INT: CITY COUNCIL ROOM, DUSK, BUT ALL THE
LIGHTING'S ARTIFICIAL ANYWAY SO WHO CARES.

UNNAMED COUNCILWOMAN
The Save Our Streets committee would like to propose additional funding for community policing, citing the recent rise in break-ins, vandalism—

GIDEON (M, 16, about to be a local hero) bursts in through the main doors.

GIDEON
And murder!

UNNAMED COUNCILWOMAN
Uh—

UNNAMED COUNCILWOMAN #2 cuts in.

UNNAMED COUNCILWOMAN #2:

We're not to the community statements
portion yet—

GIDEON

A man was murdered on the floor of
Triggerfish Brewery, in cold blood.

LILY

(F, 16, looking horrified for some reason)
Oh my God. Oh my *God*—

GIDEON

And the murderer is right here in this room
tonight. . . . He's sitting at that table.

The CAMERA PANS around the city council table.

GIDEON

This murderer is very clever. He might have
not wanted for this to happen, but he
figured out pretty quickly how to cover it
up. Isn't that right, Mr. Willets?

The CAMERA STOPS on FRED WILLETS (blond, 40s,
murderer)

UNNAMED COUNCILWOMAN

(to camera guy) Jordan, cut the feed. *Cut the feed!*

GIDEON

He planned the whole thing beautifully. What better way to boost his campaign for mayor than with a tough-on-crime, save-our-streets crusade? The only problem was, there wasn't enough crime. That would have stopped a less ambitious man, but not Fred Willets.

UNNAMED COUNCILWOMAN

Someone call security!

GIDEON

He conspired with the local criminal element—small-time mob lords and petty criminals—to *create* a crime wave. With the help of men like Paul Vince and Charlie . . . the bartender to sacrifice their employees, their patrons, to preplanned property crimes. These break-ins and arsons made the papers, and they gave credence to his constant speeches about the city's downfall.

UNNAMED COUNCILWOMAN

Young man—excuse me, young man, security
has been called! You need to—

GIDEON

But why kill Marco Vince? All he wanted was
his own cut, Mr. Willets. All he had was
evidence of the conspiracy, to loosen your
purse strings? How much could he have
wanted? Too much for you, clearly. He asked
you to meet, and you suggested your own
brewery. Out of the way, no one looking in.
Somewhere you felt safe. And when he
threatened to blackmail you—you killed him.

UNNAMED COUNCILWOMAN

Where the hell is Mark? *(Beat)* Well, call
him again, this is nuts, this is—

LILY

Gideon, Jesus, stop!

GIDEON

I don't think you meant to. If you'd meant
to, it would have been cleaner. Smarter. But
the man was dead, and you had a problem.
You knew of his drug use, and sure enough,

in his bag, there was his stash. So you set
the scene to look like an overdose, and
because you didn't want him ID'd too fast,
you took his credit cards, his driver's
license . . . and his watch. That watch
you're wearing around your left wrist right
now.

You almost got away with it. You might have
just walked away, a free man. But you've
always thought of yourself as a winner. And
you couldn't resist taking a trophy.

This is a bombshell. And it's just burst.

I take a deep breath and wait for the next inevitable part.
When Fred Willets, guilty as sin, admits what he's done or rages
against the accusation to no avail. It doesn't matter. He just has
to react.

But Fred Willets doesn't look angry. He doesn't even look
scared. He looks . . . amused.

That isn't right. That isn't how this is supposed to go at all.

"Are you done?" he asks me, and the casualness in his voice
rocks me worse than if he'd shouted. "I don't want to interrupt
before you're done."

"I'm—" I stutter. "I'm done. And you can't deny it, can you,

Mr. Willets?" I finish, but my voice isn't steady anymore.

Fred Willets smiles. This is so not going according to script.

"Come here," he says, waving me toward him.

"Fred!" the woman next to him says, alarmed, but he brushes her off.

"Relax, Sheila, he's a kid." He gestures at me again. "No, come on up here."

Slowly, cautiously, and feeling a lot like a fox who just got his ankle snapped in a snare, I walk to the center of the room. Right in front of Fred Willets.

"I had the wildest imagination as a kid," he tells me. "You wouldn't believe. Or maybe you would. Created these whole worlds. I knew how everything worked in them, and there were no surprises, because I made the rules."

Behind me, the doors swing open again, and a panting security guard stumbles into the room. When he spots me up front, his eyes zero in on me.

"You," he says. "Come with me."

But Fred Willets holds up his hand. "No, we're all right, Mark. Just a moment." He turns back to me. "The problem was, that world was too real to me. You know? I'd tell people about these elaborate fantasies, and then couldn't understand why they didn't believe in them. The way I did. I'd let my own brain trick me into mistaking stories I made up for reality."

It doesn't take a genius to see the parallel he's trying to draw. But this isn't me coming up with a fantasyland of unicorns and dragons. This is *real* and I'm *right*, I have to be right, because if I'm not—

"Eventually, I came to terms with that. I stopped letting my imagination control me, and I started focusing on the world that was actually around me. And what I could do to make it better. That's how I ended up here."

Oh my God, I realize. He's *using* me. That's why he didn't have me hauled out immediately, that's why he had me come up, he's using what I'm doing to make himself an election ad clip. I'm not destroying him. He's not going to let that happen. He's spinning it. He's transforming it.

He wouldn't do that unless he was sure.

He wouldn't do that unless he was certain I had nothing on him.

He knows something I don't.

"But—" I take a sharp, shallow breath. "You—you have—"

"It's the watch, right?" He holds up his hand, showing me the gold watch face. "That's the linchpin. For this whole wild scenario you've built in your head, it all comes down to my watch." He pauses. "Correct?"

He knows something I don't. And I think I'm about to be told what it is.

"Come on, you had so much to say before. What changed? You starting to realize your head ran away with you?"

No, I want to say. *I'm just not stupid. I can see what you're doing, and I know talking now is a mistake.*

Drawing the moment out, he slowly undoes the watch's bracelet clasp.

"This is a dead man's watch." He holds it up. "According to you. And I'm going to let you see it."

Then he holds it out to me with a smile. Like it's a gift. Or like it's a trump card.

I take another three steps forward—I count them—and he drops it in my open hand. The first thing I do is turn it over, and from the way his smile widens, he knew I would.

It could be new, I try to convince myself. *He could have done this last week.* But it's not true, and I know it. This engraving isn't fresh. It's been smoothed and battered by time and wear, just like the watch itself.

"Go ahead," Willets says. "Tell everyone what it says."

"'To Fred,'" I read. "'With Love, Mom.'"

CHAPTER 22

"YOU DON'T HAVE to drag me," I tell the security guard as he propels me down the hallway, toward the front entrance. "Can't you tell I'm going willingly?"

Case in point: it's my coat collar he's got balled up in his thick fist. If I really wanted to, I could slip right out, leaving my coat behind. He doesn't respond.

"Or do you consider getting to drag people places one of your job perks?"

That makes his eye twitch. "You're funny."

"Thank you."

"We'll see how funny you are when the cops get here."

And *that* makes my stomach drop. "Wait, no—"

"Oh," he says, "yes."

"I'll leave," I promise. "Right now, I'll walk out the door and you'll never see me again, you don't need to call the—"

"Gideon Green?" says an unfortunately familiar voice behind us.

Oh, as if this day couldn't get any worse.

The security guard turns, swinging me around with him. And there, in front of us, like I knew he would be, is—

"Deputy Chief Garcia," the security guard says. Then nods his head toward me. "You know him?"

"We have met."

"Twice," I say.

"Twice," he agrees.

"Is disturbing the peace a hobby for you?" the security guard asks me.

"First time," I say. "I think I'll go back to knitting."

"Wait," Garcia cuts in. "Disturbing the peace how?"

"He stormed the city council meeting, basically—"

Stormed. He makes it seem like Normandy Beach.

"Started rambling about all this crazy stuff, like that Willets has—you know Willets, right?"

"Yes."

"Yeah, so about how there's this big conspiracy, and Willets has been paying people to commit crimes, and he even killed some guy and stole his watch."

Garcia stares down at me. He shakes his head. "You've got to be kidding me."

"No," the security guard says, "that's actually what he went with."

Garcia doesn't look away from me. "I told you to keep yourself out of this, didn't I?"

I drop my eyes to my shoes and say nothing.

"You know what, Mark, I'll take it from here," Garcia says, which makes my head snap up.

"Really?"

"Yeah, I'm on my way out, and the kid's a frequent flier, so . . ."

Reluctantly, Mark the security guard lets me go. Just as reluctantly, I smooth out my coat collar where he creased it and step over to Garcia. He gestures at the front door but lets me walk out of City Hall under my own power.

As he walks me in the direction of the parking lot, I ask: "What's a frequent flier?"

"Somebody the whole department knows, because they show up in the back of a squad car so often."

"I think that's an exaggeration."

"I think you should just be quiet."

So I am. But the silence gnaws at me. Every second I'm quiet, all that plays in my head is a relentless drumbeat of *you were wrong, you got it wrong, you got it completely wrong*, until I can't take it anymore and blurt out:

"Don't you have to tell me what you're arresting me for?"

"I would," he says, "if I were arresting you."

"Fine, detaining, whatever."

"I'm not detaining you. It's not actually disturbing the peace to interrupt a city council meeting. Even if you did accuse a public servant of murder."

"Then—"

"I'm going to take you to your dad. Let him handle it from there."

That's simultaneously the worst news I've heard all day and the best outcome I could have hoped for. "Yeah. Okay."

He looks surprised. "Just like that? No half hour of stone-walling this time?"

I shake my head.

In the parking lot, Garcia opens the back door of his squad car and, once I've buckled myself in, says, "Why don't you call your dad, figure out where he is."

"I don't have my phone."

"A teenager without his phone. You really do break the mold."

"I had to leave it at home because he checks the tracking sometimes." I pause. "I shouldn't have told you that, though."

"Is he more likely at your house, or at his restaurant?"

I check the dashboard clock. Almost six p.m. "Restaurant."

"Flores Street, right?"

I nod miserably. This is going to suck.

"So you don't think I'm involved?" I ask as he drives. He can't, if all he's doing is delivering me to my parent's custody.

"I never thought you'd killed anyone, if that's what you're

asking. I thought you knew more than you were saying." He shrugs. "But if Willets was your theory . . . clearly I was wrong about your level of knowledge."

I wait a beat, then ask: "So who do you think killed him?"

"Do you really think I'm going to discuss that with you?"

"No, but—"

"All I can say is we're pursuing leads. And there are plenty of them."

"Because of who his dad is."

He sighs. "Of course you know that."

It was in the paper. That's not even detective work. It's just reading.

"But I always wondered if that was really it," I add. Garcia doesn't say anything. "That he got killed because of who his dad is. I thought maybe, it was because of who *he* was." He's still quiet, and for a moment, so am I. "I wondered if he died because he was the fuckup."

"Excuse me?"

I don't know if he's responding to the swearing or the statement. "He was the screwed-up kid, the one who got arrested for public intoxication and stuff, the one with the drug problem, the one who couldn't even manage a furniture store that was just a money-laundering front to begin with."

Another sigh. "Of course you know that, too."

"So I wondered if he died *because* of that. Because he was so reckless and stupid and brought the whole situation down on himself. Or—" I don't like thinking about this theory. But I have thought it. "Or if his dad let it happen."

Garcia reels back. "Jesus. This was not a human sacrifice."

"I don't mean a sacrifice," I say. "I mean, what if he didn't *care* if he put his son in a dangerous situation, what if he just *let* the chips fall, because he was so sick of putting up with this kid who only brought him trouble. His fuckup son who was never going to be useful, never going to take over the family business—"

"Business? It's a crime syndicate—"

"That he'd just have to stare at him day after day with that look of disappointment and that feeling of, of, *loss*."

"Kid," Garcia says quietly. "Gideon—stop. This is . . . stop."

But I can't. "No, I mean that—*loss*, real loss because he had this idea of what his son was going to be, and it didn't happen. It just didn't. And when he figured out that it wasn't ever going to happen, that he wasn't going to *get* the kid he wanted, that's a loss. He lost the future he pictured." I swallow. "He lost it twice."

It's quiet. I can be quiet, now. It's like I spit out every word I had in me. And now I'm empty.

The streets and sidewalks and houses blur as I stare out over the dashboard, and it takes me a second to notice Garcia's made a wrong turn. I wait a moment. Then another, and another, for him to realize his mistake. But . . . nothing. He just keeps driving.

Shit. *Shit.* He's taking me back to the station. I must have said something that makes him want to question me, or maybe he's changed his mind and wants to throw me in a holding cell for a while, just to make sure I never again crash a city council meeting.

As if I could. This case is dead. And as if I would. Those people were the human equivalent of sleeping pills.

"Where are you taking me?" I ask.

"Isn't your house on Daybreak?"

I blink. "Yeah."

"That's where I'm taking you."

I don't get it. Did he decide Verde is too far out of his way? That doesn't make sense; it's closer to the station than my house. And if he's planning on having Dad meet us there, then why not call him now, from the car?

This is really not my finest day as a detective.

Garcia clears his throat. "You like mysteries. From what I've seen—and what the chief told me—you like them to the point of obsession."

"Obsession" makes it sounds so negative. Couldn't anyone ever just go with "enthusiasm"?

"I liked mysteries, too, when I was a kid," he continues. "Less investigative, more . . . brainteasers, I guess you'd call them. I liked solving those."

A little low stakes for my taste, but I'm not going to say that.

"I liked that to figure them out, you always had to forget what you knew."

"What do you mean?"

"Your biases. Preconceptions. You had to be willing to let go of the things you assumed were true in order to figure out what actually was. You might assume the doctor mentioned in the brainteaser is a man, but . . . have they said that? No. That's your assumption."

"I wouldn't assume that."

"Well. Kudos to the new generation, then."

"I mean, *my* doctor's name is Carolyn, so—"

"My point is, you had to figure out what your assumptions were and then consider a world in which you were wrong."

"Isn't that what all detectives do? Analyze the crime scene with an open mind, explore vantage points."

"And you like doing that," he says. "You did do that, at Triggerfish."

"I tried to."

He pauses. "Do you do it for people, too?"

"You mean . . . suspects?"

"No," he says. "I mean people."

I shake my head. "I don't understand."

"People can be mysteries, too. Confusing, complicated, just these *tangles* of feelings and motivations and choices, and not a single one makes any sense. Not to you, anyway. Because you're tangled up yourself. Only with different knots."

We've pulled up outside my house now, and he stops the car but doesn't stop talking. I don't stop listening, either.

"What do you do to solve a mystery?" he asks. I think it's rhetorical. So I don't answer. "You let go of what you think you know. You try to see what's actually there. But you have to let yourself see it."

I've always thought I could see things so much better than other people. But maybe it's not true. Maybe there are angles I haven't ever tried to see. Because I was so sure of my own.

"Do you understand what I'm saying?"

"I'm not sure," I say. Simply. Honestly.

"Sometimes it's a good thing," he says as he waves me out the car door, "not to be sure."

No sooner do I finally drag myself back to my room, switch off the still-running TV, and collapse on my bed than the doorbell rings.

I ignore it, hoping against hope it's just our mail guy dropping off a package.

But it rings again. And then again, heavy and unrelenting, like someone's taking out all their rage on the doorbell.

"Hi," I say when I open the door.

Lily glares back at me, one hand on the doorbell, the other in a death grip around her bag strap. "That's all you're going to say? Hi?"

"I feel like that's what most people do when they answer a door."

"Most people," she repeats, so calmly it terrifies me. "Okay.

Let me tell you what *most* people do, because I don't think you know."

"Wait, I—"

"Most people would warn their friend when they're about to blow the lid on something she's been working on for months. Most people would get her opinion before they did that." Her voice rises and rises with each word. "Most people would *tell her* about the big solution they'd come up with, not let her find out as they're sharing it with the entire city council on *local fucking television!*"

I swallow. "I . . . don't think most people end up in that situation."

"*You* shouldn't have been in that situation!"

"Can you please stop yelling at me?"

"No!"

I open the door farther. "Then can you at least yell at me inside?"

"Fine!"

She stomps in, dumps her bag on the ground, and barely waits a second after I've closed the door to launch in again.

"I can't believe you did that! That's all I can think about, how I can't *believe*—"

"I thought I'd figured it out."

"Based on what? A watch?"

"Not just the watch, he only made it seem like—he's an owner of the brewery, he's got short blond hair, just like the ones I saw on Marco's jacket, and he had every reason to want those crime statistics to go up—"

"But he wasn't even *here*!"

I stop short. "What?"

"On the night Marco Vince was murdered, Fred Willets was hundreds of miles away in Palo Alto, attending a benefit dinner for cancer research. It was written up. There are pictures."

If I had any shred of hope left, it vanishes now.

"How did you—?"

"I do my research," she snaps. "And if you'd let me in on your theory, I could have told you why it was impossible."

I didn't think it was possible to feel worse about today. But Lily comes in clutch, like she always does. None of this had to happen. None of it *would* have happened if I'd thought for a second before I did it.

"I'm sorry," I say. "I really am. But I really thought I'd solved it."

"The point is you didn't even call me! You didn't even *care*. You just burst into the meeting—a meeting you knew I was at—and blew it all to smithereens."

I cringe, because . . . she's right. "I wasn't trying to blow it up."

"No, you were trying to imitate fake detectives in fictional movies and have a big reveal where you ended up the hero. Weren't you?"

I look away.

"Weren't you?" she asks again.

"I would have given you credit," I say. Not confirming her suspicions. But not lying. "I was getting there. I just thought if people saw I was right—"

"It's not about credit! It's about you ruining everything I worked so hard for because of your own stupid ego!"

"Lily—"

"You embarrassed yourself," she says. "You embarrassed *me*."

Something clicks, in my head, when she says that. Like a gear snapping out of place.

"That's really it, isn't it?" I ask.

"What is?"

"That I embarrassed you."

Like a gear scraping against a wall, getting ready to break.

"You also cut me out of my own investigation," she says, "and acted completely without thinking—"

"But it's the embarrassment," I say. "That's the part you really, *really* can't handle."

"I have no idea what you mean by—"

"We stopped being friends when you started being embarrassed by me."

For the first time since I opened the door, Lily has nothing to say. But only for a second. She always could bounce back fast.

"It's normal for people to drift apart. Make new friends.

Especially in middle school."

We didn't drift apart. She set me adrift. On an ice floe to nowhere.

"Okay. Let me tell you what's *normal*," I grind out, "since I don't think you know."

"Oh, God—" she groans, clearly already over this. But I'm not. I'm just getting warmed up.

"It's not normal for your best friend to go away for the summer and come back wanting nothing to do with you. It's not normal for the person you used to spend every day with to suddenly ignore you in the hallways and not tell you why. It's not normal to have Mia fucking McElroy act as a go-between to explain that your *best friend* doesn't want to hang out with you or even see you, ever again!"

"I didn't know that's what she said." Lily's mouth crumples. "I never told her to say that."

"It didn't matter how she *said* it—you ditched me!"

"And I feel terrible about it!"

"Do you?"

"Of course I do."

"Then it's weird that you've never apologized."

Lily folds her arms across her chest. Is it protective? Or defensive? I can't tell.

"Haven't I made up for it?" she asks. "I know I hurt you, but haven't I made up for it yet?"

I scoff. "How?"

"I brought you into what I was doing, I let you help with my investigation. I got you on the newspaper—"

I turn away, because that sets my teeth on edge. The way she talks about it, like it was charity. "Don't act like you did me some big favor."

"If I hadn't come over that day, you'd still be in your room surrounded by black-and-white movies instead of living a real life."

I whirl back around on her. "You didn't do it for me. You did it for yourself."

She takes a step back. "What?"

"It wasn't out of the kindness of your heart. I don't even think it was guilt. You needed something from me. *Let* me help with your investigation, bull*shit*. You wouldn't *be* anywhere in this investigation without me."

"Oh, without the boy who just cratered the whole thing at a city council meeting? Yeah, whatever would I do without you?"

"You would have researched and looked at stats from the comfort of your bedroom and gotten exactly nowhere. You talk this big game about being ambitious, and I guess you are, but I've known you since you were six, so I also know that you're always going to take the easy way out."

"Stop it."

"You've been taking the path of least resistance since seventh grade, when you figured it would be easier to stop *talking* to me than deal with the *horror* of having an uncool friend!"

"I didn't stop being friends with you because you weren't cool," Lily snaps. "I stopped being friends with you because you were a *jerk*."

Then it's me who's taking a step back.

"Do you know what it's like, to feel like a sidekick in your own life?" she says. "No. Of course not. You've always been your own main character."

I didn't do that. Did I? Make her feel like I took her for granted, like I was more important? That isn't the truth. It's not my fault if she bought into a lie, even one in her own head.

"We were partners," I say.

"No, Gideon, we were not partners. We were little kids playing detectives, and it was fun until it wasn't. It was fun until I started to realize how much smarter you thought you were and how little you cared about what I thought."

"That's not true."

When Lily locks her eyes on mine, they're hard and flinty and hurt. "It's still true."

It's not. Is it? I know what's true and what isn't. Don't I?

"You could have told me," I say. "You could have talked to me. But that would have been hard, right? It was easier—for you—to just go ahead and abandon me."

"I didn't know what to do, I was a kid! We both were. You're mad at someone who doesn't exist anymore."

She can't just absolve herself because she got older. Twelve or not, she did what she did.

"All you did was trade up."

"Trade up—?"

"Are you telling me Mia *listens* to you? That she treats you like anything *other* than a sidekick?"

Lily bites her lip but doesn't say anything.

"You can't pretend you ditched me because I was a jerk when you turned right around and found an even bigger one. You can't pretend that's the only reason."

She's biting her lip so hard it's turning white, but she still doesn't say anything.

"I'm always going to be who I am. I'm always going to like the stuff I like even if nobody else does. I'm always going to dress the way I want to even if everyone stares." I swallow. "And I'm so sick of feeling bad or guilty or . . . *alien* because other people don't like who I am!"

"That's not—"

"You being embarrassed of me didn't make me a bad person." I take a breath. "It made you shallow."

"God." When she blinks, two parallel tears streak down her cheeks. "Gideon."

"I'm just being—"

"Honest, yeah, I know," she says, grabbing her bag and stalking past me toward the door.

"I won't apologize for not being a liar."

Lily stops, then turns around to face me. "You care so much more about what's true than what's kind."

"The truth is important."

"Kindness is important, too." She jerks the front door open. "And without it, all your honesty just looks like cruelty."

Before I can think of a single thing to say back, she's gone.

CHAPTER 23

IN ANOTHER LIFE, Lily would have been an excellent military general. She's got the whole scorched-earth strategy down pat.

Or maybe she would have been a good hermit. She's got the silent-treatment thing perfectly honed, too.

Tess pulls me aside one Late Night. "What's going on with you two?"

Clearly, Lily hasn't told Tess anything. And I don't think she'd be any happier with me if I broke her confidence. Again. "We're . . . kind of in a fight."

"Oh." Tess frowns. "Well, please make up, because this is *super* uncomfortable."

She's not wrong. But every time I try to go to Lily, she walks away. She even gets Noah to deliver her pages to me for copy editing. I don't think making up is on the menu.

With the investigation over, any day I'm not spending at the *Herald* or with Tess is a day I'm spending in my bedroom, again.

It takes Dad about a week to notice, but when he does, he's on the case.

"Do you want to tell me what's wrong?" he asks one day before work. Just like he has for the past three days.

I keep my eyes on *Double Indemnity*. "No."

"Gideon."

"I said, no."

"Don't use that tone with me."

Don't keep asking the same question, then. "I told you. I don't want to talk about it. It's fine."

He walks over and turns off my TV. "It doesn't seem fine."

"Well, it is!"

"Again with the tone," he says. "If something's going on, I need to know about it."

"Why? You'd only get mad."

"Should I be?"

I take a mental inventory of my most recent sins. Getting driven home by a cop. Ruining my friendship with Lily. Publicly accusing a city council member of murder.

Yeah. He probably should be mad. Definitely *would* be. "What's it matter? You're always mad at me."

"You have done some pretty stupid stuff lately."

I know that. I wouldn't be sitting by myself in this room having this *agonizing conversation with him* if I hadn't done such stupid things. I'm mad at myself, but I can't tell him why, which only makes me madder at myself and somehow madder at him, too, and it heats and burns right under my skin until I boil over. "Yeah, well, I guess that makes it fine, then, right?"

"Makes what fine?"

"That you don't *like* me!"

His jaw drops.

"I'm sure you're going to say something about how you love me, and fine, whatever, but that doesn't mean you like me, and you *don't*."

"Whoa, hold on—"

"You think I'm weird, and you think the stuff I like is weird, too, and you wish I was somebody way different than I am."

"Gideon . . . ," he says, sitting down on the bed, but I move so there's the same distance between us.

"It's like you think I don't know that, which . . ." I throw up my hands. "Of course I know! Of course I can tell! I notice everything, it's what I do, not that you like *that*, either. I notice the way you look at me. The way you've always looked at me. And I am sorry—trust me, nobody is sorrier than me—that I am such a fucking disappointment to you."

He doesn't yell back. He doesn't tell me to stop. He doesn't even call me out for swearing. He just looks down at his hands and asks:

"Do you hate me?"

This time, it's my jaw that drops. "What?"

"I hated my father," he says. "When I was your age. I really did, I . . . *hated* him, so fully and deeply, and I thought: When

I have a kid, I'll never treat him like this."

That's not what I meant. That wasn't what I was trying to say.

"But you didn't," I tell him. "You didn't treat me like . . . that."

"You don't have to hit someone to hurt them."

That's true. You can hurt someone in a million different ways. Like Lily hurt me in seventh grade. Or how I hurt her.

"I wouldn't have wanted to talk to him, either, if something was wrong," Dad continues. "Not that we talked a lot anyway, even when nothing was wrong. But I wouldn't have wanted to tell him anything, ever, because I didn't trust him. And I don't think you trust me."

The truest thing I could say is: *No, I don't.* Or maybe not. Maybe the truest thing I could say is: *I wish I did.* But then I think—what will it help? To say either of those things? He already knows, or he wouldn't have said it.

"You said you hated him."

"Yeah."

"Past tense."

He nods. "Yes."

"So what changed?"

"I grew up." He smiles a little sadly. "I had you."

Me? What do I have to do with it? And maybe he can read the question on my face, because he keeps going.

"The older you got, the less I could hate him. I couldn't really forgive him, either, but . . . I couldn't hate him."

"Why, though?"

"Because I saw how easy it was to become someone you didn't want to be, just because it was the only thing you'd ever seen." He shakes his head. "I keep thinking about that day at Verde— the way I talked to you."

I haven't thought about that in weeks. I can't believe it's been stuck in his head longer than mine.

"He's been dead for almost twenty years, but the second I get mad at you, what comes flying out of my mouth? His words. His phrases. Without even meaning to, I'm throwing them at you. And then how can I be surprised when you think I don't *like* you? When you don't trust me?" He shrugs helplessly. "That's exactly how I would have reacted. And you're exactly like me."

He could have told me aliens had landed on the roof, and I wouldn't be more shocked than I am right now.

"What are you talking about, we don't like any of the same—"

"So you like movies I don't, and I like cooking things you won't eat, okay. I'm talking about what we're *like*, Gideon, not *what* we like."

I frown. He keeps going.

"I was ready to leave my hometown, too, about the second I turned thirteen. I was independent, like you, and passionate about the things that mattered to me, and so unbelievably frustrated by the world." He looks down at the bedspread. "I know what it's like to feel the way you do. Maybe not in every way. But . . . some."

A tiny sliver of shared space. In the least expected place.

"I'm sorry," he says, "that I've made you feel the way you do. I'm sorry that you feel like you can't trust me. I'm trying, though," he says. "I'm going to keep trying, harder, and I want you to know that."

Dad's hand twitches—almost like he was going to reach for something—but then he lowers it back onto his knee. He clears his throat and gets to his feet.

If this were a movie, I'd stop him before he got to the door, because I know I should say something. I know this is the moment I'm supposed to say something. I just don't know what it is.

"We can't change who we are," Dad says with his hand on the doorknob. "But maybe we can change how we treat each other."

He closes the door gently behind him, but I don't move. It almost feels like when I know I've found a clue or heard something I can tell is going to be important, if I can just figure out why.

We can't change who we are.

Nobody knows that better than me.

We can change how we treat each other.

In movies, a character is their traits and their backstory. What they're like, and what's happened to them.

But—no. That's not right. That would only be right if they were locked in time, in a single moment, and that's not what movies are. They're stories, and it isn't a good story if a character never makes a decision. A story isn't just what *happens* to the heroes. It's the things they do, too.

A person is more than their traits and their backstory. A person is their choices.

Some of the things I've done can't be altered, because real life doesn't have reshoots. And they can't be forgotten, either, edited out of my memory frame by frame.

I can't change who I am, and even if I could—I don't want to. But maybe I can change how I treat people . . . even if they don't understand me.

CHAPTER 24

IT'S NOT THAT I don't like going to Tess's house, because I do. Her grandma won't let us go anywhere without putting a week's worth of calories in front of us first (refusal is not an option) and her conchas are even better than Dad's (not that I would ever tell him that). It also presents ideal opportunities to gather valuable intel about Tess. Like, for instance, that her childhood nickname was—adorably—Conejita.

"I really liked carrots," Tess explains, long-suffering.

But it is a true and honest fact we have infinitely more privacy at my house.

So that's where we are this afternoon—in my room, curled up together on my bed, watching *Call Northside 777* on my TV.

It isn't necessarily a classic, and there's some debate over whether it's noir at all, but it's a newsroom mystery, so I thought Tess might like it. She identifies with it, for sure. Especially the no-nonsense editor-in-chief character.

"Sometimes I wish I could do that," Tess says wistfully, during a scene between the editor in chief and his star reporter.

I squint at Lee Cobb on the screen. "Chain-smoke a pack a day?"

"Stick around," she says. "On the paper. Real editors in chief don't work for just one year, they get to really build something."

I pause the movie. "Are you saying you don't want to graduate?"

I don't want her to graduate, but that's only because I don't want to be at this stupid school without her. And sure, she'll only be about ten miles away at UCSD in the fall, but we both know it'll be different. Even if we haven't talked about it . . . we both know.

"I'm ready to leave high school," Tess says. "But that doesn't mean I'm ready to leave everything about high school, the *Herald* especially. I'm . . . worried."

"What about?"

"That I have to just toss all my hard work at the feet of the next person in line and hope the paper survives."

"It'll survive," I promise her. "Lily will do great."

Tess looks away quickly. Too quickly. I work to catch her eye again. "Are you not picking Lily?"

She looks uncomfortable. "I'm . . . not sure."

"But she'd be good. Don't you think she would be? She's a great writer, I've heard you say so, and she's organized and smart and—"

"A pushover."

I stop. "What?"

"Haven't you noticed?"

I don't want to tell the truth. And I don't want to lie. "She stood her ground with the investigation."

"No, she didn't. She could have fought for that piece. She could have argued with me. But that would have been hard. So instead, she went behind my back and brought you into it. Add that to her Model UN Club article—"

"Wait," I interrupt. "What article?"

"At the beginning of the semester, Lily had this Features piece about Model UN. She pitched it, she wanted to write it herself. I said go for it. She turns it into me a few weeks later, and it's great. Well written, super thoroughly researched, and way more nuanced than I expected. Turns out their last treasurer had to step down but there was evidence she'd sort of embezzled funds. *She* said the whole club was in on it and kicked her out to save themselves—scandal. So I'm like, great, done, we're teasing it on the front page. That Thursday Late Night, I come into the *Herald* room and pull up the front page, and there's just a giant blank space where her article should be. Then Lily tells me the president of Model UN, I guess a friend of hers, got wind she'd interviewed that former treasurer and demanded Lily pull the piece."

I feel like I can see where this story is going. "And she agreed?"

"She *caved*. At the slightest hint of confrontation, she just . . ."

"Folded like a cheap suit?"

"I was going to say 'lay down and died,' but sure," Tess says. "Anyway, I got the Model UN president on the phone, explained the article was going to be printed with or without their approval, and welcomed them to write a letter to the editor if they felt wronged."

I shrug. "So it sounds like you fixed it."

"Right! *I* fixed it, not her! If Lily can't stand up to me, or to her friend, is she going to be able to push back if Ms. Flueger wants to change something next year? Can she stand by a controversial article, if she gets called down to Principal Wallace's office? Or will she do what she always does?"

Take the path of least resistance. Just like I told Lily. And now I feel even worse for saying it. Because it was true . . . but it wasn't kind.

"Can we put the movie back on?" Tess asks apologetically.

"Yeah," I say, feeling bad for having even brought up the subject. "Of course."

I turn it back on, and Tess nestles against me, her head leaning on my chest. It's different, watching a movie together with someone, instead of alone. Scarier, in a way, because you want them to love it the way you do, and you don't know if they will. But better, too, because not only do you get to watch the movie, but you get to watch *them* experiencing it for the first time.

The two hit men of *The Killers* ominously sitting down at the diner counter. Rita Hayworth on *Gilda*'s nightclub stage, peeling off a long black glove inch by inch. Humphrey Bogart cradling the lead Maltese Falcon in his hands and calling it "the stuff dreams are made of."

I pause the movie again.

"Tess."

She looks up at me through dark, delicate eyelashes. "Yeah?"

"Did you have a special thing, when you were a kid?"

"A what?"

"Something you were really into. It feels like most kids did, when we were a lot younger. Like, fire trucks, or frogs, Disney princesses, or—" I think back. "Lily's special thing were these ponies. These hyper-realistic plastic horses that were also super delicate. You just looked at one and its ankle snapped in half."

"Then what?" she says. "You had to pull out the tiny plastic shotgun to put it down?"

"No, you had to run, because Lily was about to murder *you*."

She laughs. Then thinks about it for a moment. "I guess my thing was trivia."

"Trivia about what?"

"Everything. Anything. I spent a lot of time at my grandparents' house, even before I started living there, and every night at seven p.m., I'd watch *Jeopardy!* with my grandma. And the way the contestants could answer all these different questions from all these categories, I thought it was so cool. I wanted to be like that. So I checked out all these big books of facts from the library, and my grandpa got me a set of encyclopedias at a yard sale—they were pretty outdated, the maps still had the USSR on them, but—I tried to stuff as much of it in my head as I could."

"So you'd be ready, when you went on *Jeopardy!*?"

"No," she says, "so I could tell other people. I loved being the person who got to do that, who got to hand them something that might stick with them for a day or for . . . forever." She brushes a strand of hair from her face. "Maybe that's why I fell in love with journalism, too. It's the same thing—telling people something they don't know."

"Giving them a story," I say, but it's mostly to myself. "Giving them something they didn't have before."

"It's a gift," she agrees. "You have to treat it that way."

"Even though other people might not. Because they don't, always."

"Yeah." She laughs, settling herself back on my chest. "Tell me something I don't know."

I could stay like this forever, quiet and content. Or I could do what she's asked, though she doesn't know she asked it. I could give her something.

"I was a kid detective," I say, spilling the words out before I can take them back.

Tess pushes herself upright and twists around so we're facing. "Wait. What?"

I take a deep breath, look Tess right in the eyes, and tell her everything. All the way from the founding of the Green

Detective Agency, and Mrs. Cabot with her sapphires, to my last, disastrous case in seventh grade.

It's a story I've heard told a million times before—from Lily and the police chief, Dad and Channel 5 News—but it's different this time. I'm telling this story myself, without being interrupted, without being shoved into a narrative I didn't choose, without wanting anything except to be listened to.

I've heard this story a million times—and this is the first time it's been mine.

After I'm finished, she still doesn't say anything. Not at first. It's like she's waiting, to make sure I'm ready.

"Wow," she says, almost on a breath out. "I mean—wow."

And then I ask what I've been too afraid to, all along. "You don't remember any of that?"

"I've never had a great memory," she says, almost apologetic, though she shouldn't be. As much as my memory has helped me out, that might be the real gift—the ability to forget. To greet someone with a blank, new slate.

"But yeah, you'd think I'd remember a story like that," she says. "Because . . . wow."

"Okay," I say, feeling my shoulders tense. "So is that like a 'Wow, you were a very accomplished ten-year-old' or 'Wow, you were and continue to be a huge weirdo and I'm leaving now'?"

"You have a different way of thinking about things." Tess says, interlocking her hand in mine. "That's all."

All can be everything—all of you. But *all* can be the opposite, too—nothing at all. The way I see the world isn't all of me, but it's part of me, so it isn't nothing at all, either.

"It always felt like I saw the world through a totally different lens than everyone else," I say. Then shrug. "I've never been able to decide whether it's a gift or a curse."

Tess tilts her head. "Why are you so sure it's either?"

"Huh?"

"What if it isn't either of those things?" she says. "What if it just . . . *is*?"

Detectives are different, too, at least the ones in movies are. But it makes them special. If they're solitary, strange, cynical—it's a gift. It's the only way they can do what they do. Not someone to pity but someone who sees the world exactly as it should be seen.

I held on to that, because I needed to. It was like a buoy in the middle of the Pacific Ocean, just barely keeping me afloat. Fine, I was different, and so what if no one ever seemed to get me? It made me smarter than them. *Better* than them.

But what if it wasn't a buoy at all? What if it was only a rock, dragging me farther down?

I thought being different made me better, and everyone else seemed to think it made me worse, and now, for the first time, I wonder if we were all wrong. What if Tess is right, and it isn't either of those things?

Not a gift or a curse. Not good or bad. Not black or white.

It just is.

The more I let it sit in my head—get comfortable, make itself a home inside the alleyways in my brain I never let anyone enter—the truer it feels. And the truer it feels, the more I wonder why it took me so long to get here. How could I not see any of this before?

I look at Tess, sitting across from me, her eyes steady and unblinking and ready for whatever story I tell her next. I feel her hand in mine, warm and strong, both of us fit together like perfectly interlocking puzzle pieces.

Tess can't see inside my head, so maybe she wonders why I reach out across the space between us and kiss her, then. Or maybe she doesn't, because she kisses me back, long and deep and endless, until we're tangled up in the bedsheets and each other.

I have seen a thousand kisses shot in black and white, all of them rehearsed and practiced and lit just right, with a swelling soundtrack set beneath them. And none of them, not a single one, could ever be as perfect as this.

"What about the movie?" Tess asks when we come up for air.

I pull her in close again. "It can wait."

CHAPTER 25

THE BRIGHT, NOON sun beats down on my lunch table—like it always does. A month ago, I might have complained about the cheerfully oppressive Southern California sunshine, but sometimes, consistency can be nice.

My phone buzzes with a text from Tess:

Going to be late, Anatomy lab went over

This is like the third time you've had to dissect something right before lunch

NO NEED TO REMIND ME GIDEON

As I'm sticking the phone back in my pocket, I feel the footsteps—multiple—on the concrete before I hear someone—singular—clear their throat. I know who it is before I even look up, because my life might not be a noir, but sometimes it does feel like it has flashback sequences.

"No," I tell Mia before she even asks. "Come on."

"*You* come on," she says. "You're taking up a whole giant table. Again."

Her group of friends behind her all look uncomfortable with this scenario . . . but none more so than Lily. Standing at the back. Staring down at the stack of books in her arms.

"I'm not in a relationship you can destroy," Mia says with a grim smile. "So why don't you just save some time and get up?"

This isn't a flashback. It's a brand-new scene. And I can make a new choice.

"I'm not going to move," I tell her, then gesture to the empty space across from me. "But you can sit down, if you want."

She gapes at me. "What?"

"Sit down, if you want. Work here." I glance over at Lily, who quickly looks away. "I don't own this table."

"Uh yeah, that's why you should move."

"Mia," Lily says, still looking pointedly away from me. "Let's go sit on the lawn."

"No. Absolutely not."

Lily gestures at their group. "We'd barely all fit at the table anyway; why don't we go—?"

But Mia is already cutting her off. "Lily, just—shut up, I'm handling this."

Lily flinches, and her shoulders start to curl inward, like

she's trying to make herself smaller, less noticeable, just . . .
less. But then she stops. Uncurls her shoulders. Locks her eyes
on the back of Mia's unsuspecting head.

"Don't talk to me that way," Lily says.

Mia doesn't even look back. "Hm?"

"I *said*, don't talk to me that way."

"What way," Mia scoffs.

"The way you always do! Don't interrupt me, don't tell me
to shut up, don't treat me like a servant when I'm supposed to
be your friend!"

"Oh-kay," Mia says with a nervous laugh, more to the rest of
the girls than Lily. "I think you're being *kind* of dramatic."

"No, *I'm* being honest." Lily takes a breath. "Because honestly,
Mia, the way you talk to people—I know you think it makes
you look like a badass who takes no shit, but it doesn't. It just
makes you seem like an asshole."

That finally makes Mia whirl around. "What the hell is wrong
with you? You're supposed to be my *friend*—"

Then, over Lily's shoulder, side by side with Mia's gang of
friends, I see Tess. Lunch in her hands, eyes on the scene in front
of her, jaw practically on the ground.

"I *am* your friend," Lily's saying to Mia, "that's why I'm telling
you the truth, even though you don't want to hear it." And then
Lily looks at me—just for a second—out of the corner of her eye.
"That is my job, as your friend. And *your* job as *my* friend, is to
actually consider what you're saying to me before you say it."

This isn't the moment Lily and I are going to make up, because this moment really isn't about me at all. I'm not the main character in this scene. But that doesn't mean I can't make a new choice.

"Mia . . ." I clear my throat.

"What, Gideon?" she snaps. *"What?"*

"I'm sorry."

She looks briefly dazed. Then chokes out: "Huh?"

"I'm sorry I told you your boyfriend was cheating on you and embarrassed you in front of everyone. That was shitty of me. And I'm sorry. And I wanted you to know that."

"Okay," she says with a dismissive shrug of her shoulders. "I do not forgive you."

"It's okay if you don't forgive me. I did something really stupid and messed with your life, and—" I look at Lily. Just for a second. "I'm just really sorry I did it."

"What the fuck is happening?" Mia says, to no one in particular.

"What's happening is I'm telling you how I feel," Lily says, talking faster now, like if she doesn't get the rest of the words out now, she never will. "Even though it might make you mad—definitely *is* making you mad—because I needed to say it and if I kept not saying it, I was going to lose my entire mind. I needed to say it, and you needed to hear it. That's all."

Lily turns to the wide-eyed group of girls behind her. "Let's go to the lawn."

That leaves Mia and Tess, both staring at me, both shell-shocked.

I stare back. "I'm as surprised as you."

Later that week, I do something I haven't done in forever on a Thursday night: sit on my bed and pop in a movie, by myself. Normally, during a Late Night week, I'd still be at the *Herald* office with Tess, but it's like the universe conspired. In a good way. Can you conspire in a good way?

Every section got their stories in early and cleanly, so I was done with copy editing before dinner even came, and the whole paper was put to bed before seven thirty. On the one hand, this is such an unexpected miracle the Vatican should investigate it. On the other hand, it means I say goodbye to Tess at seven thirty, too. So if given the choice between a miracle and disaster—the kind of Late Night where no section is ready until ten p.m., every computer develops a different virus, and the printer spontaneously catches on fire—I'd pick the disaster.

I decided a day so easy should be capped off with one of my favorite noirs: *Out of the Past*. Dad might describe it as "the one where the gas station owner goes to Mexico," but it's so much more than that. Jeff (Robert Mitchum, at his best) is a former private eye running from the terrible choices he once made. And Kathie (Jane Greer, giving new meaning to femme fatale) is the woman who led him to those choices.

"Is there a way to win?" Kathie asks Jeff as they stand by a casino roulette table.

"Well, there's a way to lose more slowly," he tells her.

I sit up straight.

Rewind. Replay.

There's a way to lose more slowly.

Wait.

Wait.

I've been thinking about this all wrong. I've been assuming that this whole case—the paid-off criminals, the planned arrests, all of it—happened because of what someone could gain. What someone could *win*, just the same as if they were at a roulette table.

Black or white. Right or wrong. Win or lose. Even those words are an assumption. The world—or people—can't fit neatly into something so simple.

I assumed that was the key. Who benefits? Whoever could win, of course. And who had something to win? If Willets could plant that story about rising crime, he would get what he wanted. The mayor's office. He would win.

But what if that's not why it happened at all? What if whoever planned all this didn't do it to *get* something—but to prevent something? Not to topple someone, but to keep things as they were. Not victory, but inertia.

What if . . . they were only trying to lose a bit more slowly?

The more I turn it over in my head, the more sense it makes. Even as my brain's in overdrive, my body's on autopilot once again. Shoes, on. Jacket, in my hand. Phone, under the pillow.

I'll go to O'Hara's house, again, see what I find—or maybe I'll go down to the station, because if I could just—

Then I stop, midloop on my left shoelace.

Think, I order myself, but it's different this time. *Think*, I tell myself—not about unraveling the case or putting the pieces together. *Think about the choices you have.*

I could do this alone. I wouldn't have to explain myself to anyone, or convince anyone, or even risk getting hurt by anyone.

I could do this alone.

But I shouldn't.

With both shoes tied but only one arm in my jacket, I run out the door, only barely remembering to lock it behind me.

Fifteen minutes, one mile on suburban sidewalks, and a potential burst right lung later, I run past a mailbox that used to be pink, step onto a porch that has always been covered in shoes, and knock on the door without stopping until I see someone peek through the curtains.

"Gideon," Lily gasps when she opens her front door. "What are you *doing* here?"

"What if—?" I pant. "What if I wasn't wrong?"

CHAPTER 26

"EXCUSE ME?" LILY says.

"What if I wasn't wrong?" I repeat. "About the investigation. What if I wasn't wrong?"

"But you *were* wrong," she says. "Willets wasn't here. The watch was his, not Marco's. I know this is tough for you to accept, Gideon, but you weren't right."

"I know," I say. "But what if I wasn't all the way wrong?"

She stares at me for a moment, then steps out of the doorway. "You'd better come inside."

Her house is weirdly quiet as we walk to her bedroom. "Where are your moms?"

"Dinner and a movie. It's their anniversary."

In her room, she takes a seat on her desk chair, folds her arms across her chest, and waits.

"Cui bono," I say. "You taught me that."

"Yeah, well, glad to know you occasionally listen to me."

"I thought I'd found the person who benefited," I say. "It all made sense. Willets paid off petty criminals—or people who knew them—to artificially inflate the crime rate—some of it—so he could run on a law-and-order platform."

"I know all this," she reminds me. "I had a front-row seat to your performance, remember?"

"How many of the crimes were unsolved?"

Her eyebrows knit together. "What?"

"Did *any* of the crimes you flagged all the way back when you first came to my door—all the crimes in the police blotter— did *any* of them go unsolved?"

Lily stares at me. Then she swivels to her desk, grabs her notebook, and begins flicking between the pages rapid-fire. Finally, she looks back up at me. Shakes her head. And says: "No."

"That's a one hundred percent conviction rate."

"Atypical, for sure," she admits. "But—"

"Willets wouldn't benefit from a one hundred percent conviction rate." I pause. "If he were part of this scheme, he'd want the conviction rate to be low, because that would make the police department look worse."

Lily takes a moment to consider that. "If anything, this only makes them look better."

"Right." I pause. "And who, of all the people in the world

right now, would *benefit* from the San Miguel Police Department looking *better*?"

Lily stares at me. Then through me. Then, slowly, she tilts her head.

In noir, there's this type of shot called the Dutch angle. The camera rolls to one side, slanting the horizon line so it's not horizontal anymore, but angled, and odd, and completely off balance.

I think that's what's happening inside Lily's head as the truth slowly, but certainly, dawns on her. The world is shifting on its axis.

"No." She shakes her head, harder this time. "There's. No. *Way*."

"There's no way that a police chief who's been under constant fire for being incompetent, for not being tough enough on crime, might buy some easy wins for himself?"

I should have seen it before. What was that mock ceremony he staged for me, except a cheap way to get some good media coverage? Hadn't I already seen that he'd do anything, as long as it was self-serving? *Use* anyone?

"But he's literally the law. Or—the order? The law *and* the order—?"

"He's also about to lose his job because Fred Willets wants to be mayor and he's in the way. He's also the guy who keeps defending himself by pointing to how many criminals they've gotten off the streets. He's the guy who would know O'Hara could be bought, who would want a dead body to show up in a brewery Fred Willets owned and would have perfect cover to do it all, because—like you said—he's the law."

"That's why O'Hara was mad about Luke," Lily murmurs, more to herself than me.

"Luke?" It's hard to remember that's how this all started, for her and me.

"He's a minor, and minors have privacy rights. An underage perp means a very vague news story, if there's one at all."

I nod, because it's all clicking into place. "And a diversion program means a sealed record. O'Hara got upset when he saw that ID because he knew Luke wouldn't even *count*."

"But what about Paul Vince?" Lily asks. "Where does he fit in?"

"You said he was trying to push his territory into San Miguel." It can still be the quid pro quo I thought it was, just with different terms. "Maybe the chief looks the other way."

"So you're saying the San Miguel Police Department," Lily says slowly, "*paid* for people to commit crimes so they could *catch* them in those crimes?"

"I'm saying—" I hesitate, trying to think of a more articulate way to put it. I fail. "No, yeah, that's pretty much it."

"It's just . . ." Lily frowns. "I've watched dozens of interviews with that guy, Gideon. The chief is a blowhard, and a bully, but he's not . . . crafty."

"Maybe he just wants you to think that," I say, but I have to admit she's totally on the mark. Who could have guessed he'd be sly enough to pull this off? Or even come up with it?

But that was the problem from the beginning. I'd already slotted him into the role I chose for him in fifth grade, so I nearly missed what was right under my nose. For all the complaining I did about him never taking me seriously . . . what did I do, except turn around and make the same mistake?

"He can barely string a decent sentence together at press conferences. I'm sure that—what's her name—Penny? Something Overway. She writes everything for him."

I stop short. "What did you say?"

"The chief's secretary. I don't remember her first name, I just kept seeing her behind him during press statements, so I looked her up." She wrinkles her nose. "I know, secretary sounds so fifties. I can't remember her actual job title—"

Oh my God.

Oh my *God*.

I grab the dossier and flip through the notes.

23:15 PV met with PO @ V LTD warehouse

$ from PO delivered to Dr. H

Request via PO for new job: Thurs. night btwn 16:00 and 20:30

PO arranged the meetings. Made the requests for new sacrificial criminals and set the time they'd be caught. Delivered the cash to pay off the bartender at Doc Holliday's and Paul Vince and probably people we don't even know about.

"PO doesn't stand for police officer," I say. "It stands for *Phoebe Overway.*"

Lily nods. "That makes sense."

She's taking the news of a giant criminal conspiracy a lot better than I thought she would. "It does?"

"I mean that if you're right—and we don't know that you are—it makes sense she would be the go-between. She's way less recognizable, which makes her way less risky."

"And she's his assistant," I add. "From what I saw in the station, she keeps track of his whole life. Why wouldn't she keep track of this, too?" Something else dawns on me. "Paul Vince had records. Emails, texts, receipts—"

Lily catches on quick. "She'd have her own set, too."

"And if they can't keep anything incriminating at the station house . . ."

Lily looks at me. Then at her notebook. She swivels her chair to her computer.

"Okay, Phoebe Overway," Lily says, typing it in. "Let's meet you."

"Are you sure that's the right house?"

Lily double-checks her phone. "Yes."

All the curtains are open in Phoebe's dark, two-story condo, but there isn't a single light visible, at least from across the street, where we've parked. My hands are sweating, half from nerves, half from being shoved into a pair of rubber dishwashing gloves from Lily's kitchen. Lily thought that was over-the-top, but after I reminded her *both* our fingerprints are in the system, she found a pair of winter gloves for herself.

"She's got to be out," I say. No better time to try to get inside and see what we can find. Something incriminating, something that really, truly ties the chief to the dossier, which is sitting safely in Lily's back seat.

Lily looks less sure. "Let me take a walk around the block," she suggests. "Make sure she's not in the back, or something."

She goes, and I wait, alone except for the thought that's been nagging in the back of my mind the whole way here. Lily left a note for her moms on the kitchen table, in case they got home before her. I don't know what it said. But she left one. And I . . . just left.

I didn't know what to say to Dad when he came into my room last week. I didn't have the words. And maybe it's only because I know what I'm about to do is dangerous, and pretty stupid, and maybe also an actual felony . . . but I think I have the words now. And I owe him the words I have.

Lily left her phone unlocked on the driver's seat, and I dial Dad's number as quickly as I can, given the rubber gloves. He doesn't pick up, which doesn't surprise me. It's still the middle of a dinner service, and he's probably frantic and pissed off and stressed out . . . and that's not even counting what he'd feel like if he knew where I was.

Leave a message, his voice says through the phone. So I do.

"Hi, Dad," I start off. "It's Gideon. Obviously. This is Lily's phone. I left mine at the house because I didn't want you to know *I'd* left the house—" I pause. "Shouldn't have told you that part."

But then I shake my head, even though he can't see it. "No, you know what, that's wrong. I should have told you a *lot* of things. Like that Lily and I found that dead body not because we were stupid kids exploring a creepy brewery, but because we were investigating something for the paper and it got super out of hand, and I don't know exactly—" I swallow. "I don't know exactly what's going to happen, so I needed to call you." I take a breath. "Because I needed to tell you something.

"Not about the case," I clarify. "And please don't call the cops, or anything, because it's not going to help and I can't tell you why yet, but you'll just have to trust me. I know I haven't given you any reason to trust me, lately, but I hope you can. I hope you can try, anyway, because I know you're trying, in general. And . . . I'm going to try, too."

If I don't die tonight, I add in my head. But I'm not going to die tonight. There's no chance. Maybe like a 1 percent chance.

"I know I didn't tell you about any of this. I know I keep scaring the shit out of you, and . . ." I breathe out. "I'm sorry. I'm so sorry. I never really considered that I might be hurting you, and I think it's because I didn't think you *could* be hurt. You know? I don't know."

I'm rambling now, but with each stupid, stumbling word, I'm getting closer. I can tell. I'm getting close.

"You've always seemed . . . invincible. Like you could do anything. And I mean, you opened restaurants, you raised me by yourself, you *did* do everything."

And then, there it is. Like a light flicking on in a dark room, there it is. What I wanted to say.

"I don't hate you. I'm not going to pretend like this has been perfect, or you've been perfect, or that you haven't made me feel like shit sometimes, but I still never, ever hated you. I know we don't say it a lot, but . . . I love you, Dad. A lot. All the time, every day. Even when it seems like I don't."

It's so simple, and it's so small.

"I don't know if that's how you felt about your dad. I know you worry about being like him, turning into him, but I don't think you could. Not really."

So simple. So small. And so true.

"You're not your dad. You're mine."

I end the message there. But it isn't until after I've hung up that I realize my mistake—I didn't dial his cell phone at all. I called the *home* phone.

I'm considering whether to try again, with the right number this time, when Lily appears by the car window. I open my door, and she leans down.

"Totally dark," Lily says. "Oh—thanks." She takes her phone from my hand and sticks it in her pocket. "There's a gate to the back, it's just a latch, so I think that's our best bet."

The latched gate, it turns out, leads into a tiny backyard—more like a fenced-in patio than anything else, just enough room for a chair, a table, and—

"A dog," Lily whispers.

"What?" I follow her pointing finger to the back entrance of the house. Sure enough, there's a dog door. And not a small one.

"Okay," Lily says in a voice much higher than normal. "I'm having second thoughts."

"It hasn't barked. Maybe she took it with her."

That seems to calm Lily down. "Yeah. You have to take dogs out at night, right? They're on a walk."

That's an assumption, but it isn't a bad one. "Then we need to go fast," I tell her. "We might not have a lot of time."

The back door is locked, and there's no key under the mat. Lily studies the dog door.

"I can do that," she says.

"Huh?"

"I can fit in there."

"Are you sure?" I ask, picturing Lily stuck halfway through, the firefighters cutting her out before they helpfully deliver her to the cops for attempted B&E. It's the kind of thing that really ruins your day. I would know.

She nods. "Yeah." Crouching down, she angles her body and

then slides herself through with ease. So much ease, I know I'll be able to fit, too.

But as I bend down, a butter-colored blur appears in the doorway behind Lily, inside the house. Before I can warn Lily, it's sprinting toward her, nails skittering on the floor as it runs. Lily opens her mouth to shriek, but before she can, the dog jumps right on her chest—

And starts licking her face.

"Ufgh—" Lily shoves at the dog, but he's undeterred from his desperate attempt to french kiss her. "Get *off*."

When I crawl in the dog door, less gracefully than Lily, the dog bounds over to me with just as much enthusiasm. He looks like he's half yellow Lab, half harbor seal—basically a giant wriggling tube of fur and slobber.

"Hello," I say, rubbing his happy, drooling face. "Who's a good dog?"

Lily wipes at her wet cheeks. "Some guard dog."

I look at the metal tag on his collar. "Yeah, I don't think you'd name your guard dog 'Toast.'"

At the sound of his name, Toast thumps his tail even harder.

"We better start looking around," Lily says. "We don't know when she'll be back."

"Maybe Toast can help us. Labs are supposed to be smart, right? They're guide dogs." I slap my hands on my knees. "Where's the secret stash of evidence? Where is it? Where is it, boy?"

Toast licks his own eyeball in response.

Lily gets to her feet, shaking her head at me. "Oh my God."

"It worked for Lassie."

"Lassie is a fictional character. That—" She points at Toast. "Is a potato with eyes."

"Don't listen to her," I tell Toast as I stand up. "She's a cat person."

Lily pokes her head around the corner of the kitchen door, then waves me on. "Where do we start? It's not like it's a mansion, but . . ."

We wander around the ground floor, Toast trotting along beside us, but there's only the kitchen, a living room with a couch and a TV, and a little half bath.

When we've made a full loop, I stop at the staircase. "If there's anything to find, it's going to be upstairs."

"How do you know that?" Lily asks, but she follows me up the hardwood staircase.

"People keep really important things close to them. In the place they feel safest, and most secure. Like an office—"

Lily peeks inside an open door. "Or a bedroom?"

I look in, over her shoulder. The room is kind of a mess—bed unmade, clothes on the floor—but in a different way than Marco's office was. With the closet door open, I can see the neatly labeled baskets for different clothes categories, the built-in shoe organizer. Marco was always a mess. Phoebe didn't use to be.

Something changed. And it made *her* change.

"Be careful," Lily warns as I start to poke through her bedside table drawers. "If she notices things are out of place—"

"She won't." It's too chaotic in here. And probably too chaotic in her own brain. "But I'll be careful."

Toast nibbles at my ankle. I brush him off. "No, Toast. That's my sock."

"This is a needle in a haystack," Lily complains from inside the closet.

"We have to think like Phoebe. What can we tell about her, from the closet?"

"She has expensive taste in shoes."

"I don't mean *what* she likes," I say, coming over and starting to search the opposite end of the closet. "I mean what she's *like*."

"I can tell you she's got no sense of interior design." Lily steps around me and out of the closet. "What a waste of good space."

I stop. "What do you mean?"

Lily gestures to my left, into the corner she just came from. "She put an armoire in the corner. Who does that?"

"That depends," I say. "What's an armoire?"

"A wardrobe," Lily says, clearly willing herself not to roll her eyes. "If you pull back all the dresses, you'll see it."

I push the dresses aside and sure enough, shoved into the closet's farthest corner is a wooden wardrobe. Lily's right. It takes up a bunch of space, it's totally out of place, it's—

"It's weird," I say. "It's weird she'd put it here."

"Like I said."

Lily's already moved on, poking gingerly under Phoebe's bed, but I don't move. Weird matters. Weird is important.

Phoebe lives alone—there's only one bedside table, and I clocked only one toothbrush in the upstairs bathroom as we passed by. That means, in all likelihood, she put that piece of furniture in the closet by herself, too. It looks heavy. It would have taken effort. And that tells me . . . this mattered.

It's not until I take a big step back, trying to figure out how she could even have angled it to fit inside, that I spot them: four identical, L-shaped marks on an oddly empty patch of beige carpet. Just outside the closet and right next to the bedroom door.

"She moved it."

Lily looks over. "Huh?"

"The arm—wardrobe thing, it used to be here, up against the wall. See the marks?" I point them out to Lily. "She moved it."

"So?"

"So why would she go to the trouble?" I pause. "Unless . . . every time she came into this room, she had to see it. And she didn't want to. So she put it in the only place she wouldn't have to see it."

I rush back to the closet, with Lily on my heels.

"I already looked through it, though," Lily says as I fling open the doors. "There isn't anything inside."

Empty. Totally empty. Even weirder. I kneel down beside it and sweep the bottom with my hand, but there's nothing there, either. It's not until I let my hand drop to the wood floor below that I feel it: a rough, wide half-moon scratch on otherwise polished floorboards. I trace it with my fingers, and while geometry was never my strongest subject, I'd bet money the arc of this scratch matches the angle you'd get if you dragged that wardrobe away from the wall, on one side.

Maybe she had trouble getting it into place. Maybe she needed to readjust it a couple of times, before it was right. Or maybe—

I scramble to my feet. "She keeps checking it."

"Checking wh—be *careful*—" Lily says as I grab one corner of the armoire and drag it away from the wall. Just a couple of inches. Just wide enough to snake my arm into the gap.

My fingers sweep along the backside of the armoire, brushing against the coarse, unvarnished wood. I'm about to reconsider my theory when my thumbnail bumps against something smooth.

I grope around more. Whatever's on the back isn't just smooth, it's smooth and crinkly and bigger than my hand, and—

Full.

I feel like ripping it right off the wood but don't. That would only be the first choice I thought of. Not the best choice. Instead, I force myself to feel around for the tape holding it on, and slowly, carefully, peel it away.

"Oh my God," Lily gasps.

It's a clear plastic bag. And inside it are four plastic cards, none of which I can read and none of which I need to read, because the other thing in the clear plastic bag is a gold men's watch.

And it's covered in blood.

"Is—is that . . . his?"

I don't have to ask who she means. And we both know it is. But still, I turn the bag over to see the back of the watch.

"'MLV,'" I read. "Marco L. Vince."

"Oh my God," Lily repeats as I sink back against the armoire, onto the floor. "Oh my—"

"He didn't stand her up," I whisper to myself.

She stops. "What?"

"When I was in the police station, I saw Phoebe give O'Hara this look—I thought he'd stood her up, but . . ." I shake my head. "No, he *did* stand her up. Just not for a date." I look up at Lily. "For a *meeting.*"

"At Triggerfish?" Lily drops down to the carpet with me. "You're saying she was there, with whoever killed Marco?"

I sit there, with a pile of evidence in my lap and a whirlwind in my head.

Someone with access to police tape . . . but no clue how to put it up.

Someone who knew enough to take the watch and the IDs . . . but not enough to realize they'd ID him anyway.

Someone who knew the cops might overlook an overdose . . . but had never seen a real overdose scene in their life.

"No," I say. "I'm saying she killed him."

I watch the truth of it dawn on Lily, just like it dawned on me. I've never thought about that phrase before—how right it is. The moment, this moment, when all the confusion and doubt slip away like night giving way to a bright, hot morning sun. No shadows. Only light.

Until, of course, the next thought dawns: if we have found the murderer, then we are also in a murderer's house.

When I breathe out, it's shaky. "We have to get out of here."

"Yeah," Lily says, swallowing down the fear she must be feeling, too. "Right. Yeah."

With one last look at the bag, I snake my hand behind the armoire and reattach it to the back.

"Wait, we're not taking it with us?" Lily asks. "We have to turn that in to someone."

"We can't. There's no way to explain how we got it."

"Gideon, we have to tell somebody," she insists as we inch the armoire back into place. "She killed him; she kept his stuff like a trophy hunter—"

If it were a trophy, it would be on the wall. I don't know why she kept it, but I doubt it was like that. Nothing about Phoebe says "budding serial killer." It screams "nervous breakdown."

"We'll figure out a way to get the cops to the house," I promise Lily. "We will. But they have to find that bag themselves."

If Lily had any more objections, I never hear them. Because just then, from downstairs, we both hear three things, in quick succession:

A lock clicking open. Footsteps on the threshold. And the front door slamming closed.

Lily gasps and yanks the closet door shut, leaving all of us—

me, her, and Toast—still inside.

"What are you doing?" I whisper-scream to her.

"I don't know!" she whisper-screams back.

"Mmm," whimpers Toast.

"It doesn't help for us to be trapped here," I whisper, gesturing at Toast, his paws wrapped protectively around a partially destroyed high heel. "She's going to notice the dog is missing!"

Lily says nothing. She just sits there, stock-still, eyes wide.

"Lily, we can't—"

She puts her finger to her lips. *Listen.*

And then I hear it. Below us—directly below us—someone is talking. And they aren't happy.

"You stalked me all night, just so you could—"

It's a man. Not Phoebe. And I've heard that voice before. Where have I—?

"What the hell was I supposed to do?" a higher voice cuts in. Phoebe. Toast whimpers more urgently at the sound of her voice. I gently wrap my hands around his muzzle. He can't bark now. He can't.

"You've been avoiding me," Phoebe's saying. "You won't talk to me—"

"There's nothing to talk about."

"Nothing to talk about?"

"We *need* to avoid each other, don't you get it?" His voice is getting louder, but he stops. Settles it. "No more meetings, no more notes by my mailbox. It's not safe."

Lily's head jerks up. She nudges me, and I nod. It's O'Hara. It's definitely O'Hara.

"We aren't done," Phoebe says, panic starting to make her voice quiver. "The no-confidence vote is next week. We need more wins."

"What about *it's not safe* don't you understand?"

"You knew exactly what this was when you started," she snaps at him. "And you got what *you* needed out of it."

"And now you're pissed at me because you might not. Is that right, Phoebe?"

"I've wasted years of my life trying to fix that man's problems. If he gets kicked out by the city council, who's going to hire me? Where the hell would I go, as the former press secretary for that clown?" She takes an audible breath. "Jesus, I couldn't even tell him what I was doing, because he'd find some way to fuck that up, too!"

I reel back. The chief didn't even *know*?

O'Hara scoffs. "You fucked it up just fine, all on your own."

I slotted the chief into *bad guy* and *guilty* fast as I could, but it wasn't that simple. I still don't think he's *good*, and he might still be guilty of a lot of shitty things but . . . this isn't one of them.

"If *you* had been where I *asked* you to be—"

"Not my fault you hitched your wagon to the worst police chief anyone's ever seen." He pauses. "And it's not my fault you went and killed someone, either."

Lily claps her hands to her mouth but doesn't make a sound.

It's one thing to realize someone is a murderer. It's another thing to hear that realization confirmed. And it's an entirely *third* kind of terrifying thing to hear it *as you're hiding in their closet.*

"I didn't mean to kill him!" Phoebe's voice is such whimpering panic, it almost makes me feel sorry for her. "You know I didn't—I shoved him, he hit his head, it wasn't my—"

She's guilty, and it was an accident. She did a terrible thing, and it's wrecked her. She didn't mean to . . . and she did it. Nothing about this has ever been black and white; I just insisted on seeing it that way. But nothing is that simple. Not mysteries, and especially not people.

"You left him there," O'Hara says. "You left him to die, it's still murder. It's just not first degree."

"What do you want me to say? I freaked out!" Her voice cracks. "He—he was lying there on the floor, eyes wide open, I was sure he was dead. And how was I going to explain that— any of this—if I called 911?"

"What you should have done was call me."

"I'm sorry that I don't have as much *experience* with *dead bodies* in front of me." She gasps for air. "They're going to figure it out. They will—Garcia is like a dog with a bone with this since the coroner's report came back. They're going to figure it out."

"You knew it was only a matter of time before they ID'd him," O'Hara says. It sounds like he's pacing. "He wasn't a transient. He was Paul fucking Vince's son."

"How many times do I have to tell you? *I panicked.*" She's breathing raggedly now. "He knew about it. The whole thing, down to the last details, things I never told his dad. He said if I didn't give him his own cut, he'd take all of us down. He said he had proof. But he never said what."

"I've gone through all the evidence in the locker," O'Hara tells her. "Everything they took from his house, from his work after the coroner's report came back. There isn't anything."

Not now there isn't, I think with a grim sense of pride. We got there first.

"It's not just me who will go down," she warns him. "If this ever gets out."

"Oh, no," he says. "I'll flip on you so fast your head will spin. Believe it."

This is starting to turn ugly. I tap Lily's arm. *We have to go,* I mouth at her.

She pulls out her phone, flicks to the notes app, and types:

How??

I rip off one rubber glove, shove it in my hoodie pocket, and type back:

We're going to be Toast

She reads it. Stares at me. Then types:

?????????????????

I snatch the phone back and type out my plan as quickly as I can. She reads it, then shakes her head so hard it must make her dizzy.

No. Fucking. Way, she mouths.

I shrug. She closes her eyes, takes a breath, and opens the closet door.

Toast immediately tries to make a break for it, but Lily holds on tight to his collar as I take off my left shoe, then my sock. When I hold it out for Toast to sniff, he—predictably—goes batshit. I toss it onto the pile of clothes on the floor, and he takes a diving leap onto it.

I stuff my foot back into my shoe as Toast happily munches on my sock, all thoughts of going downstairs having vanished from his lima bean–sized brain. Then I fish my keys out of my pants pocket, hold them to my chest with one hand, and beckon Lily forward with the other.

We creep toward the staircase. Phoebe and O'Hara are still yelling at each other, and from the direction of their voices, I know I was right—they're in the living room, which has no direct sight line from the staircase to the back door. As long as they don't get up, they won't see us.

At the top of the stairs, Lily and I share one final look. There's a lot you can say, in silence. *Good luck. I'm glad we're friends. Hope we don't die like this.*

Lily puts her hands on my shoulders. I hold my keys out, dangling, with one hand. And together, in our best impression of the world's stupidest dog, we bound down the stairs.

Toast has four legs. We have four legs. Toast has tags that jangle, and I have keys.

We're on the very bottom stair, when O'Hara suddenly pauses. Lily and I both freeze.

"What is that?" he asks.

"The dog," Phoebe snaps. "Don't change the subject."

Safely on the carpet, I keep the dog tag sound going as Lily and I tiptoe our way toward the back door. They might not be able to hear our footsteps, but I don't know how they can't hear my heart pounding in my chest or the adrenaline thrumming through my fingers and the shrill panic flooding my brain screaming *get out get out.*

I'm first to the dog door, and I scramble out just as clumsily as Toast must, then hold the flap open for Lily as she slides herself through.

And then we run.

CHAPTER 27

"WHAT DO WE do—?" Lily says, still out of breath from our sprint to her car, hands still shaking from the three blocks she managed to drive before she had to pull over again. "What do we do now, do we go to the police, do we—?"

Eventually, yeah. Of course. But right now— "You can't write your article if you're holed up in an interrogation room the whole night."

Her mouth drops open. "My *what*?"

"You have all the information you need now, and you've been writing out stuff as you go, I've seen it in your notebook—"

"Yeah, I wanted to mention, you need to stop reading over people's shoulders like that."

"This is the last piece of the puzzle. Once you fill in the gaps, you can publish your article. And you have to do it tonight."

"Tonight? But—"

"Otherwise it won't come out before the city council vote," I remind her. "And that's the point, isn't it? It's always been the point. Not you being editor in chief, or me solving a case again, but telling people something they don't know. Something they *deserve* to know."

Then we sit there, totally silent, for a long time. We sit there long enough for Lily's breathing to stop coming fast and ragged and settle into something smoother and slower. We sit there long enough that my heart stops pounding, and the adrenaline settles into my arm and leg muscles, making them ache and throb worse than running the mile.

"So what do we do?" Lily asks again.

We can't do this alone. And even if we could, we shouldn't.

"We call Tess."

"Lily?" Tess sounds a little groggy—maybe we woke her up. "It's after eleven, what's going on?"

"Hypothetically," Lily says, "what would you say if I told you that Gideon and I found out why the crime rate has been so weirdly high?"

"I'd say that's awesome, but maybe this could wait until tomorrow morning."

I jump in there. "What if we told you it was because of a conspiracy between the police department and organized crime and also we just heard someone confess to murder?"

There's a long pause on the other line. "Are we . . . still talking hypothetically?"

Lily and I look at each other. "No," we say in unison.

"Because hypothetically," Tess says, "I would think my dream had taken a *very weird turn*."

"Okay, so then practically, what would you say if we needed to get this article in the paper tonight, because otherwise it won't come out before the city council votes and—"

"Wait, wait, wait." Tess sounds like she's shifting. Like she's suddenly sat up straight. "I put the paper to bed hours ago. I sent the file to the printer. Are you saying you want to *break into* school so we can go to the *Herald* office and add this piece?"

I hadn't thought about that, but it's past eleven p.m. Of course the gates are locked. So of course—*of course*—I'm going to have to repeat the exact thing that got me in the biggest trouble of my life and hope it doesn't ruin everything all over again.

From the way Lily's eyes go wide, she hadn't thought about it, either. "You have keys, though, right?" she asks Tess. "To the newsroom?"

"Yeah, but not to the *school*."

I look at Lily. She shrugs helplessly.

"Then yeah, I guess I'm saying we need to break into school."

"Oh my God," Tess groans. "Just—just give me a second to wrap my mind around that. How will we even—?"

"Getting onto campus itself is easy, a kid could do it," I say, because, hey, a kid *did* do it. And sure, the fire department eventually had to be called, but— "It's not like it's Sing Sing, you know?"

A pause on the phone. "I don't know, Gideon, what *is* Sing Sing?"

An old prison, but— "Not important. I can get us into school, if you can get into the *Herald* room. How long would it take you to get there?"

"Depends on how long it takes you to pick me up."

"Can't you drive?"

"My car sounds like a dying hippo when it starts up. No *way* my grandparents won't wake up."

"They let you stay late at the paper."

"Not until eleven p.m.! They're pretty chill for old Mexican abuelos but they do have their limits."

"Fine," Lily says. "We'll come get you. What's your address?"

"Gideon knows how to get there."

Lily's eyes go wide, but she doesn't take them off the road. "Oh, *does* he?" she says slyly.

"Ugh," Tess says. "Yes."

"That is so *interesting* that he's been to your—"

"Would you just drive, please?" I ask her.

"It's almost like you two finally figured out you *like* each other—"

"I'm hanging up now," Tess says.

346

When she does, Lily still hasn't looked at me, but she also can't stop smirking.

"So . . ."

"Please don't," I beg her.

"I was only going to ask why you didn't tell me."

"Because—this!" I gesture at her, up and down. "All this . . . smugness."

"Nothing wrong with taking pride in being correct," she says. Then turns to me and winks. "Am I right or am I right?"

I roll my eyes. "Fine. You're right."

"Oh." She sighs, still smiling. "I know."

We park around the corner from Tess's house, and Lily texts her. The prospect of seeing Tess makes me wonder what I look like, after all that happened in the last hour. I'm probably covered in Toast slobber. I reach up and turn on the overhead light. Yep. Covered not just in slobber, but in—

Oh. *Oh.*

"Lily," I say, "do you have any plastic bags?"

She looks alarmed. "Oh God, *please* don't throw up in my car."

"What? No, a small one, like a Ziploc. And the tweezers in your purse."

"How do you know I have—?"

"Two weeks ago you went into the bathroom at my house with your purse and you came out and there were two little

347

red marks in between your eyes."

"Someday," she mutters, rummaging in her bag and producing the tweezers, "you're going to need to turn that off."

"And the plastic bag?"

"Glove compartment."

I fish one out and delicately pluck three short, yellow hairs off my sweatshirt. I place them in the bag and zip it tight.

"What's that for?" Lily asks.

"Marco Vince had dog hair on his jacket," I say. "I'd thought it was people hair, like from a short men's haircut. But . . ." I shrug. "I guess it was Toast."

"Hey," Tess interrupts us, appearing by my passenger-side door and starting to hop in the back.

"Can you drive, actually?" Lily asks, undoing her seat belt. "My moms wouldn't mind."

Tess frowns, but she does switch places with Lily in the driver's seat. "Why, did you want to stop at a bar?"

"Are you going to include us sneaking into the bar in your story?" I ask Lily.

"No."

"Whoa, I was kidding—what bar?" Tess asks.

"A terrifying one," Lily says, digging her notebook out of her bag. "I want you to drive so I can write in the back."

"You don't even have a full draft?"

"I have most of it, there are just a few details—"

"Maybe this is a bad idea." Tess shakes her head. "We don't have time to really fact-check, even edit—"

"We have to," I say. "The city council vote is next week. If we don't publish it tomorrow—"

"Then maybe we shouldn't. Maybe we should go straight to the *SD Tribune*, or something. They have resources we really don't. Maybe we let them break it."

"But it's not their story," I say. "It's *Lily's*. She's the one who saw what was happening; she's the one who did the work. She's the one who should break it."

"Well?" Tess glances at Lily in the rearview mirror. "Say something. Is he right?"

"I don't know, Tess." Lily wrings her hands. "What do you think?"

"I think . . . it doesn't matter what I think."

"Of course it does."

"I'm going to graduate soon—if this goes up in flames, that's going to be something *you* will deal with. Not me. So I'm going to ask *you*, Lily." She pauses. "Should we do this?"

Lily chews on her lip. Stays quiet for a moment. Then says: "Yes."

"If you take the credit, can you take the blame, too?"

Lily nods. And louder this time, she says: "Yes."

Tess hits the pedal and glides onto the freeway on-ramp. "I always knew you could."

"I can't believe I'm breaking into school," I mutter as the three of us stare at the hole in the fence alongside the football field. "Again."

Even in the dark, I can see Lily roll her eyes. "You've mentioned."

"What's it called when you have déjà vu, but the thing really *has* already happened?"

"Um." Tess grimaces as she lifts the broken fencing. "A memory?"

This is more than a memory. This is a full-on flashback. But maybe I'll get a better ending this time.

Lily slides herself through gingerly, pulling her arms in tight. "This is so unsafe."

"We can get tetanus shots," I tell her.

"I mean that anyone could break in." Once she's on the other side, Lily puts her hands on her hips, looking down at the hole in the fence. "We should do an exposé in the *Herald*."

"Only if we don't get expelled first."

We hang along the outside edge of campus as much as we can, darting between buildings and skirting along the walls. I'll say this for an open-air campus: it's easier to hide in the dark.

When we finally reach the courtyard door to the *Herald* office, Tess pulls her keys for the carabiner on her jeans but hesitates.

"The door could be alarmed." She looks up. "Maybe we try the window?"

I shut my eyes. "No."

"It looks big enough, I bet I could fit thr—"

"Trust me," I say. *"No."*

Tess blinks at me. Nods. Then steps forward and unlocks the door. For one long, tense moment, we wait for an alarm to go off. Nothing happens. Tess sighs with relief and pushes the door open.

Inside, Lily immediately plops down on the couch and starts scribbling in her notebook again, but Tess stops her.

"No more longhand, you need to type it," she says, then points to me. "Gideon, get on one of the computers and rearrange whatever you have to so we can get as much of this on the front page, and the rest of it in News." She pulls out her phone. "And I'm going to call the printer."

I log on to one of the computers, find this week's master file, and start. It's almost like a puzzle, moving articles, figuring out which pieces could be saved for next issue without a problem.

"Hi, Mike." Tess cradles the phone to her ear. "This is Tess Espinoza from the *Presidio Herald*." She pauses. "Good, thanks, so . . . I need to send you a new file for our print tomorrow."

She digs out her school planner. "Uh . . . account number D-387F2." She waits. "Yeah, we are a school newspaper." She pauses. "I do know what time it is." Another pause. "Let's just assume all my answers are going to be yes, okay?"

When she hangs up the phone a couple of minutes later, she rolls her eyes. "Nothing like a thirty-year-old stoner asking if your parents know you're out so late."

"Are they going to print it?" I ask.

"Yeah. We have to eat the cost of the first print, but yeah." She spins in her chair toward Lily. "What's the ETA?"

"I don't know, fifteen minutes? It's not my best work."

Lily ends up being wrong about the whole fifteen-minutes thing. It's nearly an hour later when, between Lily finishing her draft, me typing up what she's already handwritten, and Tess fitting it onto the front page, I finally start copy editing. I've never copy edited on a screen, and I know there are things I must be missing, especially because I keep getting distracted by how *good* it is.

The article is succinct and clear, managing to claim only the things she can back up with hard evidence, while letting any reader with a brain come to their own conclusion: something very messed up is happening in the San Miguel Police Department. By the time I reach the final paragraph, I decide Lily was wrong about something else: this *is* her best work.

I hold up my hands. "Done."

Tess motions me away from the computer. "Okay. Let me read it."

As Tess rapidly scans the screen, I remember there's something else I need to do in this office.

Lily's left the dossier out on one of the tables, and I gather the spread-out documents and take them all over to the big printer by the couch.

There are bigger things at stake here than me solving the case or Lily writing the important article she wanted to. There's more at play here than a school newspaper. It doesn't mean those things don't matter. Of course they do.

They just aren't the only things that matter.

It takes Lily a moment to notice. "What are you doing?"

"Copying the dossier," I say as I feed each page through.

"For security?"

"For . . . the right reasons."

"Gideon." She yawns. "You are an enigma."

"Who am I dropping off first?" Lily asks.

The article is done. The master file is sent. The printer confirmed receipt of the new version. The only thing left to do now is get home without anybody knowing.

"I'm closer," I say. "If that's okay with Tess."

She shrugs. "Sure."

It's only a little past midnight, and Dad is probably just starting to get his stuff together to leave Verde. I could still beat him home. But before that—

"We need to stop by the police station, first," I tell Lily.

She raises her eyebrows. "Are you turning yourself in?"

"No. I'm turning this in." I hold up the dossier. The original. And taped to the inside cover is a Ziploc bag of dog hair, labeled with the location where it was found.

Lily gapes at me. "Are you serious?"

"Your article is done. It's being immortalized in print as we speak—"

"Immortalized in print," Tess repeats. "The *drama*."

When you solve a murder, a little drama is justified. "You don't need this now, and I made a copy just in case you do. But they need it." I nod at the station house. "Even *if* they read your article, they can't build a case without the documents."

"This feels risky," Lily says. "And for no reason, no benefit to you—"

"I've always taken selfish risks," I say. "I think I can try a selfless one."

The station house is still and quiet when I walk through the turnstile doors. Must not be a big night for crime. Other than the multiple incidents of trespassing Lily and I did, of course. Even the receptionist looks bored, barely looking up when I tell her:

"I have a delivery."

"Cookies, brownies, et cetera have to be individually wrapped," she says. "Did you individually wrap them?"

"No, I mean, I have a delivery for Deputy Chief Garcia."

"Well, I'm sorry, hon, he's diabetic."

Jesus Christ. "It isn't—look. Can you just make sure he gets this"—I push the sealed envelope with the dossier across her desk—"first thing in the morning? It's important."

She slaps down a sticky memo pad. "You should leave a note. He gets lots of mail."

Not a bad idea.

FOR: DEPUTY CHIEF GARCIA—OPEN
IMMEDIATELY
You were right. People are mysteries. I'm not even close to solving
most of them, though I'm starting to try.
But I did crack this one.

As we round my block to my house, I crane my neck as far as I can, looking down the street to see if my house is lit up or not. When it comes into view, I heave a sigh. It's dark. Just like I left it. I can't see the driveway yet, but if Dad's car isn't there, then I can walk right in, and—

"Shit," I whisper.

As Lily pulls up, they both turn to look. The house is dark, but not only is Dad's car in the driveway . . . *he's* in the driveway, too.

"Oh," Lily groans. "That's some bad timing."

She's right. From the way Dad's standing there, keys in one hand, takeout bag in the other, he just got home. Literally. Just. Got. Home.

"Do you want us to stay?" Tess asks.

"Yeah, sure," I say. "The police will need witnesses."

"For what?"

"For when he kills me."

"You're always saying that." Lily rolls her eyes. "And yet here you remain. Very much alive."

"You don't have to sound so disappointed."

Lily nods to my door. "Better just get it over with."

Tess smiles. "Good luck."

The second I close the door, Lily peels out. And I don't blame her at all. Dad watches the car go, then slowly turns back to me with a dazed look.

"Hi," I say.

"Where the hell," he says, "did you just come from?"

So many locations to choose from, in the last couple hours. Lily's house. Tess's house. A murderer's house. I decide to go with:

"Um. School."

"School? It's—" He checks his watch. "Midnight. Your school is not open!"

"Yeah," I say, "that's why we had to break in."

"You *broke in?*"

I shouldn't have said it like that.

"It's not breaking and entering if you have keys. Right? It's just . . . entering."

I shouldn't have said it like that, either.

"I feel like I'm losing my mind here, Gideon," he says, his voice getting louder. "What are you doing outside at this hour, why did you break into your school, who drove you—?"

Who, what, why. Add *how* and *when* and he'd have written a lede.

But the story's always more complicated than the lede. If you tell it right. I look around at our block, quiet and peaceful and

356

blissfully empty. I'd like to keep it that way.

"Can we go in the house?" I ask.

"Oh, *you* are never leaving the house again." Dad turns toward the road. "Was that Lily?"

"Uh—"

"I'm calling her mothers." Shaking his head, he walks past me, keys clenched in his hand, to unlock the door. "I'm calling them right now."

"Dad, don't, it's fine."

"Fine?" He pushes the door open, then pulls me through it. "It's not fine! Nothing about my sixteen-year-old meeting me in the front yard at one in the morning is *fine*."

Thirty seconds ago it was midnight, now it's one a.m. Amazing how time flies when you're furious.

"I can explain that."

"I don't even want to hear it."

After all I've been through tonight, he could make this just a little bit easier.

"Fine." I fold my arms. "You can read about it in the paper tomorrow, if that's what you want."

"What?"

"And I can just go to bed."

"We're not done." He points at the couch. "Sit."

"I will if you're actually going to let me explain—"

"Hold on," he interrupts me, looking down at the dusty home phone. "I have a message."

Oh. Right.

"You don't need to listen to that," I tell him from the doorway.

"Why?" He leans on the counter. "Is it from the police?"

"No, it's . . . from me."

He blinks. Then turns. And hits play.

It's amazing what you notice when you can ignore one of your senses. I don't have to listen to what plays next, because I know every word. They were mine. And they were the truth. By the end, he's staring at the countertop, one hand resting on it. Like he's supporting himself. He swallows. Rubs his eye with his free hand. Looks back up at me.

He doesn't say anything. He just stares at me with an expression I couldn't decipher on my best day, and especially not now, somehow exhausted and adrenaline-high simultaneously.

"I meant to call your cell phone," I tell him. "But I misdialed."

He still doesn't say anything, so I guess I'll have to carry this conversation myself, except I don't know what to say, either. My brain is so jumbled, I barely register that he's walking across the kitchen toward me.

And then he wraps me in a hug so tight, it doesn't matter what I was going to say next, because there's no air left in my lungs.

You can be honest and you can be kind, at the same time. Truth doesn't just have to be some personal victory, like I thought when I stormed the city council meeting, or a shield, like it was when Lily and I fought. It can be something softer, too.

The truth can be a bombshell. And it can be a shelter.

"That was—" he says when we finally break away. "I, um. It means . . . a lot."

"Well. I meant it."

He laughs a little. "And I'm glad we don't have to argue about how much trouble you're in."

"Does it help that I did it for the right reasons?" I ask hopefully.

"Marginally."

"How about if I uncovered a criminal conspiracy and I'm pretty sure also solved a murder?"

He blinks. Opens his mouth. Closes it. Then turns back toward the kitchen and says:

"I'll make coffee."

CHAPTER 28

TRYING TO TELL a story through newspaper headlines is kind of a cliché—not just in film noir, but in any movie old enough that people still got their news from a real, black-and-white, leaves-ink-smudges-on-your-fingers kind of paper.

I used to roll my eyes when I'd see it in films. A newspaper, rapidly spinning and whirling until it came to a stop dead center on the screen, with some headline—much too large for a real newspaper, but big enough for the audience to read—telling the viewer exactly what they need to know. I understood why they did it. It's a quick way to give information, or to show the passage of time. But it annoyed me all the same.

I don't feel that way now. If it's a cliché, then it's a cliché not just because it works, but because it's true. Headlines can paint a picture just like oil and canvas. Or celluloid and a screen. Headlines can't tell the whole story, sure. It's just one way of seeing it. One perspective. But it can be a useful one.

If my life were a noir, these are probably the headlines that would flash across the screen:

VINCE DEATH DECLARED MURDER:
SAN MIGUEL PD INVESTIGATING

SMPD EMPLOYEE ARRESTED IN
DEATH OF MOGUL'S SON

OVERWAY MAKES FULL CONFESSION,
IMPLICATES OTHERS IN PLOT

HIGH SCHOOL PAPER BREAKS VINCE
MURDER STORY

SAN MIGUEL GIRL, 16, CRACKS POLICE
CORRUPTION CASE

INSIDE SCOOP: HOW A GIRL REPORTER AND
"BOY DETECTIVE" DUO GOT THEIR STORY

LOCAL TEEN JOURNALISTS:
"WE KNEW THIS WAS SOMETHING BIG"

Lily takes on most of the media attention that comes after the article releases, but she never fails to name-drop me in a quote—in the middle of a sentence, where it's harder to cut out. It's nice of her, but I wouldn't mind even if she never mentioned me. Not much, anyway. The glory isn't the point. It hasn't been for a long time.

You can't tell a whole story in newspaper headlines, because so many important moments will never make a front page. There are millions of little stories in between the birth announcements and the obituaries that aren't ever immortalized in print but still live on. Like Tess curled up next to me on my bed, the sun streaming through the window, on so many afternoons they blend into one golden memory. Or, in a more dramatic example, Garcia showing up at my house today and telling Dad that we all need to have a quick conversation.

Dad, at this point aware of how many misdemeanors I've committed, says: "I'd like a lawyer to be present for this."

Garcia takes off his sunglasses. "That isn't necessary."

"Yes, it is," Dad says firmly. "Gideon is not talking without a—"

"Gideon won't be doing any talking at all. *I* am going to talk and Gideon is going to listen very closely and very, very quietly." Garcia turns to me. "Clear?"

I open my mouth to say, *Yeah*, but then realize that might be a trap. So I nod.

"Great." Garcia sits down across from me at the kitchen table. "You and I both know what happened here."

I don't buy that for a second, but I've agreed not to talk, so I settle for making the most skeptical face I can. He sighs.

"I may not know every detail. I may not have the whole story. But I do know you didn't locate those documents or get that dog's fur without some serious steps outside the law. No matter what you *or* your friend have been telling the press."

No one but us ever knew Marco's dossier existed. And Lily isn't lying, technically, when she tells people someone gave her the documents. Sure, it would open up new lines of questioning if anyone knew that someone was *me*, but every time she's asked about it, Lily goes all doe-eyed innocence and reminds the interviewer that *as a journalist* she could *certainly never compromise her source.*

"You're lucky you did give me the original docs," Garcia continues, "because I can still build a case off that. You're also lucky Phoebe confessed as quickly as she did and has chosen to aid the investigation as much as she has. And you are *exceptionally* lucky that I *don't* want the bad press of sending the plucky teen-age media darlings to juvenile hall."

He leans in closer.

"But don't mistake me: you should be in lockup right now. And if I ever catch you at another crime scene, or accusing another city council member of murder—"

"Wait," Dad says. "What?"

"You won't be as lucky again," Garcia finishes. "I need to make sure you know that."

I nod.

Garcia slaps the table with both hands. "Good." He rises and turns to Dad. "See? Over and done, no need for attorneys."

"I'm sorry," Dad says, "I'm still stuck on—murder accusations?"

Thanks, I mouth at Garcia, who looks like he's fighting a smile.

"You two have things to talk about," Garcia says. "I'll let you get to it."

How benevolent.

"Gideon Green." He extends his hand. "I sincerely hope to never see you again."

"Chief Garcia." I reach out and shake it. "Congrats on your promotion."

Of all the days Garcia could have picked to visit, it had to be the day of the party.

"It's not a *party* party," Tess clarified for me. "We're all just going to hang out in Noah's backyard and eat burgers and hot dogs and whatever. Nothing major, we do it at the end of every year. Sort of a *Herald* goodbye party."

It didn't make sense to me at first, because the school year isn't all the way over. But Lily explained this is the last time we get to see each other as the current staff of the *Herald*. In a couple of weeks, the graduating seniors will pick their replacements and start training them to take over.

"And . . . editor in chief?" I'd asked, having completely

avoided the subject with Tess since that day in my bedroom.

Lily picked at her fingernail. "An email will go out to everyone. Next week."

Garcia's visit has made me late, so I'm the last one to arrive at Noah's house. And I think Lily's been waiting for me, because she spots me from across the backyard in a second.

"Hey!" She rushes up to me. "Did you also get a . . . friendly visit today?"

I nod. "So friendly I wasn't allowed to talk. You?"

"Same. But you'll do what Garcia said, right?" Lily's forehead wrinkles. "Lie low? Rest on your laurels?"

"Oh, yeah," I say. "I'll make sure my next case is outside city limits."

"Gideon!"

I hold up my hands. "I'm kidding!"

And I am. For now, anyway.

Just then, Tess sidles up alongside us, a can of soda in her hands and a big smile on her face.

"There you are. I was wondering when you'd get here," she says, and kisses me.

"Ugh, your love is so cute, it's gross," Ryan groans as he walks past us.

Tess flicks her eyes down to the mountain of food on his plate. "We're gross? You put ketchup on raw carrots."

Once everyone's gotten their fill of food, Tess gathers us all together in a circle. Lily gave me a heads-up about this tradition:

one by one, each person gets to tell their favorite *Herald* memory from the past year. I still don't know what I'm going to say, and maybe Tess can tell, because she picks Ryan—all the way across the circle from me—to start.

We go around like that, everyone adding their favorite moment. Some of them I remember, but some happened before I got there. I laugh along anyway, imagining this time next year, when I won't have missed a single moment. I can't wait.

It takes a moment for the gravity of that thought to hit me. *I can't wait.* It's so small. So simple. And so . . . new.

I've spent years counting down the days until graduation, tallying the minutes until the bell rang, the hours until I could escape to the comfortable habitat of my room, the days and weeks and months until I could escape high school itself.

Now, for the first time—the very first time—I'm looking forward to it.

Tess nudges my leg. "Your turn, Gideon."

"Oh, come on," Noah says, mouth full of hamburger. "Isn't it obvious?"

I know what he means. How could you beat cracking a local scandal? But it's not that simple, because nothing is. And it might seem obvious from his perspective, but the world has more angles than the one presented to you.

The longer I turn it over in my head, the more sure I am. Occam's razor might say the simplest explanation is usually the right one. But what kind of fun would life be without a twist or two?

"No," I say, louder than I meant but as firmly as I feel. "It's not."

"Not what?" Tess asks.

"Obvious. My favorite moment isn't obvious, because I don't have just one moment. It was every moment—every Late Night, and every dinner, and every argument over what to put on the front page. Every time I was frustrated over an article, or laughed at somebody's joke, or just sat at the table in silence, I felt like I was part of something, I felt like I was—" I swallow. "Home."

Everyone is quiet. They wait. They listen. I keep going.

"Ten years from now, I might not remember every single day on the *Herald* or any moment on its own, but . . . I won't ever forget the way I felt."

And that's what's important, isn't it? In stories and in life. Not just what happened, but what you take with you, when the movie or the moment is over. What lives on.

Tess reaches over, squeezes my hand, and picks up right where I left off. The way only she can do.

"I have a hard time picking a moment, too," Tess admits. "How can you sum up a whole year—four years, really—into just one memory? And I think it's extra hard this time, because . . . I won't get many more, of the *Herald*. There's going to be a time, really soon, when I'll turn off the lights and lock the door behind me, for the last time. I keep trying to imagine how that's going to feel." She stares into the middle distance, like she's trying to see it, right in front of her. "I'm going to lock the door behind me, and hand over the keys. I think that'll feel sad, and hard, but also hopeful and right." Tess looks around the circle, now at each of us in turn. "Because I'll be leaving the paper in good hands.

"So I think—" She takes a deep breath, and her eyes finally stop on the person right next to her. "My favorite moment is this one, the one I'm living, right now. When I get to announce Lily Krupitsky-Sharma as the next editor in chief of the *Herald*."

I've never seen a person cycle through as many emotions as Lily does in the next five seconds: confusion, shock, joy, relief, triumph. And with all those feelings all at once, it's not a surprise that she bursts into tears.

When the party's in full swing again, music blaring from the speakers, everyone soaking up the late afternoon sunlight, and Lily still wiping at her eyes but smiling wide, I find Tess perched on the back steps, watching everything from a distance.

"I thought Lily was going to pass out," I say, sitting down next to her and sneaking an arm around her waist. "Is that usually how editor in chief gets announced?"

"No." Tess lays her head on my shoulder. "But doesn't it make a great story?"

CHAPTER 29

IF I'M BEING honest, there's one thing I've never liked about film noir: the endings.

Not because they're tragic, though they almost always are. Tragedy is a part of life, and that's the point of movies, to reflect real life. It's the point of all stories, to tell us who we are. They show us what our world is like, and sometimes, how it could be better. Stories can't capture it all, not the whole truth, because nothing really can. But they can reflect it. Like a mirror. Like water.

The thing I don't like about noir endings isn't their near universal tragedy. It's that there's never any surprise.

From the very first scene, the protagonist is doomed. For all his skills and smarts, he'll leave the movie more damaged than he started. His partner may disappear. The femme fatale may betray him. He may crack the case, solve the murder, only to still find himself alone. He may walk off into a dark alley, be told to forget it, Jake, it's Chinatown, or bleed to death in the back of a '46 DeSoto. Though you don't know what the tragic ending will look like, you know it's coming.

There are lots of ways my life is not like a noir. But one of the best ways is how in the end, it's surprising.

Months ago, it would have been tough to picture myself sitting at the center table in the school newspaper office, printouts spread all around me. But that's where I am. It would have been hard to see myself happy in the middle of all the chaos—the ancient, noisy printer spitting out pages, Ryan and Noah arguing about which headline is stronger, and Lily—now editor-in-chief-in-training—reviewing the front-page mock-up spread in front of her. But that's what I am: happy. And it would have been impossible, actually impossible, to imagine Tess with her arms around me, nestling her chin into my neck as she reads over my shoulder.

That's what a surprise is, right? Something that's impossible, until it's real.

If my life were a movie—which it's not, and God, I'm so glad it's not—I think this would be one of those silent scenes. Where the action goes on, but the sound's been cut. There might be a song playing over it, quietly. The point isn't whatever the characters might be saying. The point is what you see, and how it makes you feel. Whole stories can happen in silence. Maybe everything can.

The shots would be simple. Carefully chosen. Each one important.

The bulletin board above the couch, now papered with all the media coverage from my and Lily's investigation.

Lily dropping off a new page for me to edit, with a smile.

Tess running her hand across my shoulder as she passes by.

Noah bursting in the double doors, his arms filled with pizza boxes, Ryan trailing behind him with a giant bowl of undressed salad.

All of us together, around the table, eating and talking and arguing and laughing. *A family, in a way*, Tess said once. A family in every way, I've decided now.

Then, I think, the scene would fade out.

This is one of the ways stories can only reflect life, not match it completely. Stories come to a close when the reel spins to its last frame or the final period is typeset. But in real life, stories get to tumble into each other, and that might be the best surprise of all.

The end of one story is just the beginning of another.

~~FADE TO BLACK~~

371

Acknowledgments

IF THIS WERE a movie, here is where the end credits would roll—a long list of names that scroll by so quickly and so impersonally. Luckily, this is a book, and books give you the space you need. It's one of the best things about them.

Thank you to:

Ben Rosenthal, who enthusiastically supported this idea from the very first pitch and shaped it into the book it ultimately became. Thank you for always laughing at my jokes, even when they're terrible. I couldn't ask for a better partner in telling stories, and I only hope we have many more chances to build them together.

Natalie Lakosil, who has advocated for me each step of the way and talked me off every cliff on which I found myself.

Sarah LaPolla, who has been patiently waiting on this newspaper book for years.

The entire team at Katherine Tegen Books, including David

Curtis, Tanu Srivastava, Julia Johnson, and of course, Katherine Tegen herself. Without you, this book would not be a reality.

Laura Bradford and Taryn Fagerness, for their continued and much appreciated support.

My writers' group: Brian Kennedy, Emily Helck, Michelle Rinke, and Siena Koncsol. We've seen each other through nearly a decade full of weddings, births, book deals, moves, and more—I can't wait to see what the next decade holds.

My community of fellow authors, especially the Electrics 18s, Class of 2k18, and Naomi Krupitsky. Your talent never fails to awe and inspire me.

The staff of the *Berkeley High Jacket* (2004–2008). Without every chaotic, joyful Late Night I spent with you all in H102, I wouldn't be the writer (or the person) I am today. Thank you for always leaving the salad undressed for me.

My family, both old and new, in the Bay Area, San Diego, and beyond. To Maria, Doug, Bob, Lynn, and both Marys: thank you for welcoming me with such open arms.

Leah, for understanding me in a way no other person could, and for bringing Caroline into my life.

Mom, who gave me pointers on city council procedure and cried when she finished this book.

Dad, for picking me up from the school newspaper office for three years straight and without complaint . . . even at 1 a.m.

Rob, without whom I would not have survived 2020 *or* Gideon Green. Thank you for your expertise on San Diego, Mexican food, and being a teenage boy. Thank you for sitting by my side through noir marathons, patiently helping me untangle every snarl in the plot, and for the day you looked up from your computer and said, "They should pretend to be the dog." If this were a movie, you'd get a creative consultant credit, but you'll just have to settle for my eternal love and gratitude instead.

Thank you. Thank you. Thank you.